2016

"Son of Wales Award" for best new author and poet
"Excellence of Literature Award" for the outstanding achievement of
the epic autobiography *Cave Days*

2017

"Best Adventure Autobiography" for Great Britain and
Ireland King of the Castle Publishing.

"Best Adventure and Historical Award" for the outstanding novel
Gower of the Hills, King of the Castle Publishing

Al Cole Interview, CBS radio, People of Great Distinction book
interview for *Cave Days*, 2019

I'LL MEET YOU AT PENNARD CASTLE

KINGSLEY R. HILL

Published in Swansea Wales by King of the Castle Publishing.

ISBN 978-1-7778660-1-3 (e-book)
ISBN978-1-7778660-0-6 (hardcover)

Front Cover Artwork by Sylvia Nicholson, A Touch of Art, Victoria, BC

To contact Kingsley Hill email at gowerofthehills@gmail.com

Book design by SpicaBookDesign, Victoria, BC

Printed and bound in Canada

This book is dedicated to my Dad, Roger Elliot Fitzgerald Hill, who is one of Wales' great historians, and explorers.

And to my Brother, Fraser Mark Hill, who is my great friend and fellow explorer, may we walk many more miles together, and find many more artifacts that tell us many more wonderful stories of the past.

And to my Daughter Samantha, who travels with me to our sacred places near and far, and dances upon the emerald waters of lake and sea, where Dava the Butterfly flies with you and me, dancing to your wonderful music, Jade, play another song for me.

About the Author

Kingsley Ross Hill, was born near the city of Swansea, in Glamorganshire, South Wales and grew up in the village of Pennard, on the Gower Peninsula. [The word Pennard, means "village without a gate" in the Welsh language]. Kingsley, describes growing up in Pennard, and on the Gower Peninsula, as "living this most wonderful adventure, with no gates."

It is interesting that the Gower Peninsula Series, which includes the books, *Cave Days, Gower of the Hills, Nan's Nan, and the Pirates of Port Eynon, Who Was Taliath Saren?* – all give the reader, such a sense of freedom and adventure; like walking through a land without gates or fences. The authors books are full of mystery and adventure and are extremely accurate in their betrayal of the history and geography of the Gower Peninsula itself.

The author is humble about his many awards. I am pleased that he is becoming well known in his native Wales, and throughout the United Kingdom, and more recently in Canada and the United States, for his unique style of writing and poetry.

Kingsley Hill, lives with his family in Creston, British Columbia. He is also a pastor and counsellor and works in youth outreach.

Kingsley supports a number of charities and organizations through the sales of his books, and has inspired many young writers and poets in his native Wales, by giving them literary opportunities and awards. Kingsley Hill is an ex pupil of Gowerton Grammar School, in Gowerton, South Wales, and is developing into one of the greatest writers of his generation.

Captain and Commander Horatio Tucker
Royal Navy

Table of Contents

Chapter One

The Glory of Spring

Spring waltzed across the Gower like a bride, radiant in all her glory, while people stopped and stared and smelled the fragrant air of her perfume. The warm sands of the dunes were like blankets kissing upon our bodies, while the air buzzed with honeybees, and the skylarks sung of the glories to come. June, July and August were their chorus as they sang and hovered in the deep blue above us without a distant care. Families sat and played on Pobbles Beach with their buckets and spades and coloured deckchairs, waiting for the tide to come in over the golden sands and join them in their games. Children laughed, mothers smiled, and fathers stood tall like peacocks rustling their muscles like feathers, showing off to their pale skinned wives that lay in bikinis with one eye always open as they worshipped the long-lost sun.

We swam in the sea, Samantha, Melody and Me, and ran up the dunes to get warm. Soon the refreshing chill of the May tide was gone, and we turned like the wild dune flowers to bask in the noon day sun.

The sounds of the newborn spring, rise on the breeze above the grey smiling rocks to our beds in the sand, and I dream of my Ffion to come and hold my hand. I am alone today, but the dunes, they understand, and the skylarks sing of my life so happy and grand.

Mr. Pennard Castle and Mr. Cefn Bryn, sleep lightly in the distance, occasionally opening their eyes to the sound of the din, and then close them again and grin. Winter is lonely, and January is dim, but June, July and August, they are hymns.

The sun climbs higher and higher, fleeing the shadows from the green hills, and shining upon the purple heather and the open spaces that always thrill, and when I behold them, I am King of the Hill.

There is a stillness now out across the day, as the singing surf stands still and contemplates the day. Mothers call, and fathers put down the ball, as the children run back to their dry towels, and the grey rocks become stools as they eat and drink, and dream of whirlpools.

Seagulls wait and watch for the sandwiches to drop, while Susan Smith tries to find her lost flip flop. Johnny Jones looks down from the high ancient rock and realizes that he has still got a lot! Even though Deborah Burr refused to tie the knot. He grew up on the Gower, and that is better than winning at the slot, although from up here, her bikini looks so hot, and Johnny Jones can't stop thinking about what she's got. Hot, hot, she has got a-lot!

The sea has rested now for an hour, and it is time she makes her way back up the golden sands, where a hundred people are waiting to shake her generous hand, for she, you see, is the Grand Lady of the sands!

It's time to leave our blankets in the dunes and go and meet the lady with the tunes. Let's wait until the waves reach the rocks, Samantha said, whistling one of the lady's hues, look dad I've taken off my shoes, I'll race you to the rocks, and I will take the ribbon from my hair and let the wind blow through my locks. Me too, said Melody without a care, I want to feel the sun on my back, and the moon on my head, I want to find Miss Magic before I go to bed. Me too, I said, I'll race you both to the high rocks instead, and we galloped like horses in good stead, and Samantha ran the fastest and was soon ahead. Come on Melody, you have to run like a bull that sees red, and we reached the Three Cliffs rocks that are shaped like a dinosaur's head.

Suddenly I see my Ffion, coming down the path, coming down to meet me like my other half. We will swim in the sea and have a bath, dance and kiss and have a laugh, then up to the sand dunes after our bath and make more memories that will last. She is my Spring, and in our glory, I will sing, for two people in love is a wonderful thing, when you can hear your heart go ring-a-ding-ding. For this is what makes the world go round, and the birds to sing, listening to all the hearts that ring. I love you Ffion and thank you for wearing my ring! Oh, I am so happy my King, I am so proud to wear your ring, let's make love, and sing-sing-sing!

✸

Spring whistled at summer, who turned around and they kissed. It is now the middle of July. It will soon be August the 1st, Samantha and Benjamin's Birthdays. They were born on the same day, only nine years apart. My brother Fraser and I were also born on the same day, also in August. That is two generations now, but that is another story.

I would celebrate my son Ben's birthday, when he came out to Wales again for a holiday, and I had sent him the new FIFA Soccer game for his Playstation 4. I sure missed watching football with my boys, but this was a season that we were apart, physically anyway, and it sure made us appreciate one another. I don't know if distance makes the heart grow fonder. It certainly shows a person the closeness and value of a loved one. Regardless of the distance between us, my boys and I remained close to one another, and we looked forward to the time we could be together again and go on another adventure.

When Ffion and I asked my oldest daughter Samantha what she wanted for her birthday, the answer did not surprise us. She asked if we could go on an adventure out onto the Worms Head and stay on it until the tide came in and made it an Island. I reminded her that pending the time of the tides, we might have to spend the night out there.

"That would be great", she said. "I would love to spend the night on the Rock at the End of the World! Just like you did, dad." Ffion and Melody, my youngest, were in too, so we decided to plan it.

A week before Samantha's birthday I decided to take her on a walk from Oystermouth Castle to Caswell Bay. It would give us time to talk and connect, as she had been so busy at university and spending time with her new boyfriend.

We arrived at Oystermouth Castle and walked around it's grounds. We had been in the castle a number of time's and wanted to get started on our walk. It was a beautiful day with blue sky and a light cool breeze coming in from the Bristol Channel which made a nice temperature for walking and exploring.

We walked from the castle grounds to Norton Road, where we picked up some snacks for our journey. There is a lovely view of the castle from Norton Road, as you look back at it through the trees, and the castle looks down at you from the hill, waving the flag of the Welsh Dragon. On a misty day you only see the silhouette of the castle through the trees which add to its mystery, and one feels like you could be back in medieval times in the days of the castle's youth.

The history of the castle goes back to the 13th century. And if you are interested in architecture, it is well worth a visit. It has a tracery of fine early English windows, and an old dungeon where one can feel its resident ghosts. It also has a stone pillar which is thought to have been used in the past as a whipping post. A friend of mine who visited the castle late one afternoon swore she heard crying and the sound of a cracking whip coming from the old pillar. Well, enough history and ghost stories for now. We were excited to start our journey around the cliff path to Caswell.

Samantha and I made our way down to the seafront to behold the many views one can see from the promenade. Looking eastwards in the direction of Swansea, we could see the valley gap between Town Hill on the left and Kilvey Hill, where my father lives, on the right. The valley is filled by the hill known as Mynydd Drumau, the highest point of which is 894 feet above sea level. At the center of this hill and peeping over the top is the rounded crest of Mynydd March Hywel, which is 1,391 feet high.

As one continues to look back while walking further west towards West Cross, a peak with a steep slope on the left- hand side appears from behind Town Hill and takes its place. And as we walked along, I waited for the moment that Samantha could see it.

"I can see it, Dad!" she exclaimed excitedly. "What is its name?"

"That is the peak of Fan Gyhirych," I said, also excited and happy to see Sam was enjoying the adventure as much as I was.

"It is a mountain 2,381 feet high."

"How do you know all this, Dad?"

"I have a dad who took the time to teach me," I replied.

"Just like I do," she echoed back, and I swelled with pride as we continued our way along the promenade towards Mumbles Pier.

Every fifty yards or so, Samantha stopped and looked back to see if she could still see Fan Gyhirych in the distance.

"I can still see it," she called, as I continued to walk.

"It will disappear behind Kilvey Hill at any moment," I assured her.

While she was turned around, I thought it was a good time for me to give her her birthday gift. I quickly pulled it out of my backpack, and said, "here you are, I want to give you your birthday present early, because I know you would appreciate being able to use it today," and I handed her the parcel.

"Well, open it up," I said, "and let's have a look." She quickly untied the bow and pulled away at the brown paper.

"Oh Dad, binoculars! They are just what I wanted! And thanks for giving me my present today because it's the perfect time to use them."

"I am glad you like them. Would you like me to help you get the lens in focus?"

"No, I think I can do it Dad, thanks."

She walked a few more yards and then focused them on the mountain. "Fan Gihirych has disappeared behind Kilvey Hill," she exclaimed, "and I can see the eastern slope of Fan Hir on the Carmarthen Black Mountain, just like you said, Dad."

"Good spotting," I replied, "and there is lots more to see if you know what to look for."

"The highest peak of the Black Mountain is Carmarthen Van at 2,632 feet. It should be in full view by the time we reach the old South End Station, which is now the bus terminus." Sam eagerly looked through her binoculars and said the mountain was still in plain view. I could also see it faintly with the naked eye. It soon disappeared as we reached the Mumbles Pier, but other peaks of the Black Mountain now came into view.

"Wow, Dad, there is so much to see. Anyone just walking along the promenade would never think that there is so much to see and recognize. I love my binoculars. You have no idea of how much I needed a pair."

"I think, I do, young lady, don't you think?" I smiled.

"Yes Dad… I mean no… you know what I mean. What I meant was I have been waiting a long time to get some decent ones, and these are great."

"I know what you meant," I replied laughing, "I was just teasing."

Sam then asked me if I could identify the peak with a deep western slope and a kink in its middle.

"I don't recognize that one," I said, adjusting the lens to look more closely. "But I do recognize the mountain to the right of the Neath Valley Gap. That one is called Craig-y-Lyn, and it is supposed to be about 1,969 feet high, and behind it is the pass leading from Hirwain into the Rhondda Valley."

"Hey Dad, can I have a look?"

"Sorry love, these are mine now, I really need a nice pair like this!"

"Dad, come on, stop teasing and give me my binoculars!"

"Ok, here you are then," I reluctantly said.

"There are more mountains and peaks to see, but it is time we picked up the pace" I said, and we continued our walk along the cliff path towards Caswell Bay.

We walked past the Pier and headed off to look at the Mumbles Head with its islets sticking out into the bay. The tide was low enough to walk out to the Inner Head and view the channel that runs between the Inner and Outer Head. The current was strong as we took off our shoes and waded out into the receding tide.

"It's nice and refreshing Dad," Sam said, feeling exhilarated, "but I can feel the strong pull of the current."

"Don't go in any further," I said, "you might get pulled off your feet and have to swim for it." At my word she retreated to shallower water, and we stood in the waves and refreshed our feet, ready for our walk along the cliff path.

When my father was a boy, the war office constructed a concrete Causeway out to the Lighthouse on the Outer Head, and he and his younger brother used to walk out to the Outer Head without having to scramble over the slippery seaweed stones as one must do today. Most of the Causeway has been eroded away, but one can still see parts of its structure in the conquering waves. One hot summer's day when I was a boy, my father put me on his shoulders and told me to hold on tight, while he proceeded to swim out to the Outer Head and I put my arms around his neck and held on for dear life!

We visited a cave called 'Bobs Cave' on the far side of the Islet. I never met Bob! But I remember going into the cave with my father. It was dark at first and we could not see much, but slowly our eyes became accustomed to the dark, and we saw vivid reds, greens and yellows of the lichen – coated rocks.

As we dried our feet and stood on the shore, I told Sam about the two brave Women of Mumbles Head. The 'Grace Darlings' of Wales, immortalized by the poem from Clement Scott. The two women rescued a shipwrecked mariner by tying their shawls together and pulling him from the cruel waves.

From Mumbles Head, we walked due west to Broadslade also known as Bracelet Bay. We shall call it Bracelet Bay which is the name by which my father and Grandfather introduced it to me.

Bracelet Bay is between Mumbles Head and Tut Head. When the tide is high and the sea rough, a walk along the track which goes around the foot of Tut Head will reveal some fine spectacles of waves crashing on the rocks.

Samantha and I now reached Limeslade Bay, and experienced one of the highlights of our ramble. The tide had retreated to almost its low, exposing a lovely bathing area. We stripped to our undies and raced into the waves for a swim.

"Oh, this is great, Dad!" Sam shouted at a passing gull. "I am not your dad!" The gull called back, "he's over there swimming close to the rocks." And I was.

Sam and I wallowed around in the waves for what seemed like a long time. We swam out to the swells and tried to body surf on the breakers. I managed to catch one which took me right into the beach, and Sam soon followed on one of the next ones. We walked back up the beach twisting and turning trying not to hurt our feet on the sharp rocks, and we looked like two bedraggled sailors by the time we reached the top of the beach.

"Oh, that felt so good!" I exclaimed. "A good swim washes all the cobwebs from your soul, don't you think?"

"Yeah Dad, it does."

From Limeslade we walked along the cliff path to Rams Tor. At Rams Tor, the path falls on a gentle recline to a level of about 90 feet at which level it continues around another smaller headland from the top of which you get an above view of Langland Bay. At this point in our walk, Sam informed me that she was getting tired and needed to rest.

"How about we try and make it to Langland Bay," I said, "and then we can have a good rest there. And there is also a café with sandwiches and ice cream."

"You have got a deal," she said, and we continued with a renewed spring in our steps. It is amazing how motivating the word ice cream is, especially when it's 'Joe's Ice Cream'. We soldiered on past Rother's Sker, and Rother's Tor, and then we reached Langland Bay. We made a controlled dash to the café door, beating another two people to the counter.

"What can I get you?" the lady asked.

"Two of the biggest ice creams you have and two bacon sandwiches please." We sat on a bench to eat our grub and looked out across the Bristol Channel to the hills of Devonshire in the distance.

We had had a wonderful walk so far and had enjoyed some good father daughter conversation. It is so important to engage our children and stay connected with them as they navigate the many different seasons and experiences of their lives. I thought of how wonderful it was to have a daughter like Samantha.

After we had eaten until we hurt, we continued our way along the cliff path to Caswell. Little did we know, around the next corner we were about to experience something wonderful!

We had just passed Snapple Point when we saw a cloud of brilliant blue.

"They are butterflies, Dad!" Samantha shouted. "Look at them, there are hundreds of them!" And there was! A thick cloud of dancing butterflies were right in front of us. Samantha looked at me realizing that something magical was happening, and I looked the same way at her, as we were filled with wonder and excitement. Why is this so wonderful someone may ask?

Firstly, to see a cloud of butterflies that size is very rare. And secondly, and most significant to Sam and I, is that butterflies have played a big part in our connection as dad and daughter over the years.

When Sam was three and a half years old her Great Grandmother in Devonshire, England, sent her two beautiful, flowered dresses. They were her favorite things to wear, and whenever we would spend the day together, which was at least one full day a week, she wore one of the dresses. About every second week we spent a half day in what was called the Crystal Gardens, in downtown Victoria on Vancouver Island where we were living at the time. It was as much of a 'zoo' as it was a garden, and we called it the 'jungle'. There were monkeys, penguins, many different types of parrots and macaws, and even a sloth that lived in a large classroom with bats flying around its canopy. Samantha and I would spend hours playing hide and seek around the jungle, and the 'bat cave' as we called it, was one of her favourite places to hide. She wasn't shy to hide behind a tourist or two in that dark room, and she was hard to see. Then, suddenly, she would jump out from the darkness in her brightly coloured dress and light up my world and the room. Next to visit was a parrot named Rosie, and we used to bring peanuts in our pockets to feed her until one of the staff saw us feeding her one day and explained that she was on a strict diet. Rosie would recognize Samantha with her red curls and flowered dress and climb down the tree she was perched on using her beak to balance. She would say hello and hope for a peanut. After our visit with Rosie, we walked up to the bridge that overlooked the koi carp pond and the waterfall where we made a wish. Samantha shared with me one day that her wish was that we could always come here and spend time together, and in my heart I had the same wish. We lived it out for as long as we could, until the little girl with the flowered dress whom the butterflies always landed on, grew into a big girl, and they closed the gardens down.

But our memories of the jungle and the butterflies will live in our hearts forever. One day the Kiwi got loose and chased us along the path, followed by a staff member with a net. Sam and I sat on a bench where the Kiwi proceeded to undo Samantha's shoelaces with his long curved beak. The staff member and several people stood and watched as the Kiwi undid the laces on her other shoe too, and we were all untied in wonder so to speak.

In the winter months we would look at the many chrysalises, hanging on a board inside a greenhouse, and in the early spring we would watch them turn into butterflies and fly around what we called the 'butterfly room'. There were so many of them, and all different types. Large blues ones, yellow and purple swallowtails, orange and black monarchs, just to name a few. And our favourite was a fawn and black butterfly that followed Samantha around the room, landing on her shoulders and on her flowered dress, and even hanging on the curls of her hair. Tourists would take pictures of that butterfly, hanging from her curls or riding on the palm of her hand. We named the butterfly 'Dava', and it followed and landed on Samantha for hours that day. Even today, butterflies still have a special connection for us as a dad and daughter, and we often see a 'Dava' or one of her kind.

And today on our walk, we rejoiced at seeing this blue cloud of butterflies that united our hearts again to a heritage that we would carry within us all our lives.

As the cloud of blue danced away over the cliff top, we rounded the corner of Snapple Point and then descended the path into Caswell Bay. The tide seemed fully in now, as we watched some surfers catching waves that rode high up into the cove. When the tide is out, Caswell Bay has a large area of beautiful golden sand. A great beach for building sand boats and waiting for the tide to come in and crash down the walls of your ship. And you can bath safely as the tide goes all the way out to its low.

We wadded into the waves and paddled back and forth at the top of the beach, until it was time to head back to Oyster-mouth, where we had parked the car.

By the time we got back to the car we were both tired, and glad we didn't have to wait for a bus to take us home. It takes two buses to get home to Pennard from Oystermouth. When we arrived home, Ffion had made us a lovely tea, and we all sat down to eat roast beef, Yorkshire pudding, and baked potatoes and carrots. I don't think I heard one word around the table as Samantha, Melody and I stuffed our faces. Ffion of course was the lady she always is and ate very politely.

After sharing with Ffion and Melody, our adventures, the girls went to hang out in Samantha's room, leaving Fion and I to enjoy each other's company in the living room. I made a fire, and we sat and talked over a glass of our favourite black-berry wine.

"What shall we do for Samantha's birthday?" Ffion asked.

"I know she wants us all to go and have an adventure out on the Worms Head," I replied. "But after today's long walk, I think she will be content to relax for a week or so." We would ask her when she came back downstairs. Ffion had already planned a wonderful birthday dinner for Sam next Saturday, which was the actual day of her birthday, and then we could decide on a day to go out to the Worms Head.

As Ffion and I were continuing to enjoy some time to ourselves, the girls came down from Samantha's room.

"What do you want to do for your birthday?" I asked. "Do you still want to go out to the Worms Head, and stay out there until the tide comes in?"

"Yes, Dad," she answered, "but can we wait for a few weeks, I think I am done hiking for a while."

"Yes", Ffion and I replied together, "it's your birthday and you can do what you want to, but don't plan anything for next Saturday evening."

"Okay," Sam replied, "but can we include my boyfriend?"

"Of course," I replied. "I don't think we have met this one yet." As far as I knew Glynn and Samantha were not dating any more. They had dated for quite some time. If her new boyfriend comes over for Samantha's birthday dinner, I can check him out and see what he's like, I thought, feeling protective over my daughter.

As the girls went back upstairs, I shared with Ffion that I was quite happy not to go out on the Worm next Saturday, it would be nice to have a relaxing weekend at home instead. We had done a lot of rambling and hiking over the last few weeks. It was hard to believe that we were almost into August already, and Sam's and Ben's birthdays were on the 1st.

The girls would still be on summer holidays until the first week of September, and I was still working approximately 25 hours a week at the church with my youth group. Things were still not as they should be between my boss David Griffith's and me. He still had not come to terms with the mystery of the ghost stallion that had come to Ffion's and my wedding back in the spring of last year, and we had gone from a healthy working relationship to one of suspicion, and awkwardness. I guess in hindsight I would be a bit freaked out too if it was the first time I saw a phantom horse that everyone else knew and it disappeared in front of my eyes. I was no longer enjoying my time at the church. "I still love working with the youth," I told Ffion, "but the way David has continued to treat me since our wedding, makes me not want to work at the church anymore. We can not always understand or rationalize the things that happen to us in this life, and David does not get it! He acts as if he needs to know and understand everything, otherwise there is something wrong with it. At least that is the way he is coming across, and he is becoming more critical and judgemental by the day."

As Ffion and I continued to talk, she said something that was music to my ears, and would certainly alleviate the problem at work.

"How about we sell the house in Cardiff now," she said. "The market for selling a house is good, and the rental agreement for my tenants comes to an end in September, and if we sold the house, you could retire, or work from home with your counselling. I do find the responsibility of being a landlord and having to drive up to Cardiff every few weeks is a lot of work," she continued. "It is a long way to travel back and forth every time there is a problem with the property. Besides, I would like to see more of you, my lovely man, and I would like to do more traveling now that Melody and Samantha are getting older."

Ffion and I continued to talk well into the night, and we came to the conclusion that it was the right time for us to sell the house in Cardiff.

Over the next week we enjoyed putting on a lovely birthday party for Samantha and put our house in Cardiff on the market. Things at work did not get any better, and I gave my notice to David that I would be ending my position at the church by the end of August. I would miss my youth group and would try and keep in touch with them as much as I could.

Ffion's house in Cardiff sold on the 15th of August, one day before my birthday. Ffion surprised me by booking a weekend getaway to celebrate my birthday in North Gower. It was going to be great to get away, just the two of us.

"Where are we going?" I asked, as we put the suitcases in the car. "All I can say is that we are going somewhere on North Gower. Wait and see," Ffion smiled, "don't you like surprises?"

"Oh yes," I replied, "so long as I am with you, lovely lady."

Ffion drove through Southgate village and on to Pennard, and then she turned down Sandy Lane towards Parkmill. No surprises yet, I thought. This was the quickest way to North Gower from where we lived in Southgate. "You will never guess," she said as we passed Old Parkmill School, which is now a youth outdoor center. We drove through the little hamlets of Penmaen, Nicholaston and Reynoldston, and on up to the top of Cefn Bryn.

"Now you have me wondering," I said, as we continued over the peak of Cefn Bryn.

"Ok close your eyes," Ffion giggled as she pulled over to the side of the road. "You must wear this now until we get there." She pulled out a scarf from her bag and tied it over my eyes. I began to laugh and say the names of places I thought we might be going. "I am not going to tell you, Kings, so you may as well keep quiet and relax." So, I did, and if I were a betting man, I would have placed a bet that we were going somewhere in Rhossili. And I began to get excited as I imagined us walking the wide expanse of Rhossili Bay all the way along its golden sands to Burry Holms, and around the corner to Broughton Bay and Blue Pool Corner, but it was not to be, and Ffion continued to drive. I was glad that I was sitting in the front seat with all the winding lanes and turns. I think I might have gotten car sick if I was blindfolded in the back.

Finally, we arrived at our destination, and I would have never guessed! As Ffion pulled over and untied my blindfold, the road sign read, Welcome to Llanrhidian.

Llanrhidian is built upon limestone rock and looks out onto the salt marshes.

"Have you ever been here before?" Ffion asked.

"Only once when I walked out to the marshes." I did not tell Ffion that I had walked out to the marshes with Gay. Gay was my wife before Ffion, and she had disappeared never to be seen again, and as much as we all loved her, we had to move on with our lives.

As time went by, I became more aware of how important it was for Ffion and I to explore places I had not been to with Gay, places where Ffion and I made our own memories, and sacred places as we grew in our relationship as husband and wife. This was not easy as Gay, and I had explored so much of the Gower Peninsula together.

We drove down the one street that tumbles steeply down the hill to the marshes and a church that is tucked under a wooded slope.

"Where are we staying?" I asked. I knew that there was no hotel nearby.

"We are staying in a Bed and Breakfast," she answered, "and we can do our own thing and go exploring after a cooked breakfast."

"That's wonderful!" I exclaimed. "We have never been to a B & B together! And I have always wanted to explore Llanrhidian and the salt marshes."

We drove down to the bottom of the hill to an old stone cottage, and as we parked the car in the driveway, a woman came out to welcome us and showed us to our room.

"This is perfect," I said to Ffion, as I looked around the high ceiling room. Its front window looked out across the lonely marshes. Gwen, our host, gave us our key and then left us to unpack our suitcases.

"Breakfast is anytime between 8 and 10," she said, "and do you have any food allergies?"

"No," we replied and unpacked.

Ffion, as always, had thought ahead and had packed us a nice picnic to take with us around the village as we went exploring. We had several hours before it got dark, which gave us a nice amount of time to check things out.

The village green is just before the church and is also on a slope. Two large and mysterious stones stand on the green on either side of the path that leads to the church. Ffion and I were excited to explore them. As we stood examining the stones, we could feel the past all around us, and we wondered what the significance of the stones was in relation to the ancient peoples who had lived in this part of Gower.

The top stone is a slab of quartz-conglomerate taken from Cefn Bryn and is interestingly shaped, with three short stumps sticking out of the top. As we continued to inspect the stones, a sleeping memory was awakened within me, and I remembered coming here to Llanrhidian with my father. There were also iron staples embedded into the stone, and I pointed them out to Ffion, who seemed mesmerized by the presence of the stones. It has been suggested that it could be all that remains of an old Celtic wheel cross, my father had once told me. The wheel cross is of a type that was common in Wales in the tenth century A.D. The top was likely knocked off by Puritans during the Reformation and the staples inserted long afterwards, when the old stone was used as a sort of village pillory. However, the suggestion of a pillory has been queried on the grounds that this stone was probably put in its present position around 1820 and pillories were abolished by law in 1816.

"What do you think?" Ffion asked.

"I am not sure," I pondered. "They probably did position it in its present position to commemorate a part of local history." We now studied the lower stone, which is a block of limestone. "More is known about the lower stone," I said. "There is a vivid entry in the parish register which describes the scene on the 8th day of April 1844. 'A very large stone weighing nearly 2 tons was raised on its end a short distance from the Welcome to Town public house, 10 to 12 men volunteered to do it for 1 pint of beer each'. Ffion laughed as I recalled the entry which my father had told me, and said, "it's amazing what you men will do for a pint!"

"You're right!" I exclaimed. And I looked around for the pub.

"Let's go and check out the church," I said, "I can vaguely remember going there with my father."

As we entered the porch of the church, we saw the strange Carves Stone, also known as the Leper Stone.

"Oh gosh! Look at this!" Ffion said in a loud whisper. "It's in the shape of a massive coffin and look at these grotesque human figures and animals carved on it."

Suddenly we were not alone on the porch, and what looked like a priest or father came out of the church to greet us.

"Hello," he said, "did you come in to look around?"

"Yes," I replied half startled. "Do you mind if we do?"

"No," he said. "Please feel free to have a look, I am Rev Coles," and we shook hands. "Would you like to know some of the history of the Leper Stone?" he asked.

"Yes please," Ffion answered.

"The animals look like bears with their paws held up, and we think that the stylized human figures may be representations of Mary and St. John at the cross. Some experts believe they may be figures from Viking history. The late Professor Nash Williams identified the stone as a 'hogs back' similar to those found in Northern England and dating from the tenth century."

The priest went on to explain that the church itself is dedicated to both St. Illtud and St. Rhidian. "As you can see it has a strong battlemented tower on which stands this block of masonry said to be used for carrying a beacon of fire." The priest now left the sanctuary to go back to his office leaving Ffion and I alone. We walked around meditating on the many relics of the remote past that were placed all around the church.

"This is fantastic," Ffion said. "You can feel the history all around us like a heavy air in this place."

After spending the afternoon exploring the village, we decided to have tea at the Welcome to Town Inn.

"This is medieval," I said, looking around the ancient room. "This place must be haunted," I said to the waitress who had just arrived at our table.

"It is haunted," she said, and proceeded to tell us about the Inn's invisible guest. "The ghost is quiet and harmless," she said, "and sometimes if you look in one of the front rooms you may see a coachman dressed in Regency style sitting quietly in a chair – and then he vanishes!"

"Have you ever seen it?" I asked.

"Yes once," the waitress replied. "He looked so real that I went to bring him a menu, and he vanished before my very eyes." At her words, Ffion looked around the room and then back at me. "He won't bother you," the waitress said, and she took our order.

"Ghosts are common around the Gower," I reminded Ffion, having seen several of them myself.

We enjoyed a nice supper at the inn, and then headed back to our B & B for the night.

Ffion had packed everything we needed as usual, including some bubble bath and candles, and of course our favourite blackberry wine.

"Darling you're the best! Let's have a nice bath."

Ffion ran the bath, while I poured us a glass of wine. "Bubble baths are so relaxing," she said, as she laid back against me and sipped her wine. And I pulled my fingers through her long auburn curls, and gently whispered in her ear. As we lay and relaxed and melted together, I became more aware of the deep love that I felt for her. Ffion lives in my heart now, and I could not even entertain the thought of ever being without her. She was already a wonderful wife and mother, and I am so blessed!

After our bath, I made a nice wood fire in what was our living room and bedroom all in one. The owners of the B & B had done a nice job on designing a luxurious room, and Ffion and I enjoyed lying in front of the fire and cuddling and talking until late.

On Saturday morning we went into the breakfast dining area at 9:00 am, and there was one other couple there who were staying in another room in the house. It was a full British breakfast, served with tea or coffee, and a nice fruit salad to finish.

"That was enough food to keep us going for most of the day," I said to Ffion, as we packed a few things into the car for the day.

We decided to visit another wonderful piece of local history here in Llanrhidian, the old Nether Mill. From the Welcome to Town Pub where we dined last evening, the road drops down towards the mill, and we parked the car close to the entrance of the mill.

At the time I am writing this, the mill is no longer open, and the great millstones lean against the wall, but the inscription on the slate plaque still records with pride. [Built in the year 1803 at the Sole Expense of Wm. M. Evans, Gent. John Beynon, Evan Jenkin (Masons) William Edward, George Evans (Carpenters)].

It is over **200** years since the old mill was built by the men whose names are on the slate, and the walls still looked solid and beautiful.

"What a building," Ffion proclaimed, "and it's in such good condition for being over **200** years old!" There was also a mill pond, and when Ffion and I went to investigate, we saw a flock of the whitest Aylesbury Ducks.

"Look at them," I said, "they have probably been here for many generations." Ffion was impressed by the garden of the farmhouse next door, it was full of bright flowers, and while Ffion walked down the road, I knocked on the door of the farmhouse to see if I could buy some flowers. An elderly woman answered the door and seemed most amused that I would ask to buy flowers. Come with me, she said, with a sparkle in her eyes, and she cut a beautiful bunch of wildflowers from her garden. Thank you I said, they are for a special lady. I offered her a five-pound note for the flowers, but she wouldn't take any money.

"If I know they will make someone smile, that is payment enough," she said. What a lovely lady, I thought, as I raced down the road to catch Ffion.

"Flowers! Oh, how lovely! Where did you get them Kings? We didn't see any flowers at the shop."

"They are from the farmhouse," I said, and I kissed my lady upon her lips.

From the farmhouse we walked down to the salt marshes that stretched to the horizon. And we could hear in the distance the lost piping calls of the marsh birds in the mist. What a lonely place we marveled, and it had a mysterious beauty that drew us to come and find its secrets.

"Maybe it is the remoteness of the marsh," Ffion pondered, "and the silent stillness."

"And the mysterious shrouding mists, and the lonely streams and salt pools," I added. And we vowed to walk out and explore them. And that is what we did on Sunday, we walked out for miles, onto the still and mysterious salt marsh. And both Ffion and I agreed, we had never walked such a lonely place as Llanrhidian Marsh. It is a place that seems to shine an invisible searchlight into one's heart and innermost being. For out on the marsh there is a stillness and silence, that seems to illuminate the soul to an awareness of whether it is at peace, or at strife with the world or itself. As Ffion and I held hands and walked for miles upon the marsh, we spoke not through words, but through touch in the loud silence, and we stopped and hugged and kissed every so often. We could both feel one another's hearts holding on to the awareness of our connection, as if in some mysterious way our lives depended on the connection we experienced together in this most lonely place. Somehow, we knew how much our souls needed one other. Oh, I love you Kings! My soul aches for you! Oh, I love you too my darling Ffion!

Late in the evening we headed home to Pennard.

Chapter Two

September's Tears

It was now late September, and the summer sun contin-ued to shine upon us, at least for a little while longer. I was working in the front garden with Samantha and Melody, who were helping me to mow the lawn and pull some weeds from the flower beds as we prepared for the autumn season.

"How much longer will we have to cut the grass?" the girls complained.

"Until the weather gets colder," I replied. "The grass will keep growing as long as the weather stays warm. How about you two take a break?" I said. "I sure appreciate you help-ing me," and I gave the girls some money to buy some snacks across the road at Pennard Stores.

"I am too tired to go across the road," Sam said, as she lay back in one of the garden chairs.

"I will go across to the shop," Melody said, and Sam told her what she wanted for a snack.

I sat in a chair next to Sam, and we waited for Melody to come back. As we were waiting, Sam commented on the beautiful pink and white rose bush at the bottom of the garden, and said they were the most beautiful roses she had ever seen.

"Your great grandma and grandpa planted that rose bush" I said, "and it's always been my favourite too."

"I love the combination of the pink and white together on the rose petals. How about we pick some for Ffion?" she said.

"That would be a lovely surprise," I said. "She has been busy most of the day cleaning the house. Here are some clippers, why don't you go and cut about 3 or 4 stems and you can take them into the house for her."

Sam went over to cut the roses while I lay back and relaxed in my chair. Suddenly I heard her call.

"Dad, I've found something! And it has got your name on it."

"What is it?" I shouted back.

"It is an old envelope, and it looks like it's been lying under the rose bush for a long time."

"Bring it here," I said, sitting up in my chair. Melody had also arrived back from the store with our treats.

"What's going on?" she asked. As Samantha showed her what she had found, Melody said, "aren't you going to open it, Dad? It's got your name on it."

"Okay give it to me, and I'll read what's inside."

As Samantha handed me the envelope, I could see that it still had my name faintly visible on the front, and it was creased and weathered. Obviously it had been outside for some time.

As I held the envelope in my hand, a great sense of its significance came over me, and I felt an uneasiness in my spirit.

"Open it Dad, open it," both Samantha and Melody called out together.

I opened the envelope and began to read, and it was from Gay! It was dated the day she had disappeared. As I read the letter I began to sob, and Melody, reading the expression on my face wept in tune with my sobs as her mother spoke. Samantha now cried too, as she listened to Gays words.

⤳

'My darling husband Kingsley, and my wonderful daughters Melody and Samantha, yes Samantha, I love you as my own. I must go away for a while, as I have gained knowledge of my father, and three sisters that are my siblings. I don't have time to explain everything to you now, as my family needs me. They are in danger, and I must go to them. And please Mum, take care of my loving husband and my girls, I shall return as soon as I can.'

As I finished reading, Ffion came out of the house, and saw us all weeping.

"What is it?" she said. "What on earth is the matter with you all?" In my grief I dropped the letter, as waves of sadness crashed over my soul, and I thought I would surely drown!

Ffion picked up the letter and read it, and she also wept, and then held me in her arms. And I think if it wasn't for the love of Ffion and my girls, I would have died!

"What are we going to do?" Melody asked, still crying. Maybe my mum is still alive!"

"We must go to the police," Ffion said, "and give them the letter."

⤳

And that is what we did. We all went back into the house and dried our eyes, and then we went down to the police station in Park Mill.

As we pulled up to the police station, I just sat in the car.

"I can not go through this again," I cried. "I just can't do it!"

"Don't worry Dad," Samantha said, "we are all coming with you. We are with you all the way!"

"Alright," I said, calming a little. "Let's go inside." Samantha and Melody each took one of my arms and Ffion walked in front of us carrying the envelope and opened the police station door.

As we all sat down in the waiting area, Ffion took my hand and gave me a supportive smile.

"Everything is going to be alright," she said, as we waited for the clerk to call us up to the window.

"What can I help you with Sir?" she asked.

"My daughter found this letter which was written by my wife who disappeared some years ago."

The clerk looked briefly at the letter, and then called a man whose badge read, Sgt. Bradley Evans. I recognized him as being present at one of my, shall we say interviews, no, interrogations, when Gay first went missing!

Sgt. Evans did not recognize me until we sat down in the same little interview room where I had felt so intimidated when the police first started their inquiries. And today those sad and heartbreaking memories returned. I wanted to get up and run! And then I remembered Samantha's words to me. 'Don't worry Dad, everything will be alright.' I hope so sweetie, I am just crushed inside!

Just a few hours ago Gay was still gone from our lives, a fading memory that was part of my past, and I had built a whole new life with Ffion and the girls. We were a family again now, and we had finally managed to leave the tragedy of Gay's disappearance behind us. And now she was back, back from the dead, and I could feel my heart breaking again! And I heard Ffion's voice speaking in my heart. 'This letter doesn't change anything, Kings, we are still a family, and nothing is going to change that.' And I tried to think positive thoughts.

Sgt. Evans read the letter from where he was sitting on the other side of the table, and then he asked me what I thought of the contents of the letter.

I didn't say anything at first, what could I say? Then I said, "it doesn't make sense to me, Gay has gone looking for her long lost father and sisters. We know nothing about her father, not even if he's alive or dead. And as far as we know, she doesn't have any other siblings, only her sister Pearl."

"No, it doesn't make sense Mr. Hill, it's rather confusing, and your missing spouse, or ex spouse now isn't it, sounds confused herself. I don't think this letter is going to have much influence upon our investigation, Mr. Hill. It has been over 3 years, almost 4 since she went missing, and we have not found any clues as to where she might have gone, or whether she was a victim of foul play."

"You are going to investigate where her father might be, aren't you?" I asked.

"Mr. Hill, to be perfectly honest, and I apologize for being so blunt. But it would seem to me that if your ex -wife wanted to be found, you would have heard from her by now."

"I don't think that's a very nice thing for you to say," I replied angrily. "Gay would never have just left us and not come back, unless something had happened."

"This whole situation is not very nice, Mr. Hill, and we can appreciate that, and we will pass the letter on to our investigating team, but I don't think this letter is going to shed any more light on our investigation. As far as we are concerned Gay is still a missing person, and hard as it is to hear, Mr. Hill, if she is still alive, it might just be her choice not to come back."

"No, not Gay, she would not do something like that! She said in her letter that she would come home as soon as she could!"

"She wrote this letter almost 4 years ago, Mr. Hill."

"Alright, I get the message, Sgt. Evans, but I just have one more question."

"Ok Mr. Hill, what is it, because I have an interview to do in a few minutes."

"Have you spoken to Gay's biological mother recently, her name is Armes Saren."

"Only early on in our investigation, Mr. Hill."

"Well, it might be a good idea to talk to her again, because she might know something!"

"Thank you for the advice, Mr. Hill, but we are quite capable of conducting our own investigation, and if we find anything, we will be in touch. As I said, I will hand in the letter to our investigating team."

"Thank you, Sgt. Evans," I said, feeling deflated.

"Thank you for coming in, Mr. Hill, bye for now."

"What did he say?" both Ffion and Samantha wanted to know, as I reappeared into the waiting room.

"I will tell you in a minute," I replied. "Let's get out of here."

As we left the police station, Ffion took my hand and asked again how things went.

"Where is Melody?" I asked. "Wasn't she with you two?"

"Yes Dad," Samantha replied, "she is still very upset and went back to sit in the car."

"It brought everything back," I said. "Sitting in that interview room was sad and depressing. The Sgt. doesn't think that the letter will change anything, but they will add it to Gay's file and get the original investigating team to have a look at it. Do you know what else that Sgt. said to me? He said that if Gay wanted to come back to us, we would have heard something by now! What an insensitive bloke!"

"Of course, she would come back," Ffion and Samantha both said, trying to encourage me. And as we got closer to the car, I dreaded telling Melody that her mother's letter didn't change anything, and the police were no closer to finding Gay. And I thought about all the weeks and months she had cried herself to sleep, because her mother never came back, or even told us where she was. I guess Gay had thought we would find her letter and wait for her to come back. Well, we did wait. We have waited too long!

As I reached the car, Melody opened the door and ran into my arms crying.

"It's alright," I told her, hugging her as tightly as I could. "Everything is going to be alright. Somehow it is, I know that, now stop crying my Princess," and she did. But in my heart, I cursed Gay for leaving us, and now we were going through the pain all over again!

❧

For at least a month, we all grieved as a family. Gay's letter had brought more questions than answers, but slowly our lives began to return to normal. Christmas came and went, and once we were into the New Year, we managed to put it behind us and began to enjoy life again.

❧

In early February, something wonderful happened in Melody's life, and we all celebrated the special event with her.

One evening when she got home from school, she and I went for a walk down on Fox Hole Beach. The tide was all the way out, which allowed us to walk past the rocks and onto the small area of sand that we often swam over in the summer. We talked a lot about how she was doing, and what her plans were for the following weekend.

"I don't know Dad. I just wish I had a best friend! I have some nice friends that I like at school, and Samantha is the most wonderful sister in the world, and there is Julie next door, but I don't really have a best friend who is my own age or not part of my family, Dad. All my friends at school have a best friend their own age." I didn't say much, just listened, but when we arrived home, Ffion said that someone had called for Melody. It was a girl named Destiny. She was the same age as Melody, and she had found the message that Melody had put in a bottle years before.

"Really Mum, really?" she shouted excitedly!

"Yes," Ffion replied. "She found your message and she left me her phone number so that you can call her."

"Wow Dad, did you hear that? She found my message in a bottle and I am going to call her right now!" Samantha came down from her room, and we all eavesdropped outside the living room door while Melody made her phone call.

It turned out that Destiny had found the bottle on the beach close to where she lived in Cefn Sidan, and she wanted to come and meet Melody the following weekend.

"Ask Destiny to bring the bottle with her so that we can see how long it was at sea," I said to Melody before she hung up the phone.

"Dad, Dad," she shouted! "God answered our prayers by making someone find my bottle! Dad, were you listening to my phone call?"

"Yes, of course I was!" Melody came running after me and chased me around the living room.

"Don't listen to my phone calls," she laughed jumping on my back.

"Ok I won't," I replied, "but this one was too exciting to miss. So, tell me what happened?"

"Ok everyone, listen!" Ffion and Samantha joined me on the settee, as we listened to what Melody had to say.

"A girl named Destiny found my message in a bottle, and she is the same age as me, and her mum is going to drive her out to meet me on Saturday. And maybe, who knows, we might become best friends!"

"Wow! Melody, that is great!" we all said, "and we will look forward to meeting her on Saturday."

"And yes Dad," Melody continued, "I did ask her to bring the bottle so that we can check it out."

೧

The weekend couldn't come fast enough for Melody, but soon it was Saturday morning. At 10am the doorbell rang, and it was Destiny and her mum.

"Come in," we said, and Ffion sat down with Ivy, Destiny's mum, while the girls and I checked out the bottle.

"Look," I said, holding the bottle in my hands and turning it over. "There are barnacles on both sides of the bottle, and you can see there are scrapes marks on the bottle where the tide washed it against the rocks. And look, some of the barnacles have been knocked off the neck of the bottle. Does anyone know how to read this bottle as to how long they think it has been at sea?"

Destiny looked quite puzzled at my question, but Melody quickly replied. "I think I know how to read it, Dad."

"Ok, go ahead." I said.

"Firstly, there are lots of barnacles on the bottle, which means it has been traveling at sea for some time."

"Yes, good start to our reading, Melody," I said. "And we have the added knowledge of knowing the time that we set it adrift in the sea." Melody and Samantha calculated the dates, so we were able to estimate approximately how long the bottle had been on its travels.

"It could have been stranded for a while on a beach or on the rocks," Melody said, "because there are scrape marks on the bottle and barnacles have been rubbed off."

"Good observation," I affirmed. "We do not know how long the bottle might have been stranded before it reached Destiny on Cefn Sidan Beach."

"I am just glad I found it," Destiny said, and the girls went to hang out in Melony's room while Ffion, and Samantha and I, visited with Ivy. Ivy shared with us that Destiny too was hoping to make a best friend in Melody.

"I think it was all meant to be!" Ffion exclaimed, as we all enjoyed a nice visit until late afternoon. And before Ivy and Destiny left for home, the girls arranged to spend time together next Sunday.

"We will drive Melody out to your place, Destiny," Ffion said.

Over the next few months Melody and Destiny did become best friends! And if Destiny wasn't at our home for the weekend, then Melody was at Destiny's place. It was so nice to see, and such an answer to our prayers to have Melody's need for a best friend provided for. We did not know it at the time, but Destiny was to become a vital support for Melody and our whole family in the months that followed.

Two months after meeting Destiny, Melody started having nightmares about her mother, Gay. Often, she would wake up crying in the night, having had vivid pictures within her mind and heart of Gay being trapped in another dimension and not being able to find her way back! Ffion and I found it very disturbing, especially after we had found Gay's letter not so long ago.

"The past keeps coming back to haunt us," I said. "Just when I think the influences of Gay's disappearance are behind us, they come back!"

We tried sleeping pills, and booked Melody for some counselling, but her dreams continued. I also began to have dreams of Gay trying to get back to us. And what was very unusual, was that Melody and I would have the very same dreams, sometimes on the same nights. I tried to keep my dreams a secret. I didn't want to cause Ffion any more stress in what was becoming an insecurity in herself, about Gay somehow making her way back to our lives, and Ffion losing me to her. 'They are only dreams,' I reassured her, but deep in my heart they were as real as anything! And I believed that the combination of Melody's and my dreams were a message to us, that somehow Gay was not only still alive, but was trapped somewhere, and trying to get back to us. Helen had also become depressed shortly after we had found Gay's letter, and she became frustrated with the police who appeared to be doing nothing to further investigate the disappearance of her daughter. I had tried to support Helen by driving up to Cardiff and meeting her at the market for tea and conversation just like old times. It was not the fact that Gay was still missing that was most hard for Helen to deal with, it was what Gay had said in her letter, about going to help her father and three siblings!

"Siblings?!" Helen would often say to me, "I can't get my head around Gay having three other birth sisters, I thought Pearl was her only other sister. And as for her father, no one knows where he even is, whether he is alive or dead. Unless Armes has been hiding something from us."

Armes was Gay's biological mother who lived in a Celtic Commune and gave away Gay to Helen and her husband John who were friends of Armes and more capable of looking after a young child.

I went to visit Dad a few times, to get his counsel on Melody's and my dreams, and he too, thought that Melody and I were receiving messages, that Gay was trying to return to us. I did not share with Ffion or Helen what Dad had said, and I began to feel very isolated in trying to deal with my dreams and the feelings and emotions that they evoked. Finally, I went and talked with Samantha, and I wished I had done this sooner. She was a wonderful support, and was always willing to listen, without pressing any opinion on how I should deal with things.

Destiny was an amazing help with Melody, which took a lot of the stress off Ffion and I. Melody could talk to Destiny about anything, and I do believe that she was sent into our lives for this very reason. Another event which occurred in Melody and Destiny's lives, was they both met their first boyfriends around the same time, and this was an exciting time for them, despite Melody's continuing dreams. Ffion also became more involved in Melody's 'boyfriend and girlfriend adventures', and was enjoying the motherhood she had always wanted, rather than focusing on her own insecurities around our dreams of Gay. Ffion and Ivy were also becoming good friends, and often spent time together.

Slowly but surely, the dreams went away. First Melody's and then mine, and things returned to normal in our home, as we felt happy and healthy again, and were excited about the future. Samantha was doing wonderfully well at university, and my boys were going to make another trip out to Wales to come and visit us soon.

Dad, and Ffion and I continued our translation of Taliath's diary, and it was amazing what we were learning about this woman and her family's lives, and the culture around the time of the Welsh Celtic Clans. I had found the diary when I was 12 years old on the grounds of Pennard castle and we had found it later to be written around the time of 970 AD. After Gay's disappearance, I had lost interest in translating it. Now, with Dad's and Ffion's encouragement, and us working together on the translating, I was determined for us to finish the whole diary and tell Taliath's story to the world, just like Dad had entrusted me to do, when he had given me the diary as a wedding present when Gay and I had gotten married. I also looked forward to finding more artifacts with Dad and Fion when we went metal detecting.

Chapter Three

Voices From the Past

Almost five years has passed since Gay had galloped out of our lives, and our home in my grandparent's house in Pennard continues to be such a blessing. Ffion and my marriage is rich and full, and I could not remember a time when I was more happy and fulfilled. The past had gone again, and the future looked bright.

It was a Saturday afternoon in early spring, and the girls had gone into Swansea to do some shopping. I was alone in the house when the phone rang.

"Hello, is this Kingsley?" a voice said, that seemed both strange and familiar.

"Yes, it is," I replied. "Whom am I speaking with?"

"It is Armes," she said, "from the commune in Cardiganshire."

"Armes!" I repeated involuntarily in shock. What could she want after all this time?

"I have Gay's Priestess robe, and her certificate of studies, and I was wondering if you wanted them for a keepsake?"

"Why have you phoned me now after all this time?" I asked.

"Oh, no reason," she stuttered. "I just thought one of you might like them. She worked so hard to achieve them. Or if you don't want them, maybe Helen would like them."

"No," I said, almost shouting, and I felt the hurt in my heart. "I am sure that Helen won't want them. We have all moved on in our lives and have put the past behind us."

There was a pause and then Armes continued. "How is Melody?"

"She is doing well," I said, my tone of disapproval of her calling still present in my voice. Then I said something that I might later regret.

"Look Armes, thank you for calling, but I would like you not to call our home again. I will come out to the commune to pick up Gay's stuff, and after that I see no need for you to contact my family or I again."

For a minute there was silence. And then she said, "Yes, I understand, Kingsley, but I am Gay's birth mother you know, and Melody is still my granddaughter."

"Alright," I said. "I don't mean to be harsh, but my family and I have rebuilt our lives, and it has been difficult. I will come over to the commune next Saturday and pick up Gay's things."

"Thank you," Armes said, and I put the phone down. I almost called her back immediately, as I realized what I had done. I had arranged to go to the commune and get Gay's robe and certificate. That is the last thing that Helen and Melody need, another reminder of Gay. I know what I can do, I pondered. I will go and pick up Gay's things, and then I will bury them at Gay's stone in the church yard. That way Helen and Melody won't have to see them, and nobody will be the wiser.

Interestingly enough, next Saturday was Gay's and my wedding anniversary. I'd only remembered because Melody had made a calendar at school and Ffion had put it up on the fridge. Gay and my wedding anniversary wasn't a sad day for me anymore, along with her birthday and the Christmas holidays. And as I stared at the date on Melody's calendar, it was just another day.

Helen and the girls were going to make their monthly trip to Bristol to go and visit their Aunt Pearl and do some shopping. Ffion would be going too. As always, I had been invited to go, but I enjoyed this time to be alone and to get some things done around the house. I did not need an excuse to stay home, besides, I had somewhere else to go.

Saturday morning arrived, and the girls headed off to Bristol.

"Bye, dad, see you on Sunday night."

"Bye my sweethearts, have a nice time and say hello to Aunt Pearl. Oh, and don't buy too many clothes."

"We will," they teased.

Ffion called out from the car window, "if you need me, I'll be in the shoe shop, trying on some nice sexy heels!"

I laughed and shouted, "I hope so, and don't come home without some!"

⌒

I packed the car with my hiking gear and headed off to the commune. I may as well do some exploring, I thought, if I am going all the way to Cardiganshire.

I parked the car as I had done before, outside one of the fields that led to the commune. This time there was no greeter at the fence to meet me, so I climbed over the stye and started walking towards the main commune buildings in the distance. I wondered how I might be greeted today, or would I be able to walk all the way to the buildings without being detected?

As I crossed the fields, I began to be haunted by the memories of the dreams that Melody and I had had about Gay. There was one theme that had characterized both our dreams. Gay was stuck somewhere against her will and was trying to come back to us.

Why were these dreams oppressing me again now? Was it because I was back at the commune where Gay had been so influenced by the Celtic culture and ways of life? Or was she here somewhere hiding, having started a new life?

I knew that coming back here might be against my better judgment. But here I am, having felt deep in my heart that for some reason I had to come. Was picking up Gay's belongings a final closure for me? I had not calculated the feelings and emotions that were now crashing over my soul like a raging sea!

When you know that someone has passed you can let them go, but not when a loved one remains missing! Hope always lives inside the heart and goes on searching unconsciously, even when you are living in the midst of a new life that you have built. It still searches out the faces in the crowd and follows people in the park, until you get close enough to know it isn't her. Sometimes a face on a passing bus or train catches your eye and beats your heart faster, even if only to remind you that Hope never dies!

I had thought I had finally stopped searching for Gay. But today as I walked, my eyes scanned the fields and lonely hills for the woman I had loved and lost twice.

'Come on, pull yourself together man!' I told myself, as I approached the main building of the commune.

Now I could see people in their Celtic dress, and a woman was coming towards me.

"Can I help you sir? Oh, it is you Kingsley!"

"Yes, Heulyn," I replied, feeling a strange sort of peace. Heulyn had been Gay and my body servant when we had visited the commune together and had had our first Celtic bath. And I knew that she was kind. This gave me comfort as I asked her to take me to Armes.

"It's nice to see you again Kingsley," she smiled, "and if you follow me, I will take you to Armes." As I followed behind this beautiful and graceful woman, I wondered again as I had done the first time I'd met her, why a woman like this would dedicate herself to living as a Celt and be a humble body servant to others? Maybe this is a part of what makes her so appealing, along with her obvious gentleness and kindness…

We arrived at Armes' living quarters, and Heulyn rang the bell on the large wooden door. This time Armes answered the door herself, not the two servant women as before.

"Glad you could come, Kingsley, please come inside." Heulyn bowed goodbye, and I followed Armes into the waiting area and sat in one of the wicker chairs. Armes sat in the other and waited for me to talk.

"I have come for Gay's things," I said, "and to also show you this." I had brought Gay's letter that we had found in the garden, and I handed it to Armes to read.

She read it over and over, at least three times, and then she sat in silence, contemplating and taking hold of her emotions. 'Aren't you going to say something, woman?' I said inside my head.

Finally, she spoke.

"How is Gay?" she asked.

"What do you mean, how is Gay!" I snapped. "Surely you must know!"

"Know what?" she replied.

"Gay has been missing for 5 years."

"Missing?!"

"Yes, missing!"

"I knew nothing about this, and why wasn't I told?" she exclaimed.

"I was sure the police would have contacted you," I replied, seeing that Armes was sincere as tears filled her eyes.

"The police did come and ask me some questions, and I knew she was going to write you a letter and tell you she was going to look for her father, but I assumed she had just been gone for a short while and had come back to you."

"What do you mean you assumed she had come back? She never came back! And we didn't find her letter until recently. It had been lost in the garden this whole time."

"No, I had no idea, Kingsley!"

"You had no idea?" I echoed. "Surely you wondered why she hadn't come to see you anymore at the commune."

"No, I knew nothing about Gay disappearing," Armes retorted, rubbing her eyes. "I just thought that she didn't want me in her life anymore after we had had a discussion as to why I gave her up for adoption to Helen and her husband John."

"No," I replied, "Gay wanted to develop a relationship with you, that was the reason she took the Bard training with you at the commune, so that she could get to know you as her birthmother."

"Can you excuse me for a minute?" Armes said, and she disappeared behind the thick purple curtain. From where I continued to sit in the wicker chair, I could hear her crying and sobbing from the other side of the curtain.

Suddenly the curtains pulled open and Armes re-emerged. Only this was not the 'in control and unflustered woman' that I remembered as the Head Figure of the Celtic Commune. This was a woman in pain and grief, her sorrowing emotions spilling from her usual calm repose. And a part of me that felt compassion wanted to reach out and comfort her. But wait, I thought, as I pulled my arm back, this woman was the person who had influenced my Gay to be away from me and my family, to neglect us by spending time here at the commune, when she should have been a wife and mother at home.

But eventually, my compassion won over, and I put my arms around Armes and comforted her. She wept in my arms for a long time, and then said she had something important to tell me. What could it be I thought? There was nothing more to say. She can give me Gay's things, and I can be on my way.

"What is it?" I said. "Have you got Gay's robe and her certificate for me?"

"Yes," Armes replied, "but please listen to what I have to

say. I believe that Gay is alive, and I know where she is if she has gone to find her father and sisters."

"And where is he?" I retorted! "Where did he run off to then, abandoning her when she was a baby? Did he run off to London or Manchester, or did he go abroad?"

"No, it's not like that, Kingsley. Gay has traveled to a different time and place."

"She what! Did I hear that right, you crazy woman? Did you say Gay has gone to a different time and place?"

"Yes, I did," she replied, in a hesitant voice for fear of further condemnation.

"Then you are crazier than I thought! Give me Gay's belongings and I will be on my way! No, on second thought, keep your stupid robe and certificate, I don't want any part or memory of you. I came here in good faith to pick up some things that belong to Gay, and maybe receive some solace or closure, and you tell me an outrageous story about Gay!"

"Yes, that is where she is Kingsley, just like she said in her letter, she has gone to find her father and siblings."

"Yes, I thought you might use that letter to support your crazy ideas! I wish I had never allowed Gay to come and meet you. You have been a bad influence on her life and caused us a lot of pain!" And I stood up to leave.

"One other thing before you leave Kingsley, are you and Melody still having the dreams?" Armes' words stopped me in my tracks. How could she know about our dreams?

"What dreams?" I said, trying to test her.

"The dreams of Gay being stuck in a place and not being able to get back to you." Whether I liked it or not, Armes had my full attention. "I know all about the dreams," she continued.

"How can you know?" I said angrily.

"Because I have had them too! I did not realize what they meant until now. The dreams are a message that Gay is trying to get back to us. I know that this is hard for you to understand, but will you just let me finish? Let me tell you what I believe has happened to Gay."

"Alright," I said, "I will listen, but as far as I am concerned you've lost your mind."

For a few moments she sat in silence, then continued.

"In the place where Gay's father and I come from, we were being invaded by the 'warriors that came from the sea'. They arrived on our shores in long boats with sails, killing our men, and raping our women, and destroying and burning our villages. We fought fierce and hard against them, but their weapons of war were far superior to ours. I had already given birth to three children and was pregnant with Gay when they started invading our clan lands."

"What happened then," I mumbled, pretending not to be interested. But the word 'Vikings' was resounding in my heart! I had found one of their swords and helmets with my father. But they were a people of the past, weren't they? How could Armes have lived at the time of the Vikings, that would make her over twelve hundred years old. If anyone has an open mind, I do, but this sounded ludicrous! "Come on," I said impatiently, "what happened next?" I wished Dad was here to hear this!

"The village and all the neighboring clans were in turmoil and confusion as the sea warriors plundered through our lands. My husband escaped our village with me, and sent me, pregnant with Taliath, through the portal."

I pondered for a few seconds, remembering that Taliath was Gay's birth name and it was Helen that had named her Gay.

"The portal," I echoed, "what portal?"

"The portal that leads to Pennard Castle from where we lived."

Come on, drink up, I thought! What have you been putting in your wine Armes? But she had been right about the dreams, so I continued to listen.

"I don't know if I believe you," I said. "And if you did come through this portal or what ever it is, and Gay was not yet born, how did she know about her father and sisters left on the other side? Gay was only a toddler when Helen and John adopted her."

"I told her that she had a father and sisters who loved her as soon as she was born," Armes answered. "And besides, us Celts have memory within our cells, and a knowledge of these things."

"I have heard enough," I said, starting to walk away.

"Please take these with you," Armes said, handing me Gay's robe and her bard certificate to take home. "Maybe Helen would like them if you don't want them. Thank you for listening," she called out to me, " it is up to you what you do with what I have told you. Please give my love to Helen and Melody and tell them I am so sorry about Gay."

At her words I stormed back and said, "please do not contact me or my family again!"

After walking back across the fields to my car, I was in no mood for a hike, so I headed home towards Pennard. As I drove, I pondered over what Armes had said, and most of it was surely nonsense! But I was haunted by what she knew of the dreams Melody and I had had. The fact that she had dreamed the same thing herself was disturbing to me. I decided to call Dad when I got home. God knows I needed someone to talk to. I had found it hard to share with Ffion about my dreams. I did not want to complicate our relationship anymore than it had been already by finding Gay's letter. And now there was the obvious complication of me having gone to see Armes. It's not that Ffion wouldn't give me her support in the situation, but I had just seen the strain and stress she went through when we found the letter, and then she had to go through the loss and grieving again with Melody and Samantha. Maybe I should lean on her for support. Sometimes we do more damage by trying to protect someone's heart, rather than sharing the cold hard truth of a situation. Oh well, I was in no mood to be thinking straight anyway. I would just call Dad when I got home.

I stopped in at Pennard Stores to buy a Cornish pasty for tea, and then called Dad.

∽

After explaining my experience with Armes, he said what I thought he would.

"Don't take anything seriously, other than the dreams. Obviously, you and Melody had the same dream for a reason. I don't understand what that reason is, Kings, but I do believe the dreams are messages, especially as you have all had the same dream. Try not to worry about things, but just be watchful whether you or Melody have any more dreams about Gay.

Hopefully, that is all in the past now and will soon become a distant memory. But if you have any more experiences or concerns you need to talk about, you know that I am here for you."

"Thanks Dad. I just needed someone to talk to, and as always you were there for me."

"You're welcome, Kings, that is what you're old man is here for. And of course, to go metal detecting with."

"Of course," I echoed with a smile.

After talking to Dad on the phone and finishing my pasty, I decided to have an early night. All the driving I had been doing recently was catching up with me.

I woke up Sunday morning and stared at the clock. It was 9 am already, but the girls would not be home from Bristol till at least 6:00 in the evening.

I decided that I would take Gay's robe and certificate and bury them at her stone in the churchyard as I had planned. I would also pick up some flowers to put on my old friend Maggie's grave that was nearby. After breakfast I headed off to Port Eynon Church. I stopped in the village at Maggie's old shop. Her daughter who still ran the general store remembered me from the last time I had dropped in.

"Hello Kingsley, how are you? I was so sorry to hear about your wife Gay. But I also wanted to say congratulations on your marriage to Ffion Riverstone, now Mrs. Hill of course. She is a lovely lady."

"Thank you," I replied, "she certainly is. And how do you know Ffion?" I asked. "Oh, she is my daughter's dance instructor in Swansea, and my daughter loves going to Ffion's classes."

"Yes, she is a wonderful dance instructor," I said proudly.

"Now, let me think, Kingsley. Irises for Gay, and Roses for Maggie, right?"

"That's right," I said, "you remember."

"That's four pounds for the Irises, and the Roses for mum are free."

"Thank you," I said, and closed the door. It only seemed like yesterday that Gay and I took roses to Maggie's grave together, and I gave Gay Irises to celebrate our love. How times change. When Gay and I used to walk hand in hand around Port Eynon village, we thought it would last forever! Maggie always said to make the most of every day, because even forever was not long enough! Oh Maggie, I miss you, where have the years gone?

I parked the car in the village and walked through the narrow lanes to the church. I visited Gay's stone first, and I put the Irises in the glass vase I had bought on our last anniversary.

"Well, my love, here I am again. It has been almost five years now since you've been gone. I certainly haven't forgotten you, neither has Melody and Helen. They send their love and miss you everyday. I don't know if you are with Maggie and my mum up in Heaven. Or maybe you have gone riding somewhere on your horse Blaze. I went to see your birth mother, Armes, yesterday, and she told me that you were still alive somewhere and were trying to get back to us. And a while ago, Melody and I kept having the same dream, just like Armes. Oh, I wish I knew dear love. Anyway sweetheart, happy as I am in my life with Ffion, I will always love you, and happy anniversary." I then dug a hole in front of the stone and buried Gay's robe and certificate in a small wooden box that I had used to store some camping equipment in.

Feeling sad now, I took my roses over to Maggie's grave. For quite some time I stood and remembered how God had used Maggie in such a special way in my life. She had been a second mother to me, and I celebrated the fact that I had been able to share in her lovely selfless life. "Oh, Maggie, I love you, and I miss you so much. Whenever I was troubled in my life, you would always encourage me to go and pray to God, up on Great Thunder's Hill, remember? And do you know what I'm going to do today Maggie? I am going to pray and talk to God up on that same hill. I need to hear from him, Maggie. He always hears us, you told me so. I love you Maggie and give my mum a kiss up there for me."

After I had finished at the churchyard, I drove to Penmain, and walked out across the Burrows to the dunes, and down onto Three Cliffs Bay. There amongst the other hills was the one with a flat top, named after my stallion Great Thunder! It was the place where my stallion watched over his mare Thunder Spring and his foal Little Thunder who became Roaring Thunder as he got older. And it was also the place where he and I used to end each day. And today, Great Thunder's Hill would be my sanctuary, as I cried out my heart to God!

"Dear God, it has been a long time since I laid out my heart before you, too long, and I need your help. I don't know if Gay is alive or dead, or even why she left us. Melody and I, and even Armes, her mother, have had dreams that she is still alive somewhere, and is trying to get back to us. I do not know what to believe or what not to. Dear God, if Gay is still alive and needs my help, then please help me find her. You have helped me to find her before, remember? Or if she is safely with you in Heaven, please let me know, because I don't know what to do. Help me, oh God, and speak to me on our special hill."

As I was still praying, a gentle wind blew round about me, and I heard a quiet voice speaking. 'Remember back, there was a girl you met at Pennard Castle,' the voice said. 'The girl at Pennard Castle?' I echoed back. 'Yes, Kingsley, remember the girl at Pennard Castle that you met when you were a young boy.'

I stood up as I finished my prayers and started walking down the hill and back up the dunes to the Burrows and along the sandy path to my car. As I walked, I experienced a peace that I had not had for a long time. And the peace in knowing that God had heard my prayers, and that in his good time he would answer me.

As I drove along towards Pennard, I wondered what God's voice had meant by saying, 'remember the girl at Pennard Castle'. Suddenly I remembered a story that I had long forgotten!

⌒

I was ten years old when my mother took me to Pennard Castle, to play and run down the sand dune hills to the river below. My mother's best friend, Angela Jones came with us, along with her daughter, Paula, who was a year younger than me. And even though she was one of those strange species known by my friends and I as, 'a girl', we played well together.

Today Paula was a Princess, and I was a Knight! And our game was played within the talking walls of the Norman castle.

Paula would hide and wait in the one room that still had four walls standing. The castle had been destroyed by a great sandstorm late in the 12th or early 13th century we were told. And the old walls in their conversations with my soul, have never told me otherwise.

I would have my bow and arrow, and a spear that I sharpened with Paula's brother's pen knife, and armed like a knight, I searched around the walls of the castle, most often sensing that Paula the Princess was hiding in the old castle room. The doorway to the room is arch shaped, which meant that only a King or Queen, or a brave Knight of course, could enter!

We played for hours whether in the sunshine or showers, while our mothers sat in deckchairs with umbrellas and read their Harlequin romance novels. They read them, but Paula and I lived them! And our mothers never found out that Paula kissed me once when I saved her from the wicked Prince and his men. 'You saved me, King!' she said, and kissed me with her soft tender lips, which always tasted of her mother's lipstick which Paula carried in her Princess bag. And I wondered what other special girl secrets she kept in her bag.

"Come on King! Stop dreaming and count to a hundred and come and find me again. And if you don't close your eyes while you count to a hundred, then I won't kiss you!" she teased. So, I kept my eyes closed tight, and dreamed that I was a real Knight. And the walls of Pennard Castle, called out to me, and told me that I was!

Halfway through our game we had to stop and have lunch with our mothers. And then off we went back to play within the story telling walls of our castle.

"The castle is alive, King, and it hears us, doesn't it?"

"Yes, it does, Princess, I hear him calling for us to come and play."

"Do you think he is lonely without us, King?"

"Oh yes, very."

"Shall we pick flowers to put on his wall, King?"

"Yes, that will make him happy, but we must not pick the yellow flower that grows on his outside wall, because it is rare. Another knight told me. It only grows here and in one other place in all of the Gower Peninsula," I said.

"Does this mean if we pick it, King, we will make the castle sad?"

"Yes, it will."

"But its flower looks so bright and lovely, King, it is yellow like the sun. Can we maybe one day, just pick one?"

"Listen, Princess Paula, to what my father once told me. The sacred yellow flower only blooms once a year, usually in March or April, and it has magic powers! Some years the flower blooms in May, and if a person picks one of its flowers in May, then that person is given special powers that are called a 'second sight'."

"Second sight King, what does that mean?"

"It means a person can know and understand things that happened in the past and also what is going to happen in the future."

"Like a special wisdom, King?"

"Yes, that's right. But if a person picks one of its flowers in March or April, then the person is not given the plants special powers."

"Wow King, I wish we could pick one of the flowers, just one, so that we can know what happened in the days when Pennard Castle was young."

"Well, maybe one day we will pick just one of its flowers,

but not today, because it is only March, and we have to wait for a time when the plant blossoms in May."

I closed my eyes and counted, as we played another game, and I hoped none of my friends would find out, not even my mother, that I wanted another kiss from Paula Jones.

I walked around all the walls of the castle, and finally came to the castle room. "Coming ready or not," I said, and I went inside. To my surprise, Paula was sitting with another girl on the sand. Paula was enthralled by the story her new friend was telling her.

"This is Tally," Paula announced, with a reverent and protective tone in her voice. "She is my friend, King." And I sat in the sand and listened to this strange little girl, who told us a story about her life back in the time when Pennard Castle was young.

"There was a real Prince and Princess then," Tally said. "And the King's horseman wore the prince's colours of green, purple and white as they rode their horses into battle against the invaders. There was a village and a church," she said, pointing to the old ruin a short distance away from the castle. "Only one part of the wall remains of the church," she continued, "as the sands came and covered it."

Apart from speaking as if she lived in the time of the castle, what was most strange to me about that first meeting with Tally, was that she wore strange looking clothes. Clothes of long ago, Paula called them.

"Why do you wear such strange clothes?" Paula asked, as Tally finished telling us the story.

"They are not strange clothes," she protested! "You both are wearing strange clothes, not me!"

Just then my mother and Auntie Angela came into the castle room and said it was time to go. "And who is this girl sitting with you in those old -fashioned clothes?"

"I am not old-fashioned!" Tally shouted angrily at my aunt Angela. "Your clothes are stupid!"

How bold to speak to an adult like that, I thought, and inside I admired her courage. Paula sat there with her mouth open in amazement that someone her age would speak to her mother like that!

"Don't speak so rudely!" Aunty Angela spoke back. "And where do you live, and shouldn't you be at school?"

My mother spoke next and said, "what are you doing here on your own, and where are your mother and father?"

"They live in the castle," Tally replied, "and I am not alone!" She sounded so convincing that my mother and aunty Angela shouted out, "hello, hello, there is a young girl here all alone!"

We waited for what seemed like a long time, but nobody came.

"We can't just leave her, Joy," aunty Angela said to my mother.

"No, she will have to come home with us, and then we can phone the police to find her parents."

"Who are the police?" Tally asked.

"Have you run away from home?" my mother asked.

"No, I have not! This is my home in the castle, and my mother and father will be back soon to take me to the village."

"This castle is just a ruin now," Angela continued, "it's thousands of years old, you can't live here!"

"Tell us where you live," I said, entering the conversation, "and we will help you find your way home, won't we mum?"

"Yes, we have to get going, and we don't want to leave you here on your own."

"You just do not understand, do you! Again, I say, I am not on my own! This castle is my home!" she shouted. And she stood up and then started to run.

Paula and I quickly jumped to our feet and started to run after her.

"Wait, wait," we both yelled after her. "We are your friends, and only want you to get home safe." Paula stopped running now, as we had chased her through the castle grounds and half-way to the old church wall. I continued in pursuit, and shouted, "wait, please wait!" I could see that I was gaining on her now, so I ran all the faster, even though my legs were getting tired. Suddenly she stopped and turned around in my direction. Surprised that she had stopped running, I stopped too, and we stared at one another for a minute, and then she shouted something? It sounded like, "Chichester." Suddenly there was a shadow flying above me in the sky, and it looked like a hawk or a falcon.

"Come on Chichester," she called again. And the bird landed on her shoulder! And she turned around and started running again. Wow, I thought, she has a tame falcon! And I started running after her again.

She now reached the old church wall. I have caught her now, I thought, as I slowed to a walk, and then snuck up slowly to the wall. She must be hiding on the other side. Slowly I pushed my head around the wall, but she was nowhere to be seen! She was gone. The bird was sitting there on the ground, and I could see now that it was a falcon, and it had something in its beak. It was Tally's blue headband that I had seen her wearing in the castle room.

"Chichester," I shouted! "Where is Tally?" At my words, he dropped the headband and took to the air. "Chichester, where is she?" I shouted again. As I lifted my eyes up to the hills, I expected to see her still running. Where else could she be? She couldn't just vanish, could she?

I held her headband in my hand as the others arrived.

"Where did she go?" they all asked.

"I don't know," I answered, "she ran behind this wall, but when I got here, she was gone. And she had a falcon too, and it landed on her shoulders. I heard her call him Chichester."

"We saw the bird," mum said, "it flew right over our heads. But where is the girl, she couldn't have just vanished."

"She did mum. I looked around the wall where she stopped running and she was gone! But the falcon dropped this." And I lifted up Tally's headband for them to see.

"Can I have it?" Paula shouted.

"No, I want it," I said, "but you can look at it.". The headband evoked a sense of mystery within me, as I pictured the girl's flowing and tattered dress as she ran away. And the falcon that landed on her shoulder was obviously trusting and familiar with her.

"Did she really vanish King?" Paula asked again.

"Yes, she did…"

"Did she have special powers?"

"I think so," I replied, "otherwise she couldn't vanish into thin air, could she?"

"No," Paula answered in a quiet puzzled tone of voice.

⌒〜〇

When we got home my mother phoned Constable Jones, the village policeman, and told him of the runaway girl, but other than that Paula and I heard nothing more about it.

"Was she a ghost, King? Or a lost girl with old fashioned clothes?"

I looked at the headband in her hand and said, "I hope we see her again and we can find out."

We asked our mothers if they would take us to the castle again. "Maybe next week if you both behave, and stop asking all the time," aunt Angela said.

At 10 years old, I was old enough to go to the castle on my own, and I had done so many times. But recently I had become afraid of one of the wild horses that had chased me on the hills, and I'd stopped going on my own.

Next week arrived, and with the added excitement of a picnic, and a clear sky spring day, we headed off to Pennard Castle.

Mum and Angela sat in their deckchairs and read, while Paula and I ran off to play our game of "Find the Princess." Paula headed off while I counted, and I pretended not to peek. She went to hide in the castle room, which we renamed 'The Arch Room', after the shape of the doorway. But the game of finding the princess was becoming boring. And if it wasn't for the anticipation and excitement of being kissed and seeing what else Paula had in her handbag, I would have given up playing a long time ago. When I became a teenager, I called this fascination 'The Power of a Woman', and I think I have felt the same ever since. But back to the story.

Paula had told me that she had found her mothers new lipstick and it was blue. And she was going to kiss me with it! And I liked watching her close her eyes when she kissed me, and I think she thought I closed mine too. I did when she was watching. Well, I could not give up playing the game yet, could I, dear reader. Not with the promise of a kiss, and blue lipstick too, I had only been kissed with red before.

"Coming ready or not, and I hope you're not in the arch room, Paula!" I shouted, having walked around the whole of the castle grounds and pretending I didn't know where she was.

I always had fun walking around the castle, and imagining what life was like in the time of the Normans and Saxons, and to be a real Knight and rescue a Princess with the use of my sword. Isn't that every boy's dream?

No boy it is not! But as long as it is your dream and you are brave, you will one day become a real Knight! Yes Sir, it is my dream! Well done boy! Yes Sir, thank you!

Arriving at the entrance of the arch room, I peered inside to find Paula, and to my surprise, Tally, both sitting on the sand, just like last time.

"Shush!" Both girls whispered, holding their fingers up to their mouths. Tally made me promise that we would not tell our mothers that she was here.

"Swear on the name of the King, that you won't tell," Tally said. "No, don't swear on the name of the King," she continued, "he's my father. So, swear on Chichester's name. And if you forsake your word, it is your honor that has been disgraced and Chichester will peck your eyes out!"

As Tally spoke, she spoke like she had authority, and yet she was only a young girl no older than Paula. Some of the words she used, and expressions were different from Paula's and mine. Our basic language was the same, yet she spoke in 'sayings of old', as Paula called them.

"Where is Chichester?" I asked, looking up at the sky.

"Oh, he is around. He is probably hunting."

"Alright," I said, "I swear on the name of Chichester, that I won't tell anyone you are here. I don't want my eyes pecked out."

As I sat on the sand with the girls, I stared at Tally's clothes as they talked. She was wearing the same old-fashioned clothes as when we saw her the first time, and her dress looked dirty, like it hadn't been changed.

"What are you staring at?" Tally retorted. Her eyes caught me staring. "Haven't you seen a dress before?"

"Yes," I replied, "sorry." Maybe she only has one dress, I thought, remembering that I had brought her headband with me in my pocket. Maybe I can make amends for upsetting her, I thought. I will give her back her headband.

"You dropped this last week," I said, handing her the headband. When she saw it, her eyes grew big, and she looked startled like she wanted to get up and run. "Don't run away Tally," I said, fearing she would. "And where did you go when I was running after you last week? Didn't you hear me calling you?"

"I didn't hear anything," she said sternly, "and I didn't see you running after me."

"Well, I was. And where did you go? I looked everywhere for you. You don't run away from your friends."

"You were not my friends then," she replied, "and I was not running away from you, I was going to be late for my father. He is the King, you know. And besides, Chichester had taken to the air, and I needed to follow because he warned me of danger. When he takes to the air, and flies directly overhead, that is my que to follow because an enemy is near." What enemy, I thought? There was only Paula and I and our mothers, but I decided not to say anything back to Tally about it.

"Chichester has warned my father many times when the Boat Men have landed on the beach. Or when other enemies have set an ambush for my father's men."

"I have dreamed of becoming a knight, one day," I replied.

"That's right," Paula said, backing me up, "King is becoming a Knight!"

"You should talk to my father," Tally said, "he has many knights that fight for him." At her words I grew excited! Who was this girl that talked of knights and battles? She is not like anyone I have ever met. Maybe she is from another time. The time of the knights!

"Where do you live then?" I continued. "There is only the sea beyond the hills. And I picked up your headband from behind the old church wall when Chichester dropped it on the ground. I saw you run behind the wall, and when I got there, you had vanished."

"Can you stop talking about this," she said with tears in her eyes. Paula nudged me to stop asking questions, so I said I would only ask one more.

"Is it true that the rare yellow flower that grows on the castle wall is magic?"

"Yes, it has secret powers, but I am forbidden to tell. Do not ask me any more questions, I shall not answer them." Paula nudged me again, and I asked no more questions.

The three of us sat and talked for a long while, and we could talk about anything, except where Tally had disappeared to, and the secrets of the yellow plant on the castle wall.

Finally, we heard aunt Angela's voice calling out, "Paula, Kingsley, come and have your picnic!"

"Come with us," Paula asked.

"No, I do not think your mum will like me being there. But I will wait here in the room until you have finished your picnic, whatever that is."

Paula and I looked at each other, and I whispered, "she doesn't know what a picnic is."

"Okay," we said, and we left the room.

We soon finished our picnic as we wanted to get back to Tally.

"What are you both in such a hurry for?" my mother asked.

"Nothing mum, just playing hide and seek."

Tally was still in the room when we got back. I had been half expecting her to be gone. But not only was she still there, she had Chichester her falcon with her. I was nervous and excited.

"Wow! It's the falcon," Paula cried out, following me into the room.

"Chichester is not a falcon," Tally replied, "he is a Sparrow Hawk! You don't know your birds."

"He's beautiful," Paula continued, "can I hold him?"

"No, he will not let anyone hold him. Chichester must be free to fly and if you put your hands around his wings, he will bite you! Father has trained him to do this, otherwise people could catch him. But I will put him on your arm if you hold out your arm and keep very still. Do not make any sudden movement or he will take to the air."

"Alright," Paula said, slowly holding up her arm.

"Remember, no sudden movements," Tally said, as she gently lowered Chichester onto Paula's arm.

"Wow! He feels heavy, look at him, King!" she said excitedly. And I asked if I could stroke his feathers.

"You may," Tally said, "but you must always approach him from the front where he can see your hand. Rub his chest with one finger only, he likes that. But never try to touch him from behind or he will bite you. And he bites hard."

Nervously, I lifted my forefinger and started to rub his feathers.

"Look, his feathers are gold and brown," I said excitedly. "And they are yellow underneath next to his down."

"Hum," Tally said, with her eyes fixed on mine, "you do know about birds." Chichester, began to ruffle his feathers now, and then he lowered his head and gently held my finger in his beak.

I looked up at Tally, who said, "don't be scared when he holds your finger in his beak, it means that he likes you, and trusts that you are not going to hurt him." Chichester held and released my finger four or five times, and I felt he was making friends with me, though I didn't say what I was thinking to Tally or Paula. This was all so wonderful!

Tally held her arms out from her body and moved her arms up and down, and suddenly Chichester began to stretch out his wings.

"Wow!" Both Paula and I said.

"Look at the size of his wings! Is that your signal for him to stretch out his wings," I asked, "to lift your arms up from your side?"

"Yes, that is right," she said, "I have trained him to do lots of things. You better give him back to me now because he is getting ready to fly." Tally held out her arm and Chichester hopped from Paula's arm to hers. She then stood up and shouted, "off to the sky," and Chichester immediately jumped off her arm and flapped his wings until he was high in the sky! He circled above us making a high-pitched shrieking sound.

"Wow!" Both Paula and I said together.

"He is wonderful!" And in my heart a dream was born that day to have a hawk of my own. I wish I could have Chichester.

Tally seemed to be staring at me now as if she liked me. And I smiled at her. There had only been one girl that looked at me like that before, and that was Fionna Ash from my class at school, but I was too shy to look back at her.

Tally said, "I must be going now, but I will meet you back here soon," and she walked over and gave me back her headband. "You can keep it for me," she said.

"Thanks," I replied, not really knowing what else to say. I would much rather have Chichester, I thought. "Where are you going, I asked?"

Tally then gave me a sad look, and she was gone! Running across the castle grounds, and then out towards the old church wall. This time Paula and I understood not to follow her, but we watched her run all the way to the church wall with Chichester hovering above.

Suddenly Chichester folded his wings and swooped down behind the wall. Paula and I looked at each other in wonderment, it was all so wonderfully strange.

It is interesting sometimes what we remember, I had not thought of the strange girl at Pennard Castle or her hawk Chichester for many years.

∽

By the time I reached Pennard, I still had a few hours before the girls got home from Bristol. I decided I would go and visit Paula and her family at their home on Browns Drive. I had not seen the Jones' since I had come back to Wales to live, and I was keen to talk to Paula and Aunt Angela to see what they remembered about seeing the strange girl at the castle.

I parked the car in the driveway and rang the doorbell. Paula's dad David answered the door.

"Good heavens, Kingsley, what are you doing here boy? I'd heard you were back from Canada! Come on in and see Angela, and I think Paula is here too."

Angela gave me a big hug and then called Paula down from upstairs. The four of us sat in the living room, and I got caught up with all the Gower news since I had been away. After about an hour, David left to go and meet a friend at the golf club, leaving Angela, Paula and I to talk.

I asked them if they remembered Tally, the strange girl we had met at the castle when Paula and I were kids.

"I remember that girl," Angela said, "she wore those old-fashioned clothes like she was from another time."

"Yes, that's right," I said, "you remember."

And Paula remembered Chichester, the girl's falcon and how it perched on her arm.

"Yes," I replied. "She said it was a Sparrowhawk and not a falcon, and it held my finger in its beak."

"Oh, and there is one more thing that I remember, King, just wait here and I will go and get it." She left the room and went upstairs. Angela and I talked for about five minutes before Paula returned.

"Do you remember this?" she said, putting an old- faded headband into my hand.

"Yes!" I exclaimed. "This was Tally's headband that she gave me, I thought I had lost it."

"No, King, you gave it to me to borrow and I forgot to give it back."

"So can I keep it?" I asked.

"Of course, it is yours."

As I inspected it more closely, I could still see a faint colouring of blue on the smooth silk. And it had what looked like little embroidered cotton flowers on the front just as I remembered.

"What did you say the girl's name was, Kings?" Angela asked.

"She called herself Tally," I replied.

"Short for Taliath," Paula said.

"Taliath!" I gulped. "How do you know her name was Taliath?"

"She told me the first time I met her in the castle room. You came in afterwards, King, remember? We were already sitting in the sand talking."

"Yes, I remember," I choked, going all quiet.

"Have I said anything to upset you King?"

"No, I just can't seem to get away from that name."

"What do you mean?" Angela asked.

"My wife Gay who disappeared, her birth name was Taliath, and it brings back a lot of feelings and emotions for me."

"Oh, I understand, and we were sorry to hear about Gay, Kings. But we had heard that you have married a lovely lady and have moved back to Pennard."

"That's right," I said, feeling happy again. "Her name is Ffion, and she is the most beautiful lady inside and out."

"I can see that," Angela said. "Your face lit up when you started talking about her."

"And where in Pennard do you live?" Paula asked.

"In my Grandparents old house in Southgate," I said proudly.

"Not Mr. and Mrs. Hill's old house?" Angela asked.

"Yes, that's right," I said. "Right across from Pennard Stores."

"Well congratulations Kingsley, that is a beautiful house isn't it."

"Yes, it is, we are enjoying it there. Thank you. I better be getting home now," I said, anxious to think things through on my own. "And thank you for the nice visit, it was wonderful to see you again."

"So glad you stopped in Kings, and all the best for the future. And don't be a stranger, pop around and see us anytime, we would love to meet your new wife."

"I will," I said, "bye for now."

"Bye King."

"Bye Paula, and thanks for giving me the headband back."

And as I waited for Ffion and the girls to get back from their weekend in Bristol, I wondered what all this meant.

What is the significance of me remembering this strange girl from my childhood? For what reason did I hear the quiet inner voice speaking in my heart to remember this story? Was this the start of an answer to my prayers in finding out what happened to Gay? It does not make any sense.

Things were wonderful in my life before we found Gay's letter in the garden. We have rebuilt our family from the tragedy of her loss. Ffion has become my wife, a wonderful wife! And a mother to my children. Why am I even looking back? My life is rich and full. Is it because of the letter and the dreams that have woken the past to come alive again in my heart? Do I need to know what happened to Gay so that I can fully lay her to rest? I believe the answer is no. I have a wonderful life! So why am I looking back?

There is a wise old saying, that says, "be careful what you ask for."

I have asked God to help me find out what happened to Gay. But at what cost to my family and me? Surely, it would only complicate our lives again if we found out what happened. The consequences of this journey of mine to find out are already having a cause and effect on my life. My mind is becoming divided again, between the present and the past.

'Don't look back,' Dad said, 'don't look back! Otherwise, you will miss the present, and the future will leave you behind. You walk with the present into the future, not back to the past.' Easier said than done, Dad.

Ffions car came up the driveway, and the girls were home.

"Hi Dad," Samantha said, giving me a big hug. "I missed you, you should have come with us. We had lots of fun."

"Hi Dad," Melody said, hugging me quickly and running upstairs to her room with a bag of clothes she had bought in Bristol. Then my Ffion came in with the most beautiful smile for me, and she landed a long soft lipstick kiss on my lips and we both sighed!

"Oh, I missed you Kings!"

"I missed you, too lovely lady."

Once the girls had finished modeling their new clothes they had bought, we all hung out in the living room. Ffion shared with me that they had been discussing a family day out on the Worms Head before the weather turned cold.

"A great Idea," I replied. "Samantha and I have been wanting to spend a day out on the Worm for a long time." So, it was a unanimous decision, next weekend we would spend the day in Rhossili and go out onto the Worms Head.

"How was your weekend, my love?" Ffion asked, before we retired for the evening.

"It was a good weekend," I said. "I did a lot of walking, and I went and visited Mr. and Mrs. Jones, my old friends and neighbours who lived next door to where I grew up on Browns Drive." I didn't mention going to Gay's stone in Port Eynon, or the trip out to visit Armes at the commune.

The week went by quickly, and it was soon Saturday morning. The girls were up early, packed and ready to go on our adventure.

Before one is tempted to scamper across the rocks of the shipway and out onto the Worm, it is important that you consult with a current tide table, or if you don't have one, call in at the Coastguard Station and talk to one of the fine staff there who can explain the daily tides and conditions, otherwise you can be in jeopardy of getting cut off by the tide, and stranded on the Worm for a good six hours before you can get off again. Local weather conditions and time of day must also be a factor in your decision to go. The rocks can be challenging enough when the weather is dry and there is ample light, but crossing the rocks when slippery and wet, or when the light is fading, can make the journey precarious. Too many people have been swept out to sea and drowned, either by being swept off the rocks by the waves or attempting to swim after being cut off from the mainland. The currents around the Worms Head can be strong and dangerous. Good walking or hiking shoes along with a warm jacket are also a must when navigating the rocks and walking out from the Inner Head to the Outer Head, as there can often be a strong wind blowing over the hump of the Worm.

I am not in any way attempting to put people off from experiencing one of the most rewarding and exhilarating walks in all of Britain. But having a friend work in the Coastguard Station and tell me about the "almost weekly rescues" they perform in the spring and summer months is quite staggering! And sadly, there are tragedies almost every year out on the Worm, most of which could have been avoided.

Right, let's get back to our journey.

We parked our car at the National Trust car park, and then walked out along the cliff path.

"We will take turns carrying the backpacks," I reminded everyone, "and remember it isn't a race across the rocks," I said, looking at Melody, who gave me that knowing smile.

"What about the Blow Hole?" Samantha asked. "Will it be blowing today?"

"I don't know," I replied. "It is most active when the wind drives in from the west, making the spray leap up from the blowhole on the Outer Head. I will never forget the first time I heard the Worm speaking," I said, as both Ffion and Samantha gave me an inquisitive look. "It does speak," I continued, "by making a strange booming sound that can be heard as far as the village. Whose job is it to read the tide table and keep an eye on the time?" I asked.

"Me Dad," Samantha said with a look of pride. She knew how seriously I took our safety, and I was pleased she had taken the responsibility to be our timekeeper and read the tide.

As we reached about the halfway point along the cliff path to where we climbed down to the shipway, I began to feel an irresistible urge to walk out to the very furthest point on the worm.

"It is here at this very place on the cliffs, that I hear the Worm calling out to me."

"I can hear it calling too," Ffion said, taking my hand and giving me a gentle kiss. What a day, I thought out loud. The sky is blue, there is only a light wind, and the Worm is calling us to come and have an adventure.

As we reached the end of the cliff path, I decided to test Samantha on her knowledge of the tides. Over the summer months she and I had taken a lot of walks along the cliffs at Pennard and had explored some beaches where it was easy to get cut off by the tide. She had become excellent at reading the tides by the different phases of the moon, and the variants of winds and currents, all without using a tide table. I want to read the tides like you Dad, she had said, and become a great explorer. I was pleased about that, shy of her living in a cave that is!

"Read the tide and conditions for us, Sam," I said.

"Listen up everyone," she replied. "We have one hour before the tide is at its low, and as you can see the shipway is exposed so that we can make our way across the rocks to the Worm. It is going to take us about an hour if we take our time out to the end of the Worm, by which time the tide will be at its low. It will stay dormant for an hour and then start coming in again. That gives us roughly about four hours out on the Worm itself, and then we must make our way back across the shipway, as the tide covers the shipway rocks about two hours before its high at the present rise and fall of the tides. Remember, the Worm becomes an Island once the shipway rocks are covered, so we have to start making our way back in good time before the high tide. We have a light wind, and a lovely blue sky, enjoy the hike everyone." As I listened to Samantha giving us our tide report, she sounded just like me, and I felt so proud!

"Well done for the report Sam, let's climb down the path to the shipway." As we walked along the shipway, I pointed out to Ffion the long spur of low- lying rocks known as the Crabart. "The Crabart is only exposed at close to low tide," I explained, "and it can be good for catching crabs and lobsters in the crevices and holes in the rocks." Samantha and Melody now walked ahead of us, and I shouted, "be careful as you jump over the gullies, and we will meet you on top of the Inner Head."

The girls wasted no time scurrying across the rocks, Ffion and I took our time relishing the views on each side of the shipway. As one faces the spectacular size and shape of the 'Lands End of Gower', the Worms Head always astonishes the beholder, as it looks like a vast serpent coiling its way out to the sea and rearing its huge head as it plunges westward into the waves.

"It's haunting in its appearance," Ffion said, "and so mysterious, like it is calling to us again, only now it's closer." I could see the girls in the distance, climbing up the rocks from the shipway to the Inner Head. "I hope they wait for us," Ffion said. "I'm getting hungry, and they have our backpacks." As we reached the end of the shipway, I could see the girls waiting for us up on the Inner Head, and we soon caught up with them. As one climbs up onto the top of the Inner Head, there is a wonderful view westward across the wide- open expanse of Rhossili Bay, with the Islet of Burry Holmes in the distance. Once Ffion and I had reached the girls we sat and had our picnic.

The Inner Head is the biggest of the three humps of the Worm and is quite flat on top. And we all sat like Kings and Queens as we surveyed the wondrous land and sea around us.

"Tell us a story Dad," Samantha and Melody asked, having already wolfed down their sandwiches.

"Yes darling," Ffion echoed, "do you know any stories about the Inner Head?"

"There is one," I replied, "that my grandfather told me, when he and I climbed out on the Worm when I was about eight years old…"

Chapter Four

What a Load of Sheep!

The stories my grandfather told me were still so vivid in my mind and heart. "The grass here used to be close-cropped when the farmers kept sheep on it, and the Inner Head was the only section on the Worms Head that was used for this purpose. The grass the sheep ate had a great reputation for helping to produce especially tender mutton, and the Talbot family of Penrice used to graze a flock of sheep on the Worm between September and March. One was killed every week for the Talbot table, and a local farmer had the job of crossing the shipway every Tuesday between tides and bringing one back to the mainland."

"How did he catch it and bring it back?" Samantha asked.

"He probably chased it until he caught it, and then carried it back on his shoulders," I replied.

"He must have been a strong man," Ffion said, "to climb over the rough rocks with a sheep on his shoulders!"

"Yes," I replied. I continued, "the story goes that when the farmer got the sheep back to the mainland, it was collected by a castle servant. It was killed at Penrice if the Talbot family were in residence. If they were at one of their other residences in Margam or London it was sent to them live, in a specially made traveling box. The Talbots declared that there was nothing to equal 'Worms Head Mutton', as it had been fed on grass salted by the sea winds."

"How about today," Melody asked, "do any of the farmers graze their sheep out on the Worm?"

"I don't know, but I bet the grass is good tasting and lush for sheep. It's soft and springy," Ffion commented, as she jumped up and down on the soft sod.

"Remember, we did this with mum, didn't we Dad," Melody exclaimed as she joined Ffion jumping up and down. We all joined in and held hands and jumped in a circle. "I remember this game," Melody said excitedly, "we all have to jump up and down until someone falls and breaks the circle, then they are out of the game."

"That's right Melody, and the last one still standing wins the game." So, we all jumped up and down holding hands until Ffion and Samantha were the last two standing. "Ok," I said, remembering the rules. "Once you reach the last two people, you must stop holding hands, and you can't just jump up and down, you have to twist around in the air while you jump and try to land on your feet." Ffion and Sam were both doing well, and I made a bet on Ffion to win.

"Tough luck Dad," Melody said, as Ffion fell to the ground laughing, "give me my fifty pence piece, as my bet was on Sam!"

"Ok here you are," I said, and I gave her a fifty pence piece.

After our game we sat and rested for a few minutes before making our way to the Middle Head.

"Have you ever eaten mutton, Dad?" Sam asked.

"Yes indeed," I replied, "would you like to hear a story about some sheep?" Everyone put up their hands, so I told them a story that happened years ago when I was still a teenager living in a prehistoric bone cave called Bacon Hole.

"One morning I woke up and went out to greet the new day as usual, and I sat on my stone seat outside my cave to get the weather forecast. As I looked out to sea, and then up to the top of the cliff tops, I saw a sheep stuck on a ledge right above my cave. The poor animal couldn't climb up or down, she was just stuck! I thought of climbing up the cliff and rescuing the animal, but it was on a steep rocky ledge and too dangerous to get to, so I just watched and waited. There was only one way down, and that was to fall down onto the rocks outside my cave."

"Poor animal!" Ffion said, hoping that I had a happy ending to tell.

"I'm afraid the ending is not a very happy one, unless that is, you are living in the wild and are very hungry, or you have been on a diet of just fish and rabbits to live on for months on end. Then, it is a good story. And the sheep's rather messy end was my gain."

"Come on, tell us Dad, Sam said, we can take it."

"Yeah, we can take it," Melody echoed.

"I don't know if I can," Ffion said.

And I continued.

"I waited until the sheep fell to his demise upon the rocks. I then cut off all its wool with my Bowie Knife, and then gutted it. I threw its innards into the sea below my cave, and then cut the meat into steaks. The meat was tough, and hard to cut off from the bones. And by the time I had finished I looked like I had committed a murder, and I stunk of wool and sheep blood."

"Oh Dad, gross!" both the girls said, and Ffion gave me a look of disdain.

And I continued the story at my own risk, shall we say.

"After I had cut the meat into roasting size steaks and thrown the carcass of the sheep into the sea, I built a nice large fire and cooked a piece of the mutton. Now I was hoping that it would taste somewhat like my mothers Sunday lamb dinners. I was however to become quite disappointed, as there was no comparison with mother's tender lamb chops with mint sauce and gravy. This mutton was tough as old boots and required so much chewing that I had a jaw ache for the rest of the day." Ffion and the girls laughed, picturing me chewing the cud around my campfire in the cave. "However, it was a nice change from my previous meals. And on that plea, against my aching jaw, I continued to enjoy a portion of mutton for about a week. The meat I wasn't eating I put in plastic bags and kept in my cooling pool, just below the high tide mark on the rocks."

"After eating my fifth mutton steak in a row, I misjudged the incoming tide, and the rest of my meat ended up feeding the crabs out on Hunts Bay. Now, what happened next is still something I think about 25 years later. Would you like to hear more?" And it was a full show of hands again, so I continued my story.

"About a month later, I didn't know whether I was just fed up with eating rabbits and fish again, or I was truly craving the taste of mutton with its flavourful drippings and fat, but my stomach and taste buds won the argument with my jaw. I needed to eat another sheep. So, I went about finding myself another unfortunate animal."

"Not wanting to be cruel, I searched the cliffs and ledges for another lost sheep, that I could maybe help on its way with a bit of persuasion from my bow and arrow, or if push came to shove, my caveman spear. I did not however find such an animal, so I decided to be a bad boy and take one of the sheep from the farmer's fold. Now, fortunately for me, the grazing was still good at the time, and there were a number of flocks left to graze on the cliff tops and the paths near my cave, and I did not have to travel very far to find a nice fat sheep. The farmers sprayed their animals with different colours of paint, so other farmers could tell who the sheep belonged to, when they were rounded up at the end of the grazing season. The sheep that were grazing closest to my cave had blue paint marks on them, so I decided to hunt one of them first. Sheep are rather stupid and get used to people walking along the clifftops and paths, so I was able to sneak up close to one and shoot an arrow into its side. I won't go into graphic details, but it took me three arrows to bring it down and then I finished it off with my Bowie Knife."

"Dad! Don't tell me anymore," Melody said. But Ffion and Samantha, both said, 'no you must finish the story now that you have started.' So, I did.

"This sheep either tasted better because its meat was more tender, or because I was becoming a better cook. I had not reached a conclusion on that yet, but I enjoyed a week's supply of mutton from that animal. A few more weeks of fish and rabbit went by, and I was craving another sheep. This time

I chose a sheep with red paint on its wool and managed to skin the whole animal. I made a nice woolen blanket out of the wool and had another week's supply of meat until the rest went off and I threw it into the sea to fatten up the crabs. And I will never forget one morning, I was walking back to my cave along the cliff path, I had a sheep over my shoulders, and I was covered in blood from hands to foot, and some woman was walking her dog. 'Good morning, madam,' I said, as spry as a cockerel, 'it's a lovely morning, isn't it?' And her look said it all, a combination of fear and shock! And she spoke two words, and they were to her dog. 'Come along Jason.' And that was all she needed to say! She had met the Gower Ripper!" Samantha and Melody were now giving me the look! As if to question if their father was really Jack the Ripper!

To my surprise, my dear Ffion came to my rescue, and said, "So nothing went to waste then?" And I replied, "No, never, and I needed it for survival. I needed a break from my diet of fish and rabbit, and the crabs and lobsters enjoyed the leftovers out on the bay."

I did not, however, tell either Ffion or the girls, that my sheep eating escapades carried on for 13 months. and I think I ate about two sheep from every farmer's flock within four miles of my home in Bacon Hole. And when all my arrows had been broken, I made more spears and threw them. Enough said, maybe I am the Gower Ripper! But if you ask me, I think it's just a load of sheep!

It was time for Ffion and I to take the backpacks from the girls, and we all headed off to the Middle Head of the Worm.

No matter how many times one hikes out onto the Worms Head, its unique personality of mystery and adventure makes one feel like you are seeing it for the first time! A sense of its secrets and wonders, seem to lurk and hide along the way, pouncing out at you, as you feel something reach out and stir within your soul that you have not experienced before. And if you have felt something like this before, then you find out that you had forgotten just how wonderful it is, out on the Rock at the End of the World!

∿

We now crossed from the Middle Head to the Outer Head, over the huge natural arch of limestone, known as the Devil's Bridge. Memories galloped across my mind as we walked across, for this was Gay's and my most special place out on the Worm, and we had renamed the Arch, God's Balcony! I pondered my memories for a few minutes as Ffion and I reached the Outer Head, while the girls tarried upon the arch.

"This is the most amazing place in the world!" Samantha exclaimed, not having been here before. As I have previously said about Gay's and my visit here, the Outer Head is truly a place like no other! It is a rare patch of the earth's surface, full of the wild air of the four winds, and the crying of the gulls and the thundering of the cruel sea thrashing below into rocks.

Suddenly the girls came running to Ffion and me. The Worm had woken! The strange, tormented hissing and booming noise was coming from the Blow Hole.

"My gosh!" Samantha shouted, "I've never heard anything like this, Dad! "

"There is nothing like it, I replied. "Let's continue to walk out to the end of the Worm." The girls stayed close now, as we were surrounded by the haunting booming and hissing noises of the Worm that breathed and spluttered all around us.

We reached the end of the Worm, and the cliff plunges a hundred feet into the heaving sea. "It is a restless sea," Samantha observed, and spoke as if the mysterious waters had entered her soul.

"It reminds me of lives that are not at peace," I answered back to her observation, "lost souls looking for a shore."

"The sea is almost black!" Ffion exclaimed, after listening to Samantha and my words. Just then the water leaped up from the blow hole, shooting into the air in unison with the booming sound, and Ffion grabbed my arm.

"Wow!" The girls shouted. "It must be about 70 feet high!" And we sat and watched the Worm hissing and blowing for about half an hour.

"We will have to watch the tide," Sam said, as she checked her watch and the tide table.

"I'd rather get back to the mainland sooner than later," I said, and we started making our way back to the Middle Head.

As we reached God's Balcony, gusts of wind reminded us of how exposed we were to the four winds as we stood on the limestone arch. As winds blow strong, the temptation is to run across the arch to the more tranquil Middle Head.

"Don't run," I called to the girls, "you may slip and fall."

Walking slowly across the rocks, and with the next gust of wind, Ffion whispered, "I feel like running too."

As we walked across the springing turf, our eyes turned to the north. We looked out across the full sweep of Rhossili Bay, again, and set our eyes across the golden sands, listening to the wild rollers now coming in at haste. The sands run in an arc shape for three miles long from the Worm, on under the steep slope of Rhossili Downs and out to the islet of Burry Holms. And we all vowed that this was one of the most sacred times we had spent together as a family.

'It is the Gower, boy, she has many secrets!' Yes sir, she does.

We climbed down the path from the Inner Head to the shipway and made our way back to the mainland. As we looked back from the mainland rocks, we could see now that the waves were climbing up the shipway, and we had made it back in perfect time.

We had our tea at the Worms Head Pub, just to celebrate our fate of crossing out across the shipway and conquering the Worm! Although it was never conquered, just explored, and it was a family adventure that we would remember all our lives.

～

Over the next fortnight family life continued as usual, with Samantha and Melody busy at university and school, and Ffion continuing to teach her dance classes in Swansea.

The phone rang late one night, and it was Dad, excited about what he had translated in the diary.

"Taliath affirms what Armes told you about the 'Boat Warriors' invading her village," he said. "I am positive that both Taliath and Armes must be talking about the Viking landings in South Wales, and more pertinent in the Gower Peninsula itself!" I had not heard Dad so excited since we had found a chest of artifacts, and he asked if I could come over and see the translation. It was late, and I would have much rather stayed home and enjoyed a romantic night with Ffion, but Dad was insistent that this was important.

"Alright Dad, I will be there in about forty -five minutes."

When I arrived, Dad had the Viking sword and helmet that we had found together sitting on the table.

"Remember these Old Son?" he said. "We found these when you were only ten."

"Yes, I will never forget finding these," I said, picking up the sword in my hand and swinging it. And I startled Mary as she walked into the room.

"What are you two up to at this time of night," she said, suspicious that we were up to no good.

"We are just running a reference to the diary," Dad replied, "and can you make us a cup of tea?"

Mary smiled at me and shook her head, "you're becoming more like your father every day, Kings," and she left to make the tea.

"Look at this," Dad said, handing me some historical documents that he had loaned from the Swansea Museum.

And I quote this abridged version of these documents into my father's words. "The word 'Swansea' is derived from the Scandinavian word 'Sveinn' – a personal name – and 'ey', an island. It is therefore Sveinn's Island, and indeed there was a small island at the mouth of the River Tawe until the eighteenth century. Who Sveinn was we shall never know, but the Dane;s certainly sailed continuously up the Bristol Channel leaving names behind them from Skomer Island to Worms Head, and it is likely that there was a small Norse Settlement here." End of quote.

"Do you remember where we found this sword and helmet, Kings?"

"Yes , we found them on the islet of Burry Holms, which lies at the other end of Rhossili Beach, due north from the Worms Head."

"That's right, Son! And the origin of the sword and helmet are Viking! Remember Kings, between 350 A.D. and 400 A.D. came disaster. The unbelievable happened and the Roman empire collapsed."

"Disaster for them, Dad, not us! I would have fought the Romans as well as the Vikings, to protect the people of Gower."

"I know you would, Son. I remember the day when you lifted up this sword and stood on the end of Burry Holms, and swung it at the French, wishing you had been born in the days of Lord Nelson, so you could have fought against Napoleon."

"I remember doing that," I laughed, and Mary returned to the room with our tea.

"What are you two planning now," she said, "I hope you're not going out to dig up Vikings this time of night!"

"No Mary," I laughed, "we are just discussing the history of the Viking landings in the Gower."

Mary left us with our tea and biscuits, and Dad continued to talk.

"After the collapse of the Romans, the Dark Ages were upon us. Gower was too far to the west to be ravaged by the Anglo-Saxons. It did not, however, avoid the miseries that followed the withdrawal of the legions. The Irish crossed the channel in their skin boats, and eventually settled and ruled in Pembrokeshire. By the seventh century, we find Gower is back completely under Welsh control, and Christian as well. The Celtic saints had done their work and Gower had a whole series of settlements dedicated to them. The invaders were the

Norsemen, and although it is unlikely the Vikings made any extensive settlement in Gower, they certainly landed here, Kings! And this sword and helmet are part of their landing story. And I believe that Taliath's recordings of these 'boat warriors' as she calls them in her diary, refer to the Vikings. I did skip about halfway through the diary to find any words that translated into 'boats or boat warriors', and they were there, so I believe her account of them invading to be true. The diary was also written within the time frame that the Vikings were traveling up the Bristol Channel.

I am not, however, convinced that all of what Armes said to you is true, Kings, but Taliath does record the names of her three sisters, as Gwenhwyfar, Arlias, and Tanwen. Did Armes tell you the names of her other daughters, Kings? The ones she left on the other side of this so-called portal?"

"No, she didn't tell me their names."

"Then I would go back to the commune and test her. Go back and investigate! Ask her about her three other daughters and see if they have the same names as Taliath's sisters in the diary. If they are the same, then we have made some sort of connection. But I will still not be convinced of her story of having traveled from another time and place through a portal. However, going back to the commune to investigate more, would be a good starting point."

"I think that is a good idea, Dad, I will do that, I will go and ask her some more questions."

Before I left Dad's place for home, I read his latest translation of the diary concerning the 'boat warriors', and it was very convincing!

❧

Grandfather took Arlias and Tanwen for a walk along the cliff tops, and out onto the three grey rock peaks that stand like warriors guarding the entrance to the bay where the river meets the sea. There is an arched cave that cuts through the rocks and leads up to the valley to where our settlement stands proudly upon the hill.

❧

I paused as I read, and I felt my heart beating faster. There was no doubt in my mind that Taliath was talking about the Three Cliffs Rocks and the archway where you can walk through the cliffs into the Three Cliffs valley. And the settlement must be the castle upon the hill looking down at the valley below. "It's starting to make more sense, Dad," I exclaimed. "It was in the castle grounds where I found the diary, and the landmarks that she describes are unmistakable!"

"I believe that you are right, Kings," Dad said, "please read on a bit more." And I read aloud.

❧

Grandfather and my sisters arrived back in the village and sounded the alarm! 'There were ships with sails moving across the bay! Coloured ships with sails, and shields along their lengths, and the ships were full of fierce warriors with helmets that had horns. Grandfather said to Arlias and Tanwen, quickly get down on the ground, we must not let them see us, otherwise they will land! For now, the ships have passed in a row, but they appeared to be looking for something, he said to our clan.'

⁓

I stopped reading for a moment, astounded by what Taliath was describing!

"There can be no doubt that the grandfather is describing the Vikings, Dad," I said, "what other invaders could there be? The helmets and the horns, and the shields placed on the sides of the boats!"

"My thoughts exactly, Kings, this diary is turning out to be an encyclopedia of knowledge!"

Dad went on to tell me that as he skipped ahead through the pages, he read about the 'Boat Warriors' actually landing on the beaches of the Gower Peninsula and attacking the clans!

It was getting late, and I knew that Ffion was waiting for me to get home. "Thanks for showing me, Dad," I said. "I must get going now as Ffion will be waiting for me, but I will have to read the account of the landings and the attacks on Taliath's clan."

"Alright Kings," Dad said, as he walked me to the door, "drive safely and give Ffion our love. And I will keep you posted on any more significant discoveries in the translation."

That was an amazing discovery, I thought as I drove home to Pennard. Taliath is actually recording an account of the Viking landings through the eyes of her family and clan. What an amazing piece of our history we had found!

Chapter Five

More Questions Than Answers

Another fortnight went by before I had an opportunity to go to the commune, and ask my questions of Armes as Dad had suggested.

I was feeling awkward in not telling Ffion or the girls what I was doing. I knew they would support me, but it was just so hard on Ffion and Melody, this rollercoaster of not knowing what had happened to Gay, and I felt protective of their emotional wellbeing. The thought of Gay ever returning to our lives was something that made Ffion very uncomfortable. She never said it did, certainly not to Meldoy or I, but Samantha had noticed how stressed Ffion was whenever we talked about what would happen if Gay came back into our lives. I could certainly appreciate how Ffion must feel, especially as she has bonded with Samantha and Melody so well. Melody calls her mum and loves her as her own mother now.

"Samantha and Melody are the daughters I thought I would never have," she said, "and then I married you, Kings, and we became a family." She did ask me once, what I would do if ever Gay came back to us and wanted to be part of our lives again. "If she ever came back, it would be only natural for you both to want to be together, wouldn't it?" she said.

"Never!" I replied, "not after all this time, my love is with you and what we have shared together! And look what Gay did to Melody. She abandoned her!"

Ffion is a beautiful woman, if not the most beautiful in all of Gower Land, but deep inside her lovely soul, an insecurity is brewing. Is she discerning some future event that she has an awareness of, I wondered?

Gay and I used to say, 'no secrets' in our relationship, but her life turned out to be the biggest secret of all!

I hated keeping secrets from Ffion and the girls, but I couldn't tell them about what Armes had said about Gay still being alive and having gone back to another place and time to see her father and sisters. It would really confuse Melody, and give her false hope of seeing her mother again, and I was not going to allow that to happen, not now that we have come so far as a family and share so much which is sacred and beautiful.

It was on a Saturday when I went back to the commune to see Armes. Ffion, Helen and the girls had gone to spend the day in Swansea, to do some shopping and to watch a movie in the afternoon. That would give me a full day to drive out to the commune in Cardiganshire.

As soon as Ffion and the girls left for Swansea I was on my way. This must be the last time that I keep secrets from

Ffion, I vowed, as I drove along the mountain roads. She would be so hurt to find out that I had kept her in the dark as to my visits to Armes, even if my motivation is to protect her and the girls it would fuel her insecurity. Once I understand what is going on and confirm that Armes does not have three other children and a husband hidden away somewhere, I will tell Ffion everything.

⌇

It was mid morning when I arrived at the commune, and I climbed over the sty and started walking across the fields to the main buildings. I wondered what this crazy woman would tell me this time, I pondered, and I soon arrived at the settlement.

Surprised to see me, a woman dressed in Celtic attire said, "can I help you sir?" And she bowed politely.

"Yes", I replied, "I would like to see Armes. Would you take me to her please?"

"For what reason?" the woman asked. "You are not one of our brothers." That was a term I had not heard them use before, brothers?

"No, I am not a member of your commune, but if you give my name to Armes, she will be sure to see me."

"Very well Sir, follow me."

This time I was not led to the main building and through the darkened tunnel to Arme's living quarters. Instead I was led across the fields behind the main buildings to whare Gay and I had had our Celtic Bath.

"What is your name?" the woman asked.

"Kingsley," I replied, looking across the fields at the steam rising into the air where the bathing pool was.

"What is your name?" I asked.

"Asharahh," she replied.

"And what is it that you do here at the commune, Asharahh?" I asked.

"I am a body servant," she replied.

"And what does your name mean?"

"It means 'a rising spirit'," she replied.

"An appropriate name for a body servant," I said, "and do you know Huelyn?"

"Oh yes," she replied, now smiling and obviously feeling more comfortable in my presence.

I could see now that we were approaching the Celtic Bath, and there looked to be a woman sitting in the middle of the pool. I remembered the stone seats that Gay and I had sat on during our bath. I could see now that it was Armes, who was taking a bath. Out of all the times I could have arrived, she was having her bath I thought!

As we arrived at the pool, Asharahh said something in Celtic to Armes, who then said something back and waved her hands.

"She wants you to join her, Kingsley," Asharahh said, "so please undress and I will take your clothes." I hesitated at first remembering why I had come here. I had not come to indulge in the sensuality or relaxation of having a Celtic Bath, wonderful as they are. I had come to talk of serious things with Armes, not share a bath with her. At my hesitation, Armes called out something to Asharahh, and I recognized my name among the other Celtic words.

Then Armes called out directly to me, and said, "please come on in, Kingsley, there is another seat here in the pool as you know, we can talk here."

"Alright," I said. I don't want to be here all day I thought, I will sit down in the pool and get what I have to ask her over with.

I undressed and gave my clothes to Asharahh, who then bowed and walked away. "Where is she going with my clothes?" I said to Armes, as I walked towards her in the pool.

"She has gone to get us robes and refreshments," Armes replied, "and your clothes will be returned to you later. Your seat is to my left," she said. "Please sit down and relax."

As I sat down on the warm stone seat and felt the hot bubbling spring up to my chest, I had forgotten how good and relaxing this Celtic Bath was!

"What gives me the honour of your presence, Kingsley?" Armes said, in an almost seductive voice. "Have you thought more on what I told you during our last conversation, Kingsley?"

"I have," I replied, feeling the tension of being here again at the commune leaving my muscles. "I want to ask you some questions about what you told me of your husband and daughters being in some other place and time. Or another dimension, or whatever you call it."

"You mean the other side of the portal."

"Yes, if that is what you call it."

"And what are your questions Kingsley?"

"What are your other daughter's names? I know that Gay's birth name is Taliath, and that your last name, or surname is Saren."

"Why do you ask about my other children? You left here not believing what I had told you. Have you changed your mind?"

"I don't know," I replied, "but you did tell me of Melody and my dreams about Gay, something I believe that no one else could have known. So, I would like to know, if the truth can be known, where Gay has gone… and this portal, does it still exist?"

"I am not without discernment, Kingsley. There is another reason that you want to know my daughters' names, otherwise my telling you that I had three other daughters would be enough for you to know. You have come here to test me. Do you deny it?"

"No, I do not deny coming to test you. Surely you would also under such circumstances, would you not?"

"It would rather depend on what understanding of the circumstances I had, before I would feel the need to test you, Kingsley. But you have told me the truth, the reason why you are here, so I shall tell you the names of my daughters, but then you also need to tell me something.

My eldest daughter is Gwenhwyfar, then my second born is Arlias, but they are not of my womb, but born from our Clan Queen, Abrill. I was Abrill's Body Servant, and I looked after Gwenhwyfar and Arlias while their mother performed her duties in the Temple. After Arlias was born, Abrill was not able to conceive, so I bore Tanwen, and then Taliath, your Gay, who was born on this side of the portal."

I sighed and breathed deeply as Armes told me the names of her daughters, they were the same names as Taliath had recorded in her diary. As my heart returned to its normal rhythm, I pondered in my heart and asked myself, how could their names be the same? What is the connection? There must be one! But how and where does all this connect?

"Now you have something to tell me, don't you Kingsley? And then I will tell you more about the portal."

"Yes, Armes, I have something to tell you," I replied.

"I found a diary when I was 12 years old, and my father and I, and Gay before she disappeared, have begun to translate it. It is the diary of a woman named Taliath Saren who's mother is, or should I say was, a Celtic Clan Queen. Taliath wrote about her life and the lives of her family and people in the year 970 and some time after. Taliath records the names of her sisters, and they have the same names as your daughters. I have just realised now, as you have been telling me the names of your daughters, that even their birth order is the same. Taliath is the youngest. There must be a connection."

"There is, indeed, Kingsley. I do not understand the connection yet, but all things will be revealed at the right time." I can agree with that, I thought, but again I had been left with more questions than answers.

Asharahh, now returned with our gowns and refreshments, and she undressed to enter the pool, and brought Armes and I some sandwiches and drinks on a tray.

"Thank you," both Armes and I said, bowing our heads, and Asharahh left the pool.

"Please tell me about the portal," I said. "I do believe you now, that you and Gay came from a different place and time. During our last conversation when I came to see you before, you told me of the invaders that came to your land on long boats with sails."

"Yes, what of them?"

"Well, in our most recent translation of Taliath's diary, she talks of fierce Sea Warriors arriving on long boats with sails and killing the men and raping the women of the clans. She talks very much as you talked, about how life was when your husband sent you pregnant with Gay, through the portal."

Armes, was silent at my words, closing her eyes, and contemplating deeply to what all this could mean. She was silent for about fifteen minutes, and I finished my refreshments. At last, she spoke and said, "I will tell you what I know about the portal."

"Firstly, I must tell you about my aunt, Gay's great aunt, who came through the portal before us. Her name was Taliath too, and my husband wanted to name one of our daughters after her. I promised the name to our youngest, Taliath, who of course you know as Gay. My aunt Taliath used to come back and forth through the portal and bring news to our clan as to what life was like here on this side of the portal. She described it as a safe place for our people to go to in times of trouble. A place where we could escape if our clan was invaded or if we could not find enough food during the many wars and raids we suffered at the hands of enemy clans."

"What happened to your aunt Taliath?" I asked. "Did she stay here in Gower, this side of the portal or did she stay with your people on the other side?"

"She was lost to us," Armes explained. "She traveled through the portal one March morning when she was nine years old and never returned!"

"Why did your people send someone so young to come and explore, why not an adult?"

"Taliath had special powers of discernment and prophecy, as did her mother and grandmother before her."

"Did your people send someone through the portal to rescue her?"

"It was not that easy, Kingsley. Only aunt Taliath's grandmother knew how to find the portal and what was needed to see it and travel through it."

"I do not understand what you mean, when you say, 'what is needed to see it and travel through it'."

"I will try and explain. The portal is invisible to the naked eye, and moves around at different seasons of the year, like a magic doorway that appears from nowhere."

"How can you find it then, if it moves around and you can not see it with the naked eye?"

"I can only tell you part of the answer, the rest I do not know. It is believed that there is a special yellow flower that grows on the walls of Pennard Castle. It only grows there and a few other places in all of Wales, and the flower only blooms in the early spring, usually in the months of March or April. A potion is made using only the yellow flower of the plant, and one other ingredient, that is ground together with the yellow flower and swallowed. The potion, when prepared correctly, gives the partaker a 'Second Sight', so they can see the flaming portal and walk through to the other side. Once the potion wears off the second sight is lost, so extra potion must be prepared and carried through the portal each journey, otherwise the person is stuck and unable to return. I do not know what the other ingredient is that must be mixed with the yellow flower to make the potion."

I was both stunned and excited to hear Armes talk of the yellow flower that grows on the wall of Pennard Castle. I remember Paula and my conversation with the strange girl we met in the castle room. She told us of the yellow flower but was forbidden to tell us its secrets. Is this your answer to my prayer God, when I heard your voice, I wondered? 'Remember the girl at Pennard castle', was what you whispered within my heart. Is hearing Armes talk about the yellow plant, part of me learning about what happened to Gay? I prayed under my breath.

∽

"And that is all I know, Kingsley," Armes finished.

"But how did you come through the portal? Did you drink the potion, and bring extra so that you could return?"

"My husband gave me the potion and enough to return. And he also asked me to look for my aunt who I have never been able to find. But I lost the potion I needed to return and have been here ever since. I was supposed to only stay a month, until hopefully the danger to our people was over."

"Why did your husband not come looking for you, especially as you were soon to give birth?"

At my words, Armes began to cry, and said, "I do not know why he did not come for me. I have waited all these years and fear he must have been killed by the invaders from the sea. I have built this Commune for my own people who would come after me, but no one has come!" I stood up from my stone seat and walked over to comfort Armes, who sobbed in my arms until Asharahh came back into the pool and took Armes' arm to lead her out of the bath. I held Armes's other arm and we brought her out of the pool. Asharahh dried our bodies and put on our robes, and we walked back to Armes' living quarters. I found my clothes hanging on a statue in the waiting area across from Armes' room.

"Please stay and eat with me, Kingsley," Armes, asked. "I am so happy you came to see me."

"I am glad I came too," I replied, and I agreed to stay for tea.

We ate in Armes' living quarters, and Asharahh waited on us hand and foot. We talked about many things, Ffion, Helen, and Melody, and I told Armes all about my daughter Samantha, and my hopes to have my boys come out again soon from Canada.

After we had eaten, it was time for me to go, even though I had been invited to stay at the commune until the morrow.

"Goodbye, Armes, and thank you for sharing with me what you know."

"Bye Kingsley, and please let me know what else you discover through your translation of the diary. Maybe you will discover something that will help me to be able to return home to my people."

"I will," I said, feeling glad now that I had come. I had not mentioned to Armes, the girl at Pennard Castle, and what she had said about the yellow flower. It was still a mystery to me how all this could somehow fit together. Was the young girl Armes' aunt?

I decided to drop by and talk to Dad in Swansea and tell him all the news.

We discussed in depth the connection between the diary and Armes' daughters.

"My gosh Kingsley, how does all this fit?"

"I don't know Dad! But the names of her daughters are the same. And even their birth order is the same too!"

"As far as I can see, Kings, we are left with two obvious questions. If the four sisters including Gay, that Armes claims are her daughters, are the same sisters that Taliath records as hers in her diary, then is Gay Taliath Saren? Then if Gay is Taliath Saren, was it Gay who wrote the diary in 970 A.D.? Are we translating Gays own diary?"

"Bloody Nora, Dad, I can't get my head around it!"

"Neither can I Son, neither can I!"

"And what about the chest, Dad, and the connection Gay had with that? Was Gay trying on the clothes of her own people, and looking at the artifacts of her own clan?"

"She certainly had a connection with them, Kings. Remember how you used to tell me how obsessed she was with the clothing?"

"Yes, she would wear the gowns and leather garments around the house, and she rarely took off the sandals.

And another thing, Dad, do you remember when she turned the spare room in our house into a temple? She had all the candles set up around the room and burned incense, and she put up the Rams Head that we found in the chest on a stand and made an altar in front of it. She even got me to perform Celtic ceremonies and rituals with her in front of it."

"Yes, by Jove, I remember! This is all quite astounding son!"

Yes, it was astounding alright, I thought. And I didn't tell Dad what Armes said about the yellow flower on the castle wall and the potion yet. Oh well, that was enough for now, I feel mentally exhausted trying to figure everything out.

"I don't know where we go from here, Dad."

"I think the only thing we can do, Kings, is keep on translating the diary and see if it gives us any more clues. Go and focus your energy on Ffion and your family, Kings, and don't let this consume your thoughts and time."

"That is exactly what I am going to do, Dad, I have had enough trauma and excitement for a lifetime!"

Chapter Six

The Loneliness of Broughton Sands

I arrived home in Pennard before Ffion and the girls got home from their day in Swansea. The evenings were sure drawing in again now and it was getting cooler. The weather will break soon I thought, as I prepared a fire in the living room. It will soon be November Grey on the Gower Peninsula, and the sky will be the same colour as the sea, but I have love for my Ffion and me. Our sky will be blue, and the falling leaves will be like new dreams for her and me.

The fire was rip roaring and the living room warm as my girls burst through the door like Spring in October.

"Hi Dad!" Samantha said, giving me the biggest hug.

"I missed you Dad," Melody announced, throwing her arms around me, "you should have come with us, we found another hobby shop with trains!" Next came love in high heels, as my darling Ffion lit up the room and warmed me with a lipstick kiss!

"Mmm, you taste like passion fruit," I said, gently pulling her towards me for another smooch.

"Mmm, and you smell like you, Kings," and we both laughed.

"How was your time in Swansea?"

"It was wonderful my lovely man, I wish you had come with us. We explored most of the old town and went into the market, and I bought you this. I hope you like it, and it matches your set."

"Wow! It's a Ho Scale Steam Locomotive, and a limited edition too! Thank you, my lovely lady! And take your clothes off right now!" Ffion giggled and pretended to undress until the girls reappeared into the room.

"You will have to wait till tonight," Ffion smiled and then blushed.

"What are you girls going to do tonight?" I asked both Sam and Melody.

"We are going to watch a movie in my room," Melody announced.

"And talk about boys no doubt."

"Of course, Dad, what else do you think we are going to talk about, the weather?"

Ffion laughed, and said what I so often say, "Oh, love makes the world go round." She then looked at me and said, "You make my world go round."

"And you mine," I replied, "now let's have an early night," I said winking.

"Good night girls," Ffion and I called out on the landing, "see you in the morning."

"What are you two doing," they both called out from Melody's room. "Are you just going to talk to each other?" they giggled. "I think you're going to do more than talk," Melody called out cheekily!

Ffion laughed, and said, "mind your business, and get back to your boy talk!"

Laughing I pulled Ffion onto the bed and wrestled with her. "Let's talk with our bodies," I said, holding down her hands while she laughed and pushed my arms trying to escape. "Don't you know that communication is over ninety percent nonverbal," I said, as I continued to hold her down on the bed.

"No," she blushed, "please show me!" And I did!

∽

The following Friday, Melody's friend Destiny came over to stay for the weekend, and Samantha had made plans to go to West Wales with her new boyfriend. That left Ffion and I the weekend to do what we pleased, so we decided to go and visit my brother Fraser and his wife Lynn. It had been too long since we had seen them, and Fraser suggested that we stay at his place Friday and Saturday nights, and plan day trips around the Gower on Saturday and Sunday.

∽

After breakfast on Saturday morning, we decided to walk out across Broughton Burrows to Broughton Bay. And if the tide was low enough, out to the old Whitford Lighthouse.

Fraser knew this area well, and he parked the car near the Britannia Inn.

"They serve a great pub lunch here," he said, "and if we get back early enough, we can have our grub and a pint here at the pub."

"A great plan," we all agreed, and headed off down a path towards the Borrows.

We soon reached the Burrows and trudged across the dunes towards the sea.

"I love it here," I said to Fraser, as he and I walked together in front of the girls. There are a number of paths through the dunes, each going in the same direction to Broughton Bay, and we chose the path of least resistance, as we continued to walk through the deep sand.

Broughton Bay is shared between the two villages of Llangennith and Llanmadoc since the parish boundary runs right out from the middle of the sands to the edge of the sea.

"I have always found it rather strange that no continuous lane goes around the base of Llanmadoc Hill and unites the two places on the westward side."

"Maybe they wanted to keep their communities separate," Ffion said, understanding my drift.

"I think you're right," I replied, "otherwise there would be a continuous path."

Once out of the dunes we turned north on Broughton Sands. Ffion, who was now walking by my side, whispered, "we didn't claim our territory by making love in the dunes, my lovely man."

"No, we didn't, will you take a rain check?" I replied, "because I have a rather strong feeling that Lynn wouldn't approve."

"Yes, I'll take a rain check," Ffion replied, "as long as I can cash it in next time we're here." And I sealed my pledge with a lovely long kiss on her lips.

"Get a room, you two," Lynn called out from behind us.

"See, told you," I whispered to Ffion who was trying not to laugh.

As one looks back up to the Burrows, two limestone outcrops come down and meet with the sandy dunes. The first is Prissen's Tor, also known as Spiritsail Tor but the local Lllanmadoc folk have always called it Prissen's. High up on the tor are two small caves connected by a tunnel. And I pointed them out to Ffion who was always interested in the Gower caves. I did not tell her, however, that I had eaten sheep in both dwellings! Back in my own Cave Days, I often roamed around the Gower with my spear in hand looking for fresh mutton.

Spiritsail Cave, as I have always called it, was the usual hyena's den, full of miscellaneous bones but there were also fragments of much later Roman pottery. I wondered if anyone ever found my sheep bones in the rather more modern days of the 1980s?

After spiritsail comes 'Hills Tor', "named after the 'Hill Brothers'," I said to Fraser, who emphatically agreed! After Hills Tor the higher ground takes a definite turn. From here it runs east, to form the rim of Gower that looks out over the salt marshes. At Hills Tor, we are still on the sea- side of the great low-lying spur of Whitford Point. And from here the stretch of dunes and pine plantations runs north for two miles out into the Burry Estuary. At this point in our walk, Fraser and Lynn walked ahead of us, and Ffion pulled my hand to walk slowly and let them get ahead of us. And the wonderful blushing lusting look on her face that I was becoming familiar with, was too much to resist.

"I want to cash my raincheck now," Ffion said.

"Wait," I said, as Ffion began to undress, "let them get a bit further along the sands, and let's go up into the dunes."

"The dunes are too far up the beach," she smiled, now standing in just her bra and thong. "Let's make love here, Kings, in this wild open space!" I loved how Ffion could go from her gentle prim and proper, shy looking countenance, to a wild and passionate teenage girl, who now tore my clothes off and pushed me onto the sand!

As we kissed and rolled on the flat cool sand, Fraser and Lynn were now a distant speck in our vision, and we expressed our love unto the wildness of this place. Oh, to make love in this wild and lonely place, exposed to the winds and sands, and the roar of the distant sea, that seemed to heighten our senses and the awareness of what we felt for one another. And we loved with all the rawness and trueness of our souls, two human beings on a lonely and desolate beach, where only the gulls swoop and screech. And Ffion and I fell deeper and deeper in reach, of who she is and who I am, for true love cannot lie, but fly-fly fly!

After we had dressed one another, and looked around for spectators, we walked out to the point, and looked out at the endless expanse of sandbanks that are exposed at low water. We saw flocks of oystercatchers piping through the shallow waters, as the sea, the salt air, and the exhilarating sense of space thrilled our souls as high as the blue sky above, as I held hands with Ffion my love.

Out on the furthest spit of sand, is the old Whitford lighthouse. And we could see Fraser and Lynn already exploring it. Ffion called out and waved.

The lighthouse is an elegant cast-iron tower that is 44 feet high and stands 20 feet above the water at high tide. When I was a boy, I climbed to the top of the lighthouse with an anchor and some climbing rope, and I waited for the tide to come in. A fierce gale blew up as I looked down at the brown sand filled waves with their angry white heads, threatening to drown me and sweep my lifeless body high up into the Loughor Estuary for the gulls and crabs to ravage. I still have dreams of hanging on to the top of the lighthouse and waiting for the angry waves to go out again. But that is another story.

We caught up with Fraser and Lynn and discussed what we knew about the lighthouse.

Whitford Lighthouse was built in 1854 as the coal and tin-plate industry developed out of Llanelli and Burry Port on the Carmarthenshire side of the estuary. It was certainly needed, because the channel constantly shifts and the bar into Carmarthen Bay is a welter of white water when the wind drives in from the south-west.

"When did it come out of service?" Ffion asked.

"Dad told me that the lighthouse was disused in 1933, but the tower, with its elegant iron balconies, is still intact, and due to the efforts of the yachtsmen of Burry Port, my father included, it has been put back into action again. And once more the warning light shines out over the winding sandbanks of the Loughor Estuary."

You feel very lost and lonely when you stand beside Whitford Lighthouse, and I pointed out the big power station at Burry Port that looms up across the sands away on the Carmarthen side of the estuary.

"This is a very lonely place," Ffion said, echoing the feeling I had inside as the wide open sands and dunes that surrounded me, conversed with my soul, and the hills of Carmarthenshire waved to me in the distance like long lost friends.

"My Grandfather told me that in the old days before they dredged the channel up to Llanelli, it was possible to cross the estuary by a path through the sands. John Wesley was guided from Pembrey when he came to Gower. It was a tricky crossing, Wesley remembered, and he stopped to pray before he made his way over sandbanks and quicksands, and Wesley was thankful to reach the shoreline of the Gower."

Fraser said, "one would be foolish to attempt such a crossing today!" And we all agreed with him as we looked out across the forbidding and melancholy sands.

"Dad took me out there once," I said, "and while we were talking and looking at the distant hills through his binoculars, the tide started to come in, and before we knew it, we found ourselves isolated on an ever decreasing bank of sand."

"What did you do?" Ffion and Lynn asked with concerned looks on their faces.

"Dad put me on his shoulders and we waded from sandbank to sandbank until we were safely in front of the incoming tide, which came in as swiftly as a fast paced walk."

"The tide is coming in again now," I said, "and we'd better get a move on back across the sands." As we walked back up the sands, it was not long before we looked behind us to see that the tide had already surrounded the lighthouse again.

"We timed that right," Fraser said, and we had, as the tide was flooding in fast!

We had walked around the flat sand of the point east-wards, and we came to the part of Whitford Sker known as Berges Island. As we looked to the east from the dunes of Berges Island, we could see the great expanse of the salt marshes that stretched out before us for miles.

"It reminds me of when we went out on the marshes at Llanrhidian," Ffion whispered to me, remembering the romantic time we had there.

The change from the wide seascapes on the west side of the point is significant and exciting, especially if you have an interest in bird watching.

One weekend in my early teens I spent a whole weekend here out on the sands with my father. He had bought me a pair of binoculars for Christmas, and I had not yet used them, 'not properly', he said. So, we came here on the east side of the point. And I found that the quality of the birdlife in the estuary and the marshes was quite astonishing. Like so many species of birds, it depends on the time of year that you can come and observe them. It was February I believe, when I came with my father, and we saw many different species, and some in great numbers.

I remember the wind blew raw on our faces as we waited for the first sunlight to kiss the cold sands of the Sker. Before it was light, we could hear the different sounds of the birds squawking and piping in the mist. Dad said we needed to get out early to see all the different species, and we did.

There were great black clouds of starlings that crossed from the Pembrey side of the estuary to Gower in the early morning. Starlings are such a common bird to see, but when they fly in their clouds of thousands, it is quite a sight to behold. As the sun slowly warmed the sands, we saw Dunlin,

Sanderling, and Knot, teaming along the shore. Wintering geese flew up the estuary from the open sea, with chevrons of the white-footed variety together with the commoner Brent geese in flocks of thirty and forty-strong. We also saw some Great Northern Diver, and duck in the plenty, Mallard and Teal and hundreds of Wigeon. Dad wanted to spot a Black Throated Diver or Great Crested Grebe that have occasionally been seen through the year. We didn't spot any but looking for them in the hope of seeing one was almost as much fun, as my father became like one of my friends, and I was able to get a glimpse of what it would have been like to have had my father as a friend when he was my age. To have a father who loves you and spends time with you, is one of the most wonderful gifts a boy or girl could ever have.

Today we saw several species of birds, and Fraser had brought a small pair of binoculars of which we took turns using. Ffion spotted a Great Blue Heron fishing in the shallow muddy waters of the incoming tide. We watched it for several minutes as it made its wings into a canopy and waited for a small fish to come to its shelter, then suddenly, in a split second, down went its beak, and up came its head with a fish. Ffion of course is my favourite bird, and she wore a bright shade of blue that matched her lovely eyes, and the auburn plumage of her hair. Her call can be varied from a flat monotone chirp to a loud moaning scream, but she doesn't like being looked at through binoculars.

"The heron has caught his lunch," Ffion said, as it caught four more fish.

"He's got the right idea," I replied, "we will have to pay for our lunch at the pub while he gets his fish for free." And as soon as Fraser and Lynn heard me say the word 'pub' they announced it was lunch time, and we slowly made our way back to where we had started our walk at the Britannia Inn.

As we sat at an old oak table and waited for our lunch to arrive, Fraser and I marveled at the old wooden beams on the ceiling, while the women stared at pictures on the walls that stared back and told them stories of yesterday's years.

"I have only one story to tell of the Britannia Inn," I said, keen to tell my story. "I can remember it like it happened only yesterday. I was 18 years old at the time, and there was as there still is today, only one doorway in and out of the Inn, this side of the kitchen. And in the summer months, a great big dog would sit across the entrance of the door. The owner of the pub at that time insisted that the would-be patron's step over the large intimidating dog to enter the premises. If the dog liked you, he would not stir or lift his head as you stepped over his hairy body. If he did not like you and felt you were unworthy to enter the premises, then he stood up and blocked the doorway. On my one and only previous visit to the Britannia Inn, I managed to step over the four legged hairy menace without incident, but my friend David Davies was taken exception to, and the dog suddenly jumped up and almost bit him! 'It must be the way you smell', I said to David, who took great offense to the dog and my words!

The pub's owner arrived on the scene quite quickly, and said to me, 'you may come in. But your friend is not welcome. The dog decides who comes in and who stays out!'

"What am I supposed to do?" David protested! And the man lifted his finger and pointed down the road. The next pub is five miles that way he grunted, and the dog proceeded to chase David down the road. In fear of receiving the same fate and being hungry I entered the pub and ordered a pint and a meal. It was some time until the dog returned to the pub, and there appeared to be no blood on its mouth, so I assumed that my friend David was still alive and well and may even be dining by now at the pub down the road. 'Cheers' I said to the dog as I ordered a second drink before stepping over the hairy brute and went to find David hopefully in one piece.

Needless to say, I did not return to the Britannia Inn again, that is until now, and the old dog has long gone, and probably the owner too."

After a wonderful meal at the pub, Fraser drove the four of us back to his house in Gorseinon. Ffion and I were like high school kids holding hands under a blanket in the backseat and found it difficult to control our romantic urges.

"Now we have to manage on that single bed," Ffion whispered as we neared the house. Fraser and Lynn only have one small spare room, and the bed is small even for one person, so any serious mating maneuvers would be out of the question tonight. Maybe I could contact Richard Attenborough and see if he has any advice on mating positions of orangutans. I would probably end up having to sleep on the floor, I thought feeling disappointed. Oh well, we will be back in our spacious bedroom tomorrow night.

As expected, our mating calls were subdued at best, and I fell off the bed as gracefully as I could and then slept on the hard floor using Ffion's cardigan as a pillow.

Sunday morning arrived, and I came to the breakfast table with a rather crooked neck after my disrupted sleep. Once we had finished eating, Fraser and Lynn retired to their living room while Ffion and I took a walk into town.

"We will see you this afternoon," I said to Fraser. "Ffion and I will probably have lunch in town."

It's a fair walk from where Fraser and Lynn live on Gower View Rd to the small town of Gorseinon. The town itself has only one main street and a few other branch roads with various shops and businesses, but as my brother often says, 'it's a proper little town where you can get most of the things you need'. I have gotten to know the town and some of its people over the years as I have traveled back and forth from Wales and Canada, and often stayed at my brother's house.

A town has a spirit of its own, and even a soul, very much like people.

My favourite place in all of Gorseinon, is 'Alberts Café'. For me it's the heartbeat of the town, where the locals sit around its little square tables and 'be'. They don't just sit and talk but are a part of the fabric of the place, giving the café its unique flavor and taste, just like 'Albert', who makes the best Italian coffee. The patrons are the 'news centre' of not just the town, but all of Wales and the country itself. Many times, after making the long flight from Vancouver and then a coach trip from London Gatwick to Swansea, the first place I visit once I have had some sleep is the café. The first time I visited the café, everyone in the place said "hello", and "how are you boy. Where are you from then?" a woman asked, hearing that my Welsh accent had become diluted with another tongue. "Aye, how are you boy?" said a working man having his breakfast, "are you from around here Son?"

"What are you having?" said Albert, from behind the counter.

"A coffee with two cream and one sugar, please." The wonderful noise of the steamer that makes each cup of coffee piping hot, plays like a song on the strings of my heart as I sit with my beloved countrymen, who heal my wounds with their friendliness, and welcome me back to the community I left behind, never too long ago. They speak to me with true caring and concern, that I can feel in the tone of their voices and read on their faces, like a newspaper. "You're back from Canada, are you? Then welcome home Son!"

After the first two times I had come into the cafe, and Albert had made me a coffee, I was away for two years. He lifted his head as I opened the café door, and by the time I had hung up my coat and sat at a table, there was a cup and saucer placed in front of me, and the words two cream and one sugar I heard, but they were much more than words!

My favourite seat in the café is the first seat on the left when you open the door and sit facing the window side, where I can see and feel the world outside. Old men and dogs, almost as old as Canada walk by, and there's that old lady that can hardly walk at all anymore, but she's still got that twinkle in her eye. School boys line up at the bakery door, while pretty girls stare at their figures in windows and dream that they could become more, if only one of the boys would hold open the door. Old Will and Coalman Bill drop their cigarettes on the floor, while Albert's assistant sweeps the pavement once more. Everyone is welcome through Albert's door, and the girl in the kitchen will make you breakfast and more, and a coffee and a newspaper is given to the poor, who know they will find warmth and fellowship when they walk through that door, 'hello sir, can you eat any more?'

Ffion and I opened the café door, and Albert was happy that I'd brought her on the tour.

"What are you having love," he said, while my order was already in his head.

"A coffee please."

"Two cream and one sugar as well?"

"Yes, how did you know?"

"You are both together," he said, "and some things I just know, now sit yourselves down and I will say hello, two coffees, Bronwyn, here and not to go." And the three of us sat down and talked and drank our coffees real slow. 'Customers are coming, I must go, lovely to see you both.' Yes, we know.

From my table looking out onto the street, I could see the grey stone walls of the primary school where the children play and eat. The buzzer rang and the empty playground filled up with noise and games, and I remembered my school days of playing football and hiding from bullies, playing marbles and eating sweets, and watching the girls, who in summer were in bare feet, what a treat, I'll have another coffee and something to eat.

After spending a full morning and having lunch in town, Ffion and I walked back to Fraser and Lynn's place. We spent most of the afternoon visiting and then drove home to Pennard.

That was a lovely weekend, we both exclaimed, and we had especially enjoyed walking out to Whitford Point on Saturday and seeing the lighthouse and all the birds out on the sandbanks.

Chapter Seven

Melody's Temple

On Monday morning, Samantha and Melody headed off to school and university as usual, and Ffion went to visit a friend and then to teach her dance class in the village. I had most of the day to myself, I thought, and looked forward to a quiet morning. The phone rang just before eleven, however, and it was Dad. He had some news on his latest translation of the diary, and he also gave me a bit of a hard time for losing interest in it..

"I have not lost interest," I reassured him, "I have just been busy, Dad. So, tell me what the latest discovery in the diary is."

"Taliath talks about an aunt that went back and forth through a flaming portal and had a type of reconnaissance role in which she reported the goings on of this side of the portal back to her clan."

"Just a minute, Dad! This sounds significant, as Armes told me about an aunt of hers, who is also Gay's great aunt, who crossed back and forth through this so-called portal."

"There is more Kings. Taliath also talks about a yellow flower of a plant that grows on the walls of a castle, and that it has special powers when it is mixed into a potion with another ingredient. She goes on to say that this other ingredient has been lost to her people's knowledge for many years, so no one else is able to cross back and forth through the portal."

"Wait Dad, wait! Did you say an ingredient that has been lost to her people's knowledge?"

"Yes, why?"

"Armes told me the same thing! About a yellow flower that grows on the castle wall, and that when the yellow flower is mixed with this other ingredient correctly, it gives the partaker a 'second sight' that allows the person to see what she calls a 'flaming portal' that is otherwise invisible to the naked eye."

"Needless, to say, Kingsley, between what I have just translated in the diary, and what you have told me about what Armes said about the yellow flower and the potion, there must be a definite connection!"

At Dad's words I felt shivers run up my spine, as I remembered my adventures with Paula Jones, when we met the strange girl in the castle room when we were kids.

"Dad, there is more, I said. I have never told you this before, but when I was a boy, I met a strange girl in the castle room at Pennard Castle. I was with our neighbour Paula Jones, who lived next door to us."

"Yes, I remember the Jones', continue with your story."

"Paula and I met this strange looking girl in the castle room, who appeared to be wearing old-fashioned clothes, as Paula called them. And the girl talked about living at the castle as if she lived there at the present time. She said she lived with her father and mother who were the King and Queen, and that there was a village and settlement nearby. She even talked about the old church of St. Mary's. What was strange about her, Dad, apart from her clothes was that she talked differently, like with an authority that was so different from Paula's and my speech. She also vanished when she wanted to."

"What do you mean vanished, like she disappeared into thin air?"

"Yeah, she did. I chased her out of the castle grounds and followed her as far as the old wall of St. Mary's Church. She knew I was following behind her, so she hid behind the wall. I snuck up to the wall and looked around it and she was gone! Vanished into thin air. Oh, and she did leave a headband on the ground where she vanished. Paula and I saw her a few times, Dad, and had conversations with her in the castle room, and she told us about the Yellow flower that grows on the castle wall, and its special powers."

"Did she tell you what the powers were?"

"No, she said that it was forbidden for her to talk about them."

"You never said anything about this before, Kings."

"No, I had forgotten about it. I did not know the significance of it then. It is like trying to piece together a puzzle but without all the pieces. After I visited Armes at the commune, on my way home I went to visit the Jones', and Paula remembered the girl and how she had vanished. She even still had the headband that the girl wore. And there is another thing, Dad, which really haunts me. I asked Paula if she remembered the girl's name, and she did. Her name was Tally, short for Taliath!"

"Well, Kings, we are in deep here, aren't we. There is far too much unfolding for us to ignore. The way things are connecting, and the amazing revelations we are discovering is quite fantastic! We must keep at this until everything connects in a way in which we can understand it. Only then will we have our answers. We have Gay's disappearance on a phantom horse, Armes- a woman who claims she came through a portal from another time, after drinking a potion, and a ghost girl that you and Paula Jones met at Pennard castle when you were children, and they all have some sort of connection with the name, Taliath!"

"Yes Dad, they do. And who the heck is Taliath Saren? Is she just one person or three?"

"I don't know Son, I don't know! I need a stiff drink."

"Me too, Dad," and we both laughed. There was nothing else we could do.

"I better put down the phone now Kings, Mary is calling me for lunch. Call around sometime and bring the ghost girls headband with you so I can have a look at it. Okay Dad, I will, bye for now and talk to you soon."

"Bye Kings."

∽

Over the next several months, Dad and I continued to translate the diary, but we found no clues about the portal and the potion, only the wonderful unfolding tapestry of Taliath's life and her people. We were over halfway through the translating of the diary now, and both dad and I anticipated discovering more things. But our lives were busy and full. Dad was restoring a small sailboat that he had bought on one of his getaways with Mary to Pembrokeshire. And I was enjoying one of the most wonderful seasons of my life, in my marriage to Ffion. Both the girls were doing well at university and school, and Melody and her friend Destiny had become inseparable in their friendship. Destiny spent every second weekend with us in Pennard. 'I think we have another daughter', Ffion would often say, and she continued to be a wonderful mother. Yes, I am sure a blessed man, I thought, as I meditated upon my life. I felt so happy and content.

Even though I continued to translate Taliath's diary, I didn't care about how much time I spent on it, the emotional charge I used to get doing the translation seemed to be gone, at least for now. And when I did work on the translation, it seemed less personal to me, and I read it as more of a story than something I needed a revelation of information from. Was it because I had let go of Gay and moved on with my life, that it was now only a story to me? I knew what it meant to Dad to keep going and finish it, otherwise I would have let it go long ago. Was there another revelation hiding in the pages of its future, and waiting to jump out into my life again? Who knows? I am just thankful that finally, the drama of Gay's disappearance seemed to be over, or so I had thought.

❦

A full year had gone by, and Helen was doing her bi-weekly cleaning of the house. I heard her calling my name from one of the rooms upstairs.

"What is it?" I called, standing at the bottom of the stairs.

"Come and see this," she shouted, and I headed upstairs to see what was going on. Just when I thought we had put the past behind us, she said, "I found this!"

Helen had gone in to clean the spare room and found the whole room set up like a Celtic Temple! I could hardly believe my eyes as I looked around. There were candlesticks with candles that had recently been burning. The old chest that the old mare named Nan's Nan had led us to before Gay disappeared six years ago was sitting there, and all the artifacts from inside had been positioned around the room. A Ram's head was up on a stand, and all the clothing was laid out on the floor, along with the daggers and ankle bracelets. And there were the two gold toe rings hanging on the Rams horn, I pointed out to Helen. This is exactly how I remembered Gay setting up the room six years ago! Helen and I began to look around in the other rooms.

"What on earth are we doing?" I said angrily. "Gay isn't here anymore!" But the truth was, we were both looking for her. Who else would have set up the room like this?

"It has to be Melody," we both said at the same time. But why?

"After all this time that chest has been put away, why would she bring it out?" Helen said.

"Maybe she and Samantha wanted to have a look at the artifacts," I replied. "They are interesting to look at once in a while, and they are too much of a heritage to get rid of."

"I know," Helen said with a look of frustration, "I just thought all this Celtic Clan stuff was behind us."

"I'm sure it is," I tried to reassure her, trying to make light of things. "I will talk to the girls once they get home."

But inside I felt as haunted as Helen was, and I felt knots in my stomach. It was exactly set up as Gay had it, that day when I took Dad and Mary for a tour of our house. I didn't say anything more to Helen, but I put the artifacts back in the chest and took it back to the garage.

"Please don't say anything to Ffion," I said. "I am sure it would upset her if she understood the significance of the artifacts being set up like this."

"I won't say anything," Helen reassured me, "it's fortunate that Ffion is out, so that we don't have to explain things."

"Yes," I replied, "I am glad she wasn't here."

After Helen had finished her cleaning, she went to visit her friend Deborah in the village while I waited for Ffion and the girls to come home. We had assumed that it was Melody who set up the room, and not Samantha. Who knows, maybe both of them had set things up? But my intuition spoke loudly, that it was Melody that had had the connection with the artifacts, just like her mother did.

Samantha arrived home first and knew nothing about it. Melody was in town with her friend Destiny, Samantha said, and would be home anytime. Meanwhile, Ffion arrived home from teaching her dance class in the village. Usually, she taught in Swansea three evenings a week, but this new class she taught here in Pennard.

Helen returned from visiting her friend, and we started tea before Melody and Destiny arrived home.

"Who brought the chest in from the garage?" I asked, as they sat down at the table to join us.

"Destiny and I did," Melody replied. "I wanted to show Destiny the artifacts that we found. I have been telling her the story of how Nan's Nan led us to find the chest, and that the artifacts in the chest belonged to a Celtic Clan. Was that alright to bring them in, Dad?"

"Yes, of course," I said, as Helen turned her head and looked away. "I was just surprised that you set up the artifacts in the spare room, it looked like a Celtic Temple."

"I am going to put them back," Melody continued. "Is there something wrong Dad?"

"No nothing," I replied, "you did an amazing job. I thought I was standing in a temple when I went into the room."

Melody smiled and said, "thank you Dad," but Helen excused herself to the other room. Ffion looked across at me as if she was missing something.

"What is wrong with Helen?" she asked.

"I don't know," I replied, not wanting to have to explain everything, "but I will go and make sure she is alright." I got up from the table and followed Helen into the hallway.

"What is wrong," I asked, although I was sure that I knew.

"Seeing those artifacts set up like that brought a lot of memories back," Helen said, "and I felt I was reliving what I went through with Gay."

"I hope we are not going to," I replied. "I am sure everything will be alright."

"Thanks, Kings," Helen said, and we went back to the dining room table to join the others.

"Everything alright, Helen?" Ffion asked.

"Yes, thank you Ffion," Helen said. "I'm just having a bad day."

After Samantha and Melody had retired for the evening, Helen and I were able to talk, and we felt it best that we share the significance of the artifacts with Ffion, as she could see that Helen was still upset.

"I'm sorry, Ffion," Helen said, "seeing those artifacts set up around the room again while I was cleaning, triggered memories that I would much rather forget."

"I know," I replied, and I hugged her, and told her everything was going to be alright. "The past is gone, and we have all moved on," I assured her, "and nothing is going to change that."

"That's right," Ffion said, echoing my words of support, "everything is going to be alright." Helen now smiled at Ffion and me and began to relax. But inside a voice was saying to me, has it, has the past really gone? I answered, and said, I don't know, but I hope so.

Before Melody went to sleep, I knocked on her door and explained why Helen had been feeling the way she was about the artifacts, and Melody was very understanding.

But then she said, "Dad, can I talk to you?"

"We are talking now, aren't we, sweetheart?" I replied.

"Yes Dad, I mean no. I should have talked to you and told you something earlier."

"Well, you can talk to me about it now."

"Ok Dad. Firstly, would you mind putting the artifacts back in the chest, I don't want to touch them."

"You don't eh, well you set them up in the room, and you touched them then."

"That was the problem Dad, once I finished setting everything up, I picked up the creepy dagger. You know, the one with the evil looking man's face on it, that mum felt bad things from when we first opened up the chest at grandpas and handled all the artifacts?"

"Yes, I remember that one, it is pretty scary looking isn't it."

"Yes, and when I picked it up, I saw pictures, like live pictures of things and people flashing through my mind!"

"You mean like a daydream?"

"No Dad, they were bright flashing pictures, like so real! And they frightened me. I'm scared, Dad!" Melody began to cry, and as I held and comforted her, I could feel her trembling and the fear inside her.

"Melody you don't have to be afraid sweetheart, I already packed the things back in the chest, and mum and I will put it back in the garage."

"Thanks Dad," and I smiled and kissed her.

"Good night, Dad, I love you."

"I Love you too princess, nite nite and don't let the bed bugs bite."

"Nite nite Dad, and don't let Nan's Nan... I mean the bed bugs bite."

After my conversation with Melody, Helen headed home to Cardiff, and I decided to talk more in depth with Ffion and tell her everything that had transpired. She listened carefully to what I said and thanked me for including her in the situation.

"I know it must have been very difficult for you and Helen to deal with, seeing the room set up like a temple again, just as Gay had set it up before she disappeared, but it means alot, that you would talk to me about this, as I want to support you and the girls as much as I can. It helps me to feel more secure about things when you don't try and protect me by hiding things from me."

"Thank you, my love," I replied, "I appreciate your support so much."

"Let's get rid of the chest, Kings," Ffion said, "in case Melody gets caught up in the same things as Gay did. Otherwise, she may make the same connections with the artifacts like Gay did. That chest of artifacts has only brought trouble and confusion to your lives as far as I can see, please, let's get rid of it."

"Alright," I said, I will ask Dad to keep the chest at his place, and if he doesn't want it, then we will let the museum have it."

"Oh thank you Kings for agreeing, you don't know what this means to me."

"I think I do," I replied, "and I will call Dad to pick up the chest tomorrow."

∽

Dad was only too happy to take the chest with the artifacts, and I gave him everything except the two ankle bracelets, as I wanted to take them to Armes at the commune and find out what the markings meant. It was a relief to me also to not have them around as a constant reminder of what could have been, and I told Dad so. I felt I was slowly closing chapters of my life in a book I didn't need to read anymore.

Chapter Eight

The Powers That Be

For the next few days, and for reasons I did not know, I kept thinking about the story Helen had once told me about when she and her husband John had gotten lost on a camping trip in Cardiganshire. Why was I thinking about this again, after all this time? I remembered Helen had told me that she and John had pulled over to the side of the road, to knock on someone's door and ask directions. Gay knew where they were, and recognized places and even people when she was only three and a half years old and had never been there before!

I decided to talk to Helen about it, just to jog my memory.

Helen remembered it and recited the story just as she had told me the first time.

What was I to think? Could Melody have the same powers as Gay? Was she able to recognize people and places from the past before her birth? It was all very strange and seeing her so distressed as she described her experience with the dagger the other day, I felt I needed to find out what was going on. What was her connection with these ancient artifacts? If there was something harmful afoot, then I needed to protect her and our family.

I asked Helen if she remembered the name of the place where she and John had taken Gay camping in West Wales. I thought I would take Melody and Samantha there and see if anything might happen.

"Why?" Helen asked. "It was only a campsite, and there isn't much for the girls to do."

"I want to see if Melody recognizes the place like Gay did. We can make a weekend of it, and go and stay at the Salutation Inn," I continued to say. "It has been a while since we have been to Cardiganshire as a family.

As soon as I mentioned Cardiganshire and the Salutation Inn, Helen and Ffion were in!

"When shall we go?" I asked.

"How about we take the girls there for the Easter weekend," Ffion replied. "We can stay at the Inn on the Friday and Saturday night and go up to the Preseli Hills. Samantha and Melody can hang out together while we go exploring. I'm sure Melody would love to get some advice on boys." Sister talk, Ffion called it.

"I wouldn't know about that," I joked, "I grew up with my one brother Fraser, and we only talked about girls not boys."

"Glad to hear it," Ffion laughed. "If you talked about boys, it's very unlikely that you and I would be together."

"No indeed," I said, laughing with her.

We asked the girls, and they were excited to go, so I called Innes at the Inn and booked our rooms.

"You are bringing the whole family with you this time, are you?" Innes said.

"Not quite," I replied. "I still have my two boys in Canada who haven't stayed there yet. I will have to bring them one day."

We had one more week to wait until Easter, and I was looking forward to the break, and to also see what happened with Melody. Would she remember things from the past or nothing at all? I remembered Armes telling me that on her side of the family lineage, the girls had a type of cell-memory that can remember persons and places as far back as seven generations. Not that I understand things like that but listening to Melody describe what she experienced the other day while handling the dagger, I was more than curious.

∽

We left for Cardiganshire on Good Friday morning and arrived at the Salutation Inn just before lunch.

Innes met us at the front desk and showed us to our rooms. Ffion and I were able to have our special room, and the girls got a room of their own. Helen took a room across the hall from the girls.

"Yes! I don't have to listen to the girl talk," Ffion said enthusiastically. "I much prefer the man and woman talk!"

"You do, do you?" I said, pulling my fingers through her hair and making her blush. "You turn into the most lovely colour," I teased. Ffion smiled in contemplation as we carried the suitcases to our room.

After we unpacked, we decided to have lunch at the Inn, and then go and visit the campsite and village that Gay had identified in the past.

Helen and Ffion and I had decided not to tell Melody and Samantha why we were visiting the campsite and village. We would just observe Melody's reactions to the places and see if anything happened.

"I hope she doesn't have any connection to anything," Helen said, feeling nervous. "I just want us all to have a normal family life with no more drama!"

"Me too, we have had enough drama for a lifetime," I said. Only for me it had been 'trauma' not drama!

After a nice lunch at the Inn and a quick change into our clothes for the outdoors, we headed out to find the campground, and I showed the map of the area to Helen and Ffion.

"There it is," Helen said, pointing to a place on the map which read, Temple Druid. "That's the name of the village, but it doesn't show the campsite on the map."

"Maybe it's not there anymore," I said. "It looks like it's in the middle of nowhere."

"You'd be surprised," Helen replied, "nothing much changes around these parts."

"Then we will find it," I said. "Let's go to the village first and navigate from there."

"Why are we going to a campsite," the girls asked, "when we are staying at the Inn?"

"I just want to take a walk down memory lane," Helen answered, "and visit some of the places I went to when I was young."

"You are still young," Samantha said, calling out from the back seat, "and I do understand why you want to go and explore places that you enjoyed in the past."

"Me too," Melody said, not wanting to be outdone by her sister.

"And I guess the girl talk has started," I said to Helen.

"Oh, this isn't girl talk," Helen replied, with a teasing smile. "This is merely a sisterly competition, the girl talk is something else, believe me!"

"I do," I replied, feeling I'd lived a rather sheltered life without having had any sisters of my own. But I had my Sam for a daughter, and I'd learned a lot in watching her grow up. And as Samantha and I often say, 'we grew up together', me as a dad, and she as a daughter.

Just then it all started! Not the girl-talk, but a sign in the road which read, Temple Druid, but I didn't see any druids.

"I am sure you will see some before long, Dad," Samantha said, laughing at my humour.

"Turn left at the sign," Melody said, as I was about to turn right.

"You know the way?" Helen said to Melody.

"Yes," she replied, "I do. Follow the road until we reach the top of the hill, and the campground is on the right. You drive through the two wooden pillars, and you will see the sign for the campground in front of you." Ffion looked across at me from the passenger seat, and then turned around to talk to Melody.

"I thought you hadn't been here before," Ffion said.

"I have, I mean I haven't…" Melody answered in a rather unsure tone of voice. A look of concern was growing on Helen's face, and Samantha and I were as quiet as church mice. This can't be happening I thought, no way, but it was!

"What is the name of the campground?" Samantha asked, as we started to climb the hill.

"It's called Foel-Cwmcerwyn, and it's written on a big green sign with a picture of a triangle tent on it."

Helen then looked across at me, and said, "yes, that is the name of the campground, I remember it, but how do you know, Melody?"

"I just know that it's here." We reached the top of the hill, and there on the right side of the road, were the two wooden pillars, and the big green sign in front of us read, Foel-Cwmcer-wyn campground. And I thought, bloody …

I drove to the nearest site with a picnic table, and we got out of the car. Ffion, Helen and I, still surprised, sat at the picnic table while the girls took a walk around the campground.

"What is the number of this campsite?" Helen asked me. And I looked around to see a number plaque on a tree.

"This is number 11," I said.

"John and I used to take Gay and Pearl to number 17," Helen said. "I wonder if Melody will know what one we stayed at."

We sat and waited for the girls to return.

"Would you like to walk around the campground and catch them up?" I said to Ffion and Helen.

"No," Helen replied, "if you don't mind, I'd like to just wait here, but you two can go."

"That's alright," I said. "Ffion and I will wait here with you." Helen forced a smile and we sat and waited for the girls to come back.

"We found it!" We heard Melody calling, "we found the campsite that you used to stay in, Grandma!"

"And what one is that Melody?" Helen asked as the girls arrived back at our picnic table.

"It's number 17, that's the one you stayed in," Melody said, quite undaunted. Samantha just stood there not knowing what to say. We all knew that Melody had never been here before.

"Let's walk back over there," Helen said, putting on a brave face. "Gay and Pearl used to have a lot of fun there." And we all walked over to number 17. "We used to have a fire here," Helen said, pointing to a place on the ground, "and we used to pitch our tent here next to the hedge so that we would be sheltered from the wind."

Fortunately, after a minute or two, the girls started to walk back to the car, leaving the rest of us to follow behind them. I was concerned that Melody would say more in relation to knowing the place, and Helen was feeling very vulnerable. I put my arm around her as we walked back to the car.

"There isn't much to do here," Helen said, "why don't we take the girls to the village and see if she recognizes anything else."

"Are you sure?" Ffion said. "I was thinking we should go to the seafront and find a beach; you must have had enough by now."

"I'm alright, and thank you for asking," Helen replied. "I think we can come to the conclusion that Melody has her mother's gift," I said, "but that is not necessarily a bad thing. She could do a lot of good with it, if she learns how to channel it for good in people's lives."

"I know," Helen replied, "and thanks for reassuring me, Kings. But it's okay, I feel I need to go to the village, and then we can do something else."

"Don't forget we are going up on the Hills tomorrow exploring," I said, trying to cheer her up, and she smiled.

"Come on everyone," I said as we got back in the car. "Let's go and see the village and see what's changed."

"I'm sure nothing has changed there either," Helen said, in a more cheerful voice, "as I said not much changes in this part of the world."

Melody gave us directions back to the village, as if she knew the way like the back of her hand, and the rest of us could only marvel at it. But I wondered, what the heck was going on?

We passed the sign which read Temple Druid, and Melody said, "take a left here, and drive about a mile up the road and there will be a farm on the left, it's called Rosebush Farm and the farmhouse has a red door and a thatched roof." As Melody finished speaking, Helen gave me a look as to say, 'oh well this is the way it is', and I felt that she was becoming accepting of what was happening. The look of dread and concern was slowly lifting from her face.

We reached a farm on the left side of the road as Melody had said, and the name of the farm was Rosebush Farm.

"And look! It has a red door and a thatched roof," Ffion and Samantha said. "Just like you said Melody. This is wild! How do you know all this, when you haven't been here before?"

"I don't know, I just do," Melody said, feeling awkward.

We sat in the car and looked at the farmhouse from the road for quite some time, and then Helen said, "who wants to go and check out the farm?" Samantha and Melody were quiet, and I think Samantha was picking up on Melodys discomfort.

"I want to check things out," I said, breaking the silence, and I drove the car up the driveway.

"Do you know anything about the people who live in the farmhouse, Melody?" Ffion asked.

"Why do you guys want to know!" Melody retorted, "so you can make fun of me?"

"No, of course not," both Helen and I said together. "You have a special gift, and it's nothing to make fun of."

"That's right," Samantha said, trying to support her sister. "You have a special gift that a lot of people would love to have."

"Then they are welcome to it," Melody replied, still feeling overwhelmed. "Now is there anything else you guys want to know before we get the heck out of here?" Melody continued to say.

"Only one more thing," Helen said, and I gave her a look to say, no, let's just get out of here.

"What's your question?" Melody said in answer to Helen.

"Do you remember who lives in the farmhouse, and the other house across the courtyard?"

"Yes, I do," Melody answered in an angry voice. "Aylwen and Afon live in the main farm house, and Aylwen milks the cows everyday in the barn at 4-o-clock. And Eurneid lives across the courtyard in the other house, and the pigeons shit on his roof." Samantha laughed at the thought of the pigeons, and to our relief, Melody cracked a smile.

Just then we saw the curtains move in the farmhouse window, and a face peered out wondering who we were.

"Who wants to come and knock on the door?" Helen

asked, as we all sat silent. "Come on, they are wondering what we are doing sitting here on their property."

"I'm not coming," Melody answered, "otherwise I will end up having to tell you a lot of other stuff about this place."

"I will stay with Melody in the car, '' Samantha said, and Ffion, Helen and I went to knock on the door.

As we walked across the courtyard a flock of pigeons landed on the top of the other house, and I could see the slate roof was stained with pigeon poo.

Helen knocked on the door with the heavy door knocker. Slowly the door opened with an elderly couple standing there.

"Hello," Helen said. "We are trying to locate some acquaintances of ours. Aylwen and Afan, who I believe used to live in this house."

"Ah, yes," the man said. "My wife and I are the Lllewellens, I am Cecil, and this is my wife, Morgan."

"Pleased to meet you," I said, shaking the man's hand, and the woman smiled and nodded.

"Aylwen and Afon used to live here," Cecil said. "We bought the house shortly after Afon died; about four years ago, wasn't it Morgan?"

"Yes, she's been gone about four years ago now," Morgan replied. "She was still milking cows right up until she died."

"How about the house across the courtyard?" I asked. "Does Eurneid still live there?"

"Not for quite a while now," Cecil said. "Eurneid died about ten years ago now, wasn't it, Morgan."

"Eye, about ten years he's been gone, such a lovely man. I hope we have been a help," Morgan said. "Can we offer you a cup of tea?"

"No, but thank you very much," both Helen and I said. "You have both been very helpful."

"That's all I need to know," Helen said, as we got back into the car.

"Well," Melody said, "was I right?"

"Yes," Ffion said, "you were exactly right."

"That's awesome," Samantha said, hugging her sister like a hero, and Melody smiled at the attention and praise her sister was giving her.

"It is starting to rain," Helen said, "shall we still go to the beach?"

"Why don't we rent a pizza, and have an indoor night in our rooms?" Samantha suggested.

Suddenly, Melody was laughing at her words. "You don't rent a pizza, you order one!" Samantha now roared with laughter, realizing what she had said, and we all started to laugh.

"I needed that," Helen whispered to Ffion and me under her breath. We all needed a good laugh!

We drove back to the village of Temple Druid, and we found a pizza place on the main street. Druid Pizza House, it was called, and Melody said, "I think you will find some druids in there, Dad," and I laughed, and said, "why don't you and Samantha go and find me one and order a pizza while you're at it."

Helen laughed, and said, "Come on, let's decide what we are having, and the girls can go in and get the pizzas."

"What do you guys want? Helen? Ffion? Dad?" Samantha asked.

"Get us a meat lovers pizza," I said, "and if they don't have meat lovers, a Hawaiian will do. You girls order what you want, and here's 30 pounds."

"Thirty pounds!" Melody shouted, jumping out of the car with Samantha. "We can go to London with that!"

"How are you feeling now?" I asked Helen. "Melody seems to be coping quite well."

"Yes, she is," Helen replied, "and I think you're right in what you said, this gift of hers doesn't have to be a negative thing, as long as we don't have artifacts around the house that she can connect with. Oh, I forgot to ask the girls to pick up some pepsi," Helen said, getting out of the car and running into the pizza shop.

"How are you feeling, my lovely man?" Ffion asked.

"I can't wait to get you back to our room, so we can have some wild sex and a bottle of blackberry wine. In reverse order," I replied, and we both laughed.

"That's a deal! ... and what I need is a hot bath, and you for dessert," Ffion blushed, and said, "I'm sure glad I brought some blackberry wine and some bubble bath."

Helen and the girls were back with the pizzas now, and we drove back to the Inn.

"Will you be needing reservations for tea?" Innes asked.

"No, we have pizza for tea tonight, but can we reserve our usual table at the window for breakfast?"

"Yes, it's still free," Innes said. "We will see you in the morning then."

"Thanks Innes, see you in the morning."

"Are you girls in for the night? Helen asked. "Yes," they replied and headed off to their room."

"Girl talk and a movie, I expect," Helen said, and Ffion and I headed off to our room.

We sat in front of the window and enjoyed a glass of wine. "I'm so glad we have a room to ourselves," Ffion said. "Do you remember how we had to be on watch for Melody, and not make too much noise?"

"Yes," I laughed, "this is one of the rewards when children are growing up, we can have our own room and make as much noise as we like!" Ffion blushed, and her eyes retreated away from mine, and then she looked back straight into my eyes. Oh, and the look on her face, and her exquisite blue eyes, drove me crazy!

It was 9 am, and there was a knock on the door.

"Are you coming for breakfast?" Melody called out. "Samantha and I are heading down to the dining room."

"We will meet you there," I shouted out. "The table by the window is reserved, and don't forget to knock on Helen's door too." Ffion was quickly into the shower, and I started getting dressed. "I can't believe it's 9 already," I said.

"That's what happens when we play all night, handsome man," Ffion laughed.

Ffion dressed to the nines for breakfast, and I said, "I'll give you ten. I love how you dress up and make an occasion out of mealtimes! And that lipstick and nail varnish you put on, makes me want to love you like a caveman!"

"Oh, yes please," she said, as we laughed and giggled our way down the hall. And she lit up the dining room with her smile and beauty as we walked over to the table to join Helen and the girls.

Ffion and the girls and I enjoyed a full British breakfast, while Helen had a scone with Devonshire cream and a fruit and yogurt salad.

"This is the life," Helen said, "good food and no dishes to wash!"

"What should we do today?" I asked the girls. "Are you still up for exploring the Preseli Hills?"

"That sounds great," Ffion echoed. Helen said that she was going to have a quiet morning in the village, and in the afternoon, finally read the book she had been waiting to read.

"We are tired," Samantha said. "We were up till 2 am talking. Would you guys mind if we stayed here and relaxed?"

"No, that would be alright," I said, "but you might get bored, there are only a few shops in Eglwyswrw."

"Oh, that's ok, we just want to hang out in our room."

"What about lunch?" Ffion said. "We won't be back until this evening. But if you girls want to hang out, it's fine with us, and I can give you some money for lunch."

"Are we going home tonight?" Melody asked.

"No, we are here for two nights, and we are going to spend a full day in Aberystwyth tomorrow," I commented.

Ffion changed into some outdoor clothes, and we headed off to the Preseli Hills to do some exploring. On our way we stopped at a small village called Brynberian to pick up some lunch for the day. The weather was a mixture of sun and cloud with a moderate westerly wind, but there was no rain in the forecast.

"It might be blustery on the hills," I said, and I was happy that Ffion had packed some warm jackets.

Last time we were in the Preseli Hills we explored the standing stones of Pentre Ifan burial chamber, a Neolithic

Tomb that Ffion had found particularly fascinating. Today we parked the car in the little town of Newport, and climbed up into the hills by a narrow sheep path that was steep and overgrown in places. The views on the way were breathtaking, and every few hundred yards we stopped and looked back over the wild green sea, and the villages and stone houses before it. Kestrels, and what looked like a Red Kite, flew and hovered over the hills before us, as if beckoning us to follow higher and higher, deep into the ancient hills. The air was fresh and more breezy the further we climbed, and we stopped to rest on a rocky crag and had a drink.

"I had forgotten how exhilarating the winds and the wide-open spaces were," Ffion proclaimed, taking some deep breaths and smiling at me. "I'm so glad it's just you and I,' she said. "Oh, to have you all to myself!"

From where we sat on the high crags we could see for miles in all directions, and the feeling of freedom and space lifted our spirits as high as the Red Kite, who flew in a wide circle above us, riding the thermal currents.

"You don't have to wish to be a bird up here," Ffion said. "You can feel your soul flying!" We climbed down from the rocks and lay flat on a hill watching the clouds racing on the wind and casting their shapes and shadows upon the distant calling hills, and our souls answered them with awe and thrills. And there was hardly a sound around us, and the distant farms and houses seemed to be sleeping or daydreaming in a silent dream. A dog barked from miles away, its bark muffled by the gentle whistle of the wind that blew in from the Irish Sea and found us hand in hand. "Your love is so dear to me, Kingsley, I hope you understand."

"I do, I do my love, never let go of my hand."

On a distant north hill, there appeared to be some rocks standing on end, and we had found our destination, Carreg Coetan Arthur.

Carreg Coetan Arthur is a Neolithic Burial Chamber that dates from 3000 BC. It has a 4-metre capstone and 4 smaller support rocks. As we got closer, the stones looked like the famous Bluestones of StoneHenge that are volcanic and igneous rocks, found here on the Preseli Hills, or Mountains as the locals call them.

They looked a lot bigger now as we approached their ancient presence.

"I am so fascinated by these stones," Ffion said, "and I don't know why?"

"They are raw and true, and stand strong and brave on these windswept hills, and represent these harsh and unforgiving lands, that the peoples of the past, tried to tame and carve a living from. That is part of your fascination with them," I answered. "Like me you don't just see them, you feel them, and they tell you their stories."

"Yes, they do my love, and I need to tell you one of mine."

Chapter Nine

Carreg Coetan Arthur

"I have this fantasy of taking part in a Sacred Celtic Ceremony and being murdered with my lover in front of the altar and candles, having our naked bodies slain by an evil priest, and then burned and buried together in a tomb like this. We are together in death, and travel into eternity together."

"I used to be so jealous when you told me that you and Gay practiced some of the ceremonies that Taliath talked about in her diary. And when I read about them for myself in your translations, they drove me crazy!"

"Oh, Ffion, you dark horse you! We will have to live those fantasies out, won't we, short of being murdered that is."

Ffion blushed the colour of the darkest red rose in our garden, and I began to undress her in front of Carreg Coetan Arthur, who stared at us like an evil Celtic Priest from behind the brazen grey stone altar! Ffion moaned as I lowered her jeans and pulled them off her feet. She stepped out of her underwear and stood naked before the cold waiting tomb. And she bowed to the priest who held the dagger half hidden behind the stones, and then she turned to face me.

"You must stand naked with me," she said, and she tore my clothes off like a Celtic wolf.

I grabbed her hand and pulled her under the standing stones, and I pushed her warm trembling body to the ground. She pulled me on top of her, and I found her sacred place, where we moaned and screamed underneath the mighty capstone that stared down upon us like the slaying priest. He slit our throats before the altar and stained the grey stones red with our blood, and the screams of our passions were carried on the winds, across the green sea to Ireland, where a Celtic maid and her lover made love on a lonely hill, and the Red Kite circled and said, what a thrill!

"Oh, my lovely caveman, that was wild," she gasped.

"And the priest and the stones had done their jobs," I said, "and our lusting bodies were burnt and buried underneath Carreg Coetan Arthur!"

We lay underneath the capstone, and the four supporting stones, that stood like Celtic Warriors, guarding our sacred room. And our slain bodies were resurrected by the cool breathing wind as it stirred around us, and slowly we dressed.

For the remainder of the day, Ffion and I stayed up in the hills, basking in the closeness we felt with one another, and our souls met with the adventures of the hills, and the wild Irish Sea. For hours we sat up on the ancient rocks and looked out upon an emerald sea that turned to a navy blue or black as the clouds raced with the strong winds for miles out upon the singing salt air bay.

For me the Irish sea is the most British of all our seas; it is the most enclosed, and at the same time, the most picturesque. The six countries which surround it and the one that lies in its middle, have all contrived to show their grandest and wildest of their mountains along its shores. The Snowdonian Range in North Wales, the Clwyd Hills, the Lancashire Fells, the mountains of the Lake District, the Galloway Mountains, Cairnsmore of Fleet in the Scottish Lowlands, the Manx Mountains, the Mourne Mountains, the Wicklow Mountains, and this wonderful place, where Ffion and I stand like King and Queen upon our Preseli Mountains!

"Oh, Kings, my soul is so light and free up here, I could fly to Ireland!"

"Can I come with you?" I asked, and we were on our way!

And I took Ffion with me in my memory, to County Down in Ulster, where my father and I had once sailed on his sailboat Wistful.

We sailed into Strangford Lough, which retains its Viking name of Strong Fiord. We sailed up its narrow entrance for nine miles, and the tide raced in and out with a top speed of six knots. And I shall never forget my father putting my hands on Wistful's wheel, and I sailed through what dad called, an area of disturbed water. Fierce eddies pushed the boat from side to side and thrust us forward and back as I continued to man the helm under the proud eyes of my father. After I had conquered the narrows, we passed into an immense salt lake surrounded by a rolling landscape of pasture and cultivation and woodland which carried its trees and hedges down to the water's edge. The lake is so large that it gives you a water horizon with the distant land only dimly looming over it. We sailed around islands with large farmsteads on them, and sheep dotted their green hills. On one of the islands is Nendrum, the only Celtic monastery that has ever been fully scientifically explored by excavation. My father took over the helm and then ordered me to bring in the sails, while he steered us into a small bay. We disembarked our vessel after a twenty-two-hour sailing, and went to explore Nendrum.

"Thank you, my lovely man, for taking me with you in your daydream, I felt I was right there."

After watching the sunset, it was time to find our path down through the hills to the meadows, before it got dark. We held hands as we skipped down the steep paths.

"I wonder how the girls are doing?" Ffion said.

"They are probably enjoying some down time in their room. We will all have tea at the Inn when we get back," I said, and we carried on down towards the meadows below.

Suddenly, there came a distant sound of neighing, from one of the far hills, that broke the otherwise hush of the still evening, and I slowly turned and glanced behind me. Seeing nothing I turned back, and we continued walking down the hill. There it was again, only this time it was louder, and Ffion and I both turned around to look.

"I can't see anything," Ffion said, but I felt an uneasiness come over me.

Was the horse descending towards us from one of the high paths where we had been? Maybe not, I thought as a heavy silence hung over the orange cloaked hills, and the light began fading fast.

All of a sudden, the neighing seemed louder and closer, and in the distance, I could just make out the form of a horse with no rider, and my eyes scanned the hills for the figure of a person following behind, but there was none. In my heart I was being haunted again with the thought of Gay galloping back into our lives!

A look of concern grew upon Fion's face.

"Not again," she fretted, "it can't be that wretched horse."

"I wouldn't think so," I said. "The girls saw it only last week in the Three Cliffs Valley, and that's over a hundred miles away!" Still, I felt uneasy and continued to look back over my shoulders. We had reached the meadows now, and the distant hills were almost too dark to see.

Suddenly, it was right behind us! Cantering quickly on our path!

"It's coming for us," Ffion yelled, "it's coming right for us!" I quickly stood in front of Ffion and waved my arms at the horse! It swerved around us, missing us by only a few feet, and continued on the path! But we watched in horror, as it made a wide loop and began galloping toward us again!

"What does it want?" Ffion cried, fearing for our lives, and I could see that it was Nan's Nan! I pulled Ffion back behind me, and braced for the horse to hit us, there was nowhere for us to run!

To my surprise, it slowed to a trot and then a walk, and I said to Ffion, "stand still and don't run. If it wanted to harm us, it would have by now." My heart continued to beat out of my chest, as I kept Ffion behind me.

"It's the phantom horse," she cried, "and why is it stalking us?"

"I don't know," I answered, as the horse trotted around us in a circle. It seemed to be looking around.

"It's looking for someone," Ffion said, now looking into my eyes.

"It is looking for Melody, I know it!"

"We don't know that," she replied, trying to calm herself down, but it was obvious that the animal was looking for something. Nan's Nan stopped and faced us now as if she was looking through us.

"What's it going to do?" Ffion said, having burst into tears. "Is it getting ready to charge us?" Suddenly, it's countenance changed to a fluorescent light, and it became a phantom!

"Help!" Ffion screamed. And its fluorescent colour began to flicker and then it disappeared!

Ffion wept like a child in my arms for quite some time, and there seemed no words to comfort her.

"We have to tell the authorities," she sobbed, "I have had enough! It could have trampled us, Kings, and left our children orphans! Let's drive to the police and tell them what's been going on! I know you think that no one would believe us, Kings, but we must do something!"

"Alright," I agreed, wanting to show Ffion my support, but I didn't think for one minute that the police would take us seriously.

We made it back to the car with no more encounters with the horse. I drove to the police station in Newport.

A woman Constable took a verbal statement from us both, and then we filled out a form describing again what we had told her.

"So, what happens now?" Ffion asked.

"We will send someone out to look for the horse," the Constable said, "but it won't be until tomorrow, it's too dark to track an animal up in the hills tonight. And which direction did you say the animal went?" the Constable asked again.

"I don't know, it just vanished before our eyes," Ffion said again, and the woman gave us both a puzzling look.

"She doesn't believe us," Ffion said, looking at me.

"It doesn't matter what she believes," I reassured her. "We have made a report and I'm sure they will follow it up."

As we drove back towards the Inn, Ffion seemed to be feeling better now that we had reported it to the police, but I pondered quietly to myself, how can anyone capture a phantom?

"Thanks, Kings," Ffion said. "It meant a lot to me that we went and reported it, I'm sure you would rather have not."

"I'm glad we did," I replied. "It is important that you know I support you, just as you support me with things. I do think however, it would be wise for me to go and talk to Armes about our encounters with the horse, and to ask her about Melody's powers, as they do seem to be connected to Gay's family lineage, which is something Armes has previously talked to me about, certainly when it pertained to Gay and her disappearance."

Ffion was quiet and contemplating as I spoke, and I asked her what she thought?

"If you think it would help us to understand what is going on with Melody, then I think it is a good idea," she said. "But I would really like to come with you this time."

I would have much rather gone alone, but after our encounter with Nan's Nan up on the hills, Ffion was feeling unsettled, and I wanted to support her in any way I could.

"Yes," I replied, "you come with me."

"Why don't we go for a visit to the commune next weekend? I don't think we have anything pressing on," Ffion replied, so it was agreed we would go.

When we arrived back at the Inn, the girls had had a relaxing time in their room and were now biting at the bit for something to eat. Helen had also enjoyed herself. She had a lovely walk to the village and found a farmer's market…"and I have almost finished my book," she said.

"Did you buy yourselves some lunch?" Ffion asked the girls.

Samantha replied, "we walked to the village to buy some lunch, and then we just hung out."

"It was fun," Melody added. "We had some great girl time." Ffion turned and smiled at me, and I laughed and said, 'girl talk'.

"That's right," Helen replied, "very important for us girls." And we all headed into the dining room for tea.

"Look," Helen said, "our table at the window is still free!"

"We came and reserved it after lunch," Melody said proudly. And Ffion looked at her approvingly.

"How was your day?" Innes asked, having come to take our orders.

"It was lovely," Ffion said cheerfully. "We went exploring up on the Preseli Mountains" And I gave a sigh of relief as Ffion did not mention anything about the phantom horse chasing us up on the hills. I did not want Helen and Melody to know about our experience today, at least not yet.

"How nice," Innes replied, "and you had a dry day too. It can be quite windy and cold up on the hills."

Ffion and I were tired after all our rambling and exploring on the hills, and once we had finished tea, we headed back to our room to relax. Helen and the girls stayed in the dining room for dessert, and we told them to be up and packed by 10 am in the morning as we were going to spend the day in Aberystwyth.

"We will," they all said, " nite nite."

"Nite nite," Ffion and I replied, and we headed off to our room.

"It was a lovely day," Ffion said, "in spite of the horse," and I thanked her for not saying anything to Helen or the girls about our encounter. And she kissed me gently on the lips, and said, "of course, Kings, I know it would have upset them." And I poured us a glass of blackberry wine, and we sat at our little table in front of the window. Ffion had also brought a little chocolate cake, and we had it with our wine.

"I'm looking forward to going to Aberystwyth," she said, her big blue eyes full of excitement again. "I think the girls want to go shopping, and I would like to go down to the beach if it's not raining."

"That would be nice," I echoed, as I sipped my wine, and meditated on our day.

Ffion poured us another glass, and then giggled and said, "I'll meet you in bed, my sexy caveman." After finishing my wine, I followed her items of clothing that she'd taken off between the living room and the bedroom, and I got excited as I looked down at her underwear and bra that were outside the bedroom door.

"Come and get me," she shouted, as I opened the door and saw her sleek body, waiting underneath the sheets. And I stripped off and climbed into bed.

As Ffion climbed on top of me, and we looked deep into each other's eyes, there was a wonderful awareness that said to us, no matter what happens in our lives, and the challenges that we face, things will always be alright, because we have one another.

Chapter Ten

Easter Monday In Aberystwyth

There was a knock on our door at 10 am, and Helen and the girls were up and packed and ready to go. I went and paid our bill to Innes at the front desk while the girls took the suitcases to the car.

"Thank you, Innes," I said, "we have had a lovely stay as always, and thank you for the wonderful service!"

"I'm so glad you all had a nice time, Kingsley, and we will look forward to seeing you again soon."

"Thanks Innes, bye now."

"Bye Kingsley."

"What are you girls going to do?" Helen asked, as we made our way to Aberystwyth.

"We still want to go shopping," they said, and I parked the car down on the promenade.

"Ffion and I are going to have a walk on the beach," I said, "so why don't we all meet here in about three hours, and then we can find somewhere to go and have lunch." Helen and the girls headed up the road into town while Ffion and I walked along the promenade.

We walked westward along the seafront, and a light wind blew in from the sea. The sky was a combination of clouds and sunshine, and the signs of spring were in the air. Students from the university walked along the promenade and talked about their plans for the coming season, and shopkeepers were decorating their windows and touching up their storefronts with paint after the long grey winter, and Charlee the seagull was already sitting outside the chip shop, waiting to swoop down on peoples falling chips. And as I looked across at my lovely Ffion, her big blue eyes looked bluer, like the windows in the sky.

"I love you, Kings," she whispered in my ear, as I felt her soft hand in mine, and behind her eyes, her love spoke more than words could say, and my heart shouted, 'Hurray! Hurray! I am falling in love, all over again today!'

About half-way along the promenade are some stone steps going down to the beach, and we climbed down for a walk on the sand. Just as we were arriving on the beach, a young boy began to fly his kite with his mother, who ran along the beach trying to lift the kite like the wind, but there was not enough breeze to lift it off the ground.

"The kite reminds me of our wonderful engagement," Ffion said, her eyes dancing with mine. "Our engagement was the happiest day of my life, Kings, when I read your words to me on the kite tail. You made my heart fly, Kings, higher than I have ever flown before! Then you gave me my Ruby ring and made my heart sing. And I haven't stopped singing since the day you asked if you could court me, and we fell in love."

"Yes, I remember that day," I echoed, "and the special times when we met in Mumbles or in the Swansea Market. And you would come over for the weekends, when Melody was spending time with her friends."

"Our love was so young then," Ffion smiled, with tears in her eyes. "But I love you even more now, Kings, my love for you is so deep that it has no bottom."

"Like the blue pool," I said, feeling my love for her warming my heart.

"Yes, like the blue pool," she whispered back and kissed me, and Charlee the seagull said, 'oh please get a room!'

The sea was cold, but we took our shoes and socks off and paddled our way along the beach. When we reached the far end of the beach, Ffion's feet were cold, so I piggy backed her up the beach to the little tea shop where we warmed up over a cuppa tea. My grandmother was right! Wonderful things happen when two people talk over a cuppa tea, and the warmer the tea the warmer the conversation.

"Can I top you up with some hot water?" the waitress asked.

"Yes please," Ffion said, and she filled up our teapot. And we talked of our plans for the spring and summer, and our love grew stronger.

Three hours had gone by so quickly, and it was time we walked back along the promenade to meet Helen and the girls for lunch.

When we arrived back at the car, I could hardly believe what I saw! There was Melody, waltzing down the street with high heels, white tights, and a blue and white dress like Ffion's! Our daughter looked like a younger version of my Ffion, the splitting image of her, from her hair that Samantha had styled, to her heels that Ffion thought were hers.

"No, they are mine, mum," she said. "Samantha helped me pick them out, and do you like my dress? Grandma helped me to pick it out, it reminded me of yours, Dad's favourite!" Ffion worked hard at keeping composed, as she looked in a mirror at herself. I smiled and then laughed, as Ffion's face spoke volumes.

"Both girls have gotten their nails done," Helen said, looking at me for a response.

"Your nails look great girls," I said, "and you have had your hair done, Helen, it looks lovely!"

"Thank you," she said with a blush and a smile. "We all had a nice time in town."

Ffion looked at me and then whispered, tonight you need to have 'the talk', with your younger daughter for sure, and I turned my head and tried not to laugh, though it was a serious subject and I would have to talk to her. Ffion soon saw the funny side of things, and she and Samantha and Melody walked hand in hand down the street, while Helen and I followed behind.

"Where are you going?" I shouted after them. "It's time for lunch!"

"After the shoe shop," Ffion said with a wink, and they all disappeared inside. I told my stomach that we had to wait a bit longer, and I went into the hobby shop across the road.

Forty minutes later, three women came out of the shoe store, each carrying a shiny plastic bag with a square shaped box inside. And there was no prize to guess what was inside the boxes.

I said to Helen, who had been doing some window shopping herself, "Let's go and have a pub lunch."

It was high heels all round as they examined their proud finds around the table, and even the barmaid said, "nice heels ladies, where did you get them?" And I felt like a man out of the water, as I was required to hold each sexy shoe and say something about it. And I tried to imagine Ffion's painted toes sticking out of the front, and the sexy way she walked across the market floor in her heels, and words came to me that otherwise wouldn't.

The waitress said, "it's so nice to see a man appreciating nice heels, anymore where he came from?"

"No, there is only one," Ffion said looking right at me, "and he is all mine!" Samantha and Melody smiled, and I didn't feel like a man out of water anymore, and I gave my Ffion a big smile, and said, "I do like your shoes darling." She kissed me from across the table and Samantha said, "see Melody, I told you about the power of a woman's shoes!" And Helen laughed loudly, while the waitress arrived with our drinks.

I had a beer, and the girls had some wine, and after a nice lunch we walked around the old town until late in the afternoon.

It was time to go, I informed the girls, and we slowly made our way back to the car and drove home to Pennard.

"Thanks, Dad," the girls said, "we had a great time."

"And I did too," Helen said, as we arrived at the house.

Before Melody went to sleep, she asked if she could talk to me in her room, and I sat on her bed and listened.

"There is something bothering me, Dad," she said. "It's about what happened on Saturday when I recognized those houses and knew about the people who used to live there."

"What about it, love?" I said, trying to listen to her heart as well as her words.

"Well, I'm aware that I have these powers Dad, just like my mother did, and I am worried that I will disappear like her. I don't want to ever leave my life here with you and Ffion, Dad, or my sister Samantha, or Grandma. I love you all so much and I never want to lose you!"

"You will never lose us or disappear anywhere," I reassured her. "Maybe we will lose you in the shoe shop once in a while, but only for a bit." She was smiling now, and I reassured her some more. "It does not have to be a negative thing, that you have a special gift Melody, it is something you will be able to use for good one day, when people have lost their way, or need to know about something that happened in their past. But all you need to think about now, my Princess, is being a young lady, and to enjoy this season of your life."

"You mean with high heels and boy's, Dad?"

"I don't know about boys," I said laughing, "but high heels for sure"

"No Dad, boys too, remember you and mum always told me, that love makes the world go around, and when I see you and Ffion together you make the world spin. And I want to feel what it's like to make my world go around. What's it like Dad?"

"It's wonderful," I replied. "The world stops but you don't want to get off the carousel, and you keep spinning."

"I love you Dad!"

"I love you too sweetheart, now you get some sleep and stop thinking about your boyfriend."

"Come here Dad, I want to whisper something to you."

"What is it?" I smiled.

"He's just like you Dad, that's why I chose him."

"Then he must be some kind of wonderful," I whispered back and I kissed her cheek.

"Nite nite Dad, don't let mum bite."

"Nite nite Melody, don't let your boyfriend bite."

"Oh Dad, one more thing," she called out as I stood up to leave her room, "don't worry Dad, I remember what you have taught me about boys, I'll be good I promise."

Gosh, what had I said, ..don't let your boyfriend bite? That's not the talk Ffion wanted me to have. But it was all alright, I had my daughter's love, and that alone shone a bright light!

Suddenly I heard laughter coming from outside Melody's room. It was Ffion, and she said, "nite nite don't let your boyfriend bite?"

"Hey, were you eavesdropping?" I said.

"No, just passing by," Ffion replied, still smiling.

"You should be proud of the father that you have become for Melody, Kings. I would have given anything to have had a father like you! Samantha and Melody are so open and free with you, it's so lovely to watch."

"Thank you," I replied, "and you should be proud too! You are such a wonderful mother to Samantha as well as Melody, and a wonderful wife to me."

∽

Tuesday morning was back to school for the girls, and Helen drove home to Cardiff. Ffion headed off to teach her dance classes in Swansea.

Another week had flown by so quickly, and soon it was Friday again.

Ffion and I were going to meet with Armes at the commune as planned, and on our way, we would drop Melody off at her friend Destiny's place.

As soon as Melody got home from school, she packed for her weekend, and the three of us headed off.

"Bye Sam, we will see you on Sunday."

"Bye, have a nice time."

"I think Samantha is looking forward to having the house to herself," I said, as we pulled out of the driveway.

"I'd like to have the house to myself sometime," Melody said, looking to see how Ffion and I would react.

"Not for some time yet, young lady," I answered.

"Why, don't you trust me to take care of things?" Melody asked.

"I trust you," Ffion replied, "but I don't trust all those rough and tough boys in the village."

"Good answer," I whispered to Ffion, and I could see Melody smiling at me in the rear-view mirror.

We arrived at the little village of Cefn Sidan.

"Destiny's home is almost on the seafront. It's a really nice neighbourhood," Melody said. "Everyone knows everyone and it's very friendly."

"Pennard used to be like that when I was growing up," I replied. "There were more sheep than people on the village green, which was nice on a Monday morning, but rather boring by the time Friday evening rolled around." Ffion and Melody laughed, and I carried Melody's suitcase up to Destiny's front door. The door thumped open, and Destiny and her mum were at the door.

"Nice to see you, Ivy," I said, shaking her hand. "Thank you for having Melody over, she loves spending time with Destiny."

"A pleasure as always," Ivy said, and she waved at Ffion in the car.

"We will pick you up Sunday night at 7:00, Melody."

"Okay Dad, love you."

"Love you too sweetheart, have a nice time."

It was about a forty-five-minute drive to the commune from where we had dropped Melody off in Cefn Sidan, and Ffion and I took our time driving the country roads to Cardiganshire and on to Eglwyswrw.

We arrived at the commune just after 6 pm, and I parked the car at my usual spot in front of the field that leads to the main commune buildings.

As soon as Ffion and I began crossing the field, we were met by one of the women from the commune.

"They seem to have an uncanny way of knowing someone is on their property," I said as we watched the woman walking towards us from a distance.

"She's dressed like a Celt," Ffion said, as she drew closer.

"Hello," she said, and then bowed her head to us. "Can I be of help to you?" I recognized the woman as Heulyn from one of my visits, and I said Hello.

"Oh, Hello Kingsley," she said. "Have you come to see Armes?"

"Yes," I replied, "and this is my wife Ffion."

"Oh hello, I am pleased to meet you," Heulyn replied, bowing her head again to Ffion.

"Do you think Armes will be available to see us today?" I asked.

"I think so, once she knows who is coming to visit, I am sure she will make the time."

This time we were led past the main settlement buildings towards the old farmhouse, a different way than I had been led on my last visit.

"Armes is at the farmhouse doing her meditation," Heulyn said, as we crossed the far field. And to my left I could see the steam rising from the hot spring that the commune used as a Celtic Bath. Already I have fond memories of coming here to the commune, I thought. The friendliness of the people, the food and customs, and most of all the Celtic baths, and the pampering's by body servants that I have enjoyed with Gay and when I came alone. And today, what would happen today, I thought? Maybe another bath, and certainly a meal?

We arrived at the farmhouse, and Heulyn rang the doorbell.

I didn't feel the least bit nervous, as I waited for the heavy door to open. Maybe because I had Ffion with me, or I knew what to expect, maybe both?

The door opened, and it was Armes.

"Hello Kingsley! And this must be Ffion," she said, obviously pleased to see us. "What a lovely surprise! Can you stay for lunch? I was just about to go back to the settlement to eat."

"Yes," we both replied, "we can stay."

"How about I have our food brought to us here at the farmhouse, it is quite lovely here in the afternoon light."

"Whatever you suggest, Armes," I said. "Ffion and I would also like to talk with you sometime today if you can make the time."

"Alright," Armes said, "let us eat here at the farmhouse, and then we can talk."

"Could you arrange our food?" Armes said to Huelyn, "and then bring it to us here."

"Yes," Heulyn said, and she bowed and turned, and then started walking across the field.

As I watched her graceful walk, back across the fields in her long Celtic gown, I wondered what she got out of her servanthood? What gave her life the meaning and purpose that she was obviously receiving here at the commune? Was it the way of life here? Or was it the joy of serving others? I must ask her sometime, I thought.

Armes asked us to wait in the courtyard while she went back into the farmhouse for a few minutes. She returned having changed into a long gown that was see through and revealed her wearing just a bra and a thong underneath.

"Follow me," she said, "we will eat at the stones by the hot spring, and I began to get excited as I thought it was more than likely that Ffion and I would be invited to a Celtic Bath. And we were!

"We will eat here," she said, pointing to the flat stones in front of the bubbling pool, "and then we can enjoy a nice bath."

"Thank you," I said, still peering through the steam into the mysterious pool. I could tell Ffion was excited too, as she looked at me with her pink blush which always said more than words could say.

As we sat on the stones and waited for Heulyn to return with our food, Armes and Ffion talked about life in the commune, and they seemed to be getting on well. I had wondered how Armes might receive Ffion knowing that she had taken the place of Gay in Melody's and my lives. They continued to talk, and Ffion seemed genuinely interested in life at the commune.

"Would you ever consider coming here and joining our commune for a weekend, and experiencing what life is like here?" Armes asked Ffion, and then looked over at me.

"No, I don't think so," Ffion replied and then said, "it is something I might enjoy exploring one day, but not at this season of my life as a wife and mother."

"Well, you know you are both welcome here anytime," Armes said, and we thanked her for the offer. "Well please come and enjoy a Celtic Bath," Armes continued. "And what are your plans for tonight?" Ffion and I looked at one another, thinking we had only planned to stay for the afternoon and the evening if necessary, so that we could have our conversation with Armes, but I answered, "we haven't made any plans for tonight yet."

"You can stay here at the farmhouse," Armes said, "and make a weekend of it if you like."

"What do you think?" I asked Ffion, hoping she would like to stay. I could sure do with a relaxing weekend, I pondered again, as Armes waited for Ffion to answer me.

"It's alright with me," Ffion answered, "as long as we can have our talk with Armes."

Armes looked across at me, a little nervously, as she wondered what Ffion and I wanted to talk to her about. And then I remembered I had brought the two ankle bracelets that we had found in the chest. I took them out of my backpack to show Armes.

"Oh, I remember you telling me about these on your last visit, Kingsley. Did you ever find out what the markings said on the sides of the anklets?"

Ffion looked across at me with a confused look, and whispered, "last visit?" Of course, I had not told her of my last visit with Armes, when she, Helen and the girls had gone into Swansea for the day to do some shopping, and there was an awkward silence between us.

"Let me have a look at the ankle bracelets," Armes said, breaking the silence, and I will interpret what they say." I handed them both to Armes, and she held one in each hand. She closed her eyes and began rubbing them with her fingers, and tears began to roll down the sides of her face.

"I wonder what's wrong?" Ffion whispered, as she nudged me on the arm. Armes kept her eyes closed for the longest time, and then finally opened them. A look of sorrow was in her eyes as she first looked at me and then at Ffion. What could be wrong I thought.

She now looked at the markings on the sides of the bracelets, and said, "this one belonged to my mother, it has her initials, and the number of our clan, 'one hundred and forty-two'. It also has this special mark," Armes pointed out to Ffion and I, "this is the mark of a Clan Queen. My mother and grandmother were both Clan Queens and were murdered by an evil Priest who oversaw our Sacred Ceremonies." Armes began to weep and then cried openly.

Ffion and I looked at one another, not knowing what to say.

"And this other one belonged to my grandmother," she continued, and she pointed out the markings to us. "See, she was a Clan Queen too, she sobbed, "and this is the reason that I escaped through the portal because I was next in line to be Clan Queen and the evil priest was out to kill me too!" And I could tell through her sorrow and her trembling words, that this was real! And as Ffion went over and put her arms around Armes, I battled with my thoughts inside. These ankle bracelets were the ones we had found in the chest, and Armes had previously told me the story of her mother and grandmother having been murdered by the priest, and I had not believed her. But today I did! And as Ffion rubbed Armes' back, and looked back across at me, fear was in her eyes! The fear of knowing what Armes was saying is true!

Slowly Armes stopped crying, and thanked Ffion for comforting her.

I could see two people now walking across the fields in the distance, and I thought it must be Heulyn and someone else bringing us our food.

It was Heulyn, and another woman that I had not met before. The women were also carrying towels and gowns, and I was awkwardly excited as I pictured Ffion and I enjoying the Celtic Bath.

"You can stay in the farmhouse tonight and tomorrow," Armes said, as Heulyn laid a large blanket on the ground before us. The other woman put down a large wicker basket that contained our food. Armes gestured to Ffion and me to sit down on the blanket, and then she sat down herself.

"You have met Heulyn," Armes said, "and this is Argel, who has just started training under Heulyn." Argel bowed before us, and then placed plates and cutlery in front of us, while Huelyn placed a goblet in each of our hands, and then poured us some wine.

"This is excellent," I said," smelling and then taking a sip of the wine. "Is this the same wine that is made here at the commune?"

"Yes," Armes said with a proud look, "this is from last year's bounty!"

"This is excellent," Ffion echoed after me, and Argel began serving our food.

It was chicken and rice, with a thin chutney mango sauce, which also had walnuts and blackberries in it.

"Oh, this is lovely," Ffion commented. "Thank you!" Both Heulyn and Argel smiled and then bowed their heads. One of the things I noticed about Argel, was that she was wearing an ankle bracelet that looked identical to the ones we had found in the chest and given to Armes to identify.

Once we had finished eating, Armes clapped her hands twice, and the two women began to clean up and put away our plates into the basket. Ffion looked at me, almost embarrassed, as the expression on her face asked, what sort of authority does Armes have over these women?

"They are body servants," I whispered to Ffion, but she still seemed uncomfortable. Ffion then pointed out to Armes, that Argel had a cut on her foot and wasn't wearing any sandals like Heulyn was.

I'm keeping out of this, I thought, as I listened to Armes' explanation.

"Argel is not permitted to wear anything on her feet until after the New Moon," Armes answered, "as she is learning the discipline of humility."

"Oh," Ffion said in a voice as if she felt sorry for the girl. Armes, picking up on how Ffion was feeling, explained that all the disciplines at the commune were voluntary, except for some of the training of becoming a Priestess or Bard. And I wondered what kind of disciplines that Gay had endured during her training here.

Armes then asked me if I would choose one of the women to be our body servant while Ffion and I were at the commune. I looked over at Ffion, who asked if I would choose Argel, so I did.

Armes now clapped her hands three times and said a few words in Celtic, and Heulyn left us carrying away the wicker basket. Argel stayed and poured us some more wine, and she waited a distance away until we were ready for our Bath.

Armes now stood in front of Argel, who removed her gown and bra, and then a leather thong garment that appeared to look like something Gay had worn from the items of clothing we had found in the chest. Suddenly I was back in yesteryear, in Gay's and my home in Cardiff. Gay had called the leather garment a 'Surth', and had a special connection with it. I remembered Gay parading around our house waring this leather surth which covered her vagina at the front and seperated her buttocks behind, like a sacred piece of ceremonial undergarment. Gay and I had had many wild and wonderful romantic experiences as she wore the surth and other items we had found in the ancient chest.

Suddenly, I woke from my daydream as I heard Argel and Ffion talking.

It was Ffions turn now, and she was nervous as Argel began removing her clothes. She looked across at me as if she wanted to say something to Argel in protest.

"It's alright," I said quietly, "Argel is just being our body servant like we asked."

Argel undressed me and then herself, and she led us one at a time through the hot bubbling waters to the stone seats in the middle of the pool. Armes was seated first, and then Argel came back to escort Ffion. As Ffion and Argel walked out to the middle of the pool with their backs towards me, I noticed red marks on Argel's back, and if I didn't know better, I would say they were lashes from a whip. Or did I know better? Maybe they were, and the lashings were part of another discipline she was learning.

Argel returned to the side of the pool and our eyes met. She reached out and took my hand, and then walked me out to join the others. Once I was seated, she bowed to each one of us individually, and then turned to leave the pool. She soon returned with our goblets and another bottle of wine.

It felt so good to sit back in the bubbling hot pool and relax.

"Now, what is it you want to talk to me about?" Armes said to Ffion and me.

I started to talk.

"We have become aware that Melody has a special ability to recognize places where she has not been before, and has knowledge of people, who as far as we know she has never met before. Melody is obviously aware of this ability, or gift, whatever one would call it, and Ffion and I are concerned about what it means for her life and wellbeing."

"And there is also the situation with the phantom horse, Nan's Nan," Ffion continued, "and we don't know who else we can talk to."

Armes was quiet as if meditating, and I wondered if she had even heard us? Ffion gave me a rather concerned look which said what I was thinking.

Finally, Armes spoke.

"As you found out with Gay, the women in our family lineage, have got special powers, me included." Ffion and I both looked at each other as if to say, 'what next'? I had previously had a conversation with Armes on one of my earlier visits, when she had shared that the women in her family had a type of cellular memory of people and places, but I had not been able to understand its significance, and certainly not when it came to Gay, and now Melody. What does all this mean?

"So, what do these powers mean?" Ffion asked, as frustrated as I was.

"Well, they run in the Saren family," she said, "and us women can remember people and places, for up to seven generations past."

"Yes, alright," I interjected, "but what does this mean for our daughter? It was certainly a damaging thing in Gay's life, and for her family around her!"

"Can you please let me finish," Armes said, in her calm and tranquil demeanor.

"Yes, sorry," I said. "Ffion and I are deeply concerned about Melody's safety and wellbeing, and we just want to understand what's going on."

"I will try and explain," Armes continued.

As we listened to her answer our questions, we were quite astonished by what she said!

"It's very convincing," Ffion said aloud, as we continued to listen, "even if it's not true!" Surprised by Ffion's boldness, I waited for Armes to react. And she didn't. At least, not in the way I thought she would. She was not in the least bit threatened by Ffion's words, and was calm in her repose, and her tone of voice remained gentle and empathetic, as she took into account how uncomfortable Ffion, and I were feeling about the whole situation. And I felt convinced that what Armes had said was true. Ffion did not however, and her frustrations got the better of her.

"I'm not listening to this," she said. "If I wanted to hear nonsense like this, then I can go to the library and read it in a fantasy novel!" And she stood up to leave the pool.

"Wait, love," I said, trying to calm her down, "please sit down. Who else can we talk to? Armes is trying her best to answer our questions."

"That may be so, but we are being stalked by a phantom horse that could have killed us! You had to protect us, remember, from that horse attacking us up on the hills!"

"Yes, I do," I replied, "and we went to the police, but do you think they can do anything about it; or would even take us seriously? No, they wouldn't, Ffion, so please come here and sit with me, and listen to what else Armes has to say."

Ffion burst into tears now and came and sat on my lap.

"I'm sorry Kings, I'm sorry Armes," she cried. "I am just really scared of that horse and what harm it could bring to our family!"

"It's alright," Armes replied. "It must be frightening for all of you. Would you like me to continue explaining what I know?"

"Yes," both Ffion and I said, we would, "please go on."

Armes continued to explain more about Melody's ability.

"It is not that I have a closed mind, to believe what you are saying, Armes," Ffion replied, "but what effect will this have on Melody's life?"

"That rather depends on how well she understands her abilities and learns how to apply them in her life," Armes replied. "She can live as happy and normal a life as anyone else. You must help her understand that she needs to stay away from certain artifacts and people that have a connection with her past memories unless she is ready to accept her gift. I have learned how to do this with some connections in my own life. Not everything artifact has a positive memory or attribute. And like so many other things in life, it is through trial and error that we learn. It is good that Melody has both of you to help her navigate these challenges in her life, and you also have me as a resource if you need my help."

"Thank you," we both said, still pondering what she was saying.

"So, an example of an association of something we need to help Melody protect herself from, would be the chest we found?" I said.

"Especially the chest," Armes said, "and people whose ancestry she connects with."

I shared about the dreams and visions Melody had experienced after handling artifacts from the chest.

"Yes, that is a perfect example of what I am warning you about," Armes said. "You must be vigilant in helping Melody understand this. And have you removed the chest and its artifacts from your home?"

"Yes, the chest and all the artifacts are now at my fathers house, except the ankle bracelets which I gave you."

"Good," Armes said. "You have moved the immediate source of conflict away from Melody."

"But keeping Melody away from artifacts is not going to be easy," Ffion said. "She enjoys going metal detecting with her grandfather and enjoys finding coins and relics from the past."

"We all enjoy metal detecting as a family," I said.

"It's not that she has to give that up," Armes explained, "you just have to be careful about any association she might have with certain artifacts that you find. Most of what you will find, she will have no connection to at all. And when she does have an association with something, she will know immediately, and you can dispose of the artifact. As I said, it's only certain things, like that chest and the artifacts inside, and on rare occasions, people whose ancestry she connects with that you have to be concerned about."

"How can we or she know who those people are," I said, still trying to get my head around what Armes was saying. "Those people could be almost anyone."

"You can't know," Armes said, "you don't have the gift, but Melody does, and she is immediately aware of who those people are the moment she meets them."

"Just like last Saturday, when she recognized the farmhouse, and the other house across the courtyard. She knew who used to live in those houses," I reminded Ffion.

"Yes," Ffion said. "I am making a connection now, with what you are telling us, Armes."

Armes gently smiled, and said, "I'm glad it's making some sense to you."

"How can we support Melody," Ffion continued, "if we don't know anything about these people that she has a connection to the past with?"

"You support Melody by allowing her to make choices as to who she chooses to befriend. Remember, Melody can discern much better than you can as to what a person is like, and their intent towards her. You trust her judgment and let her see that you support her in her decisions, and she will make the correct choices as to how she deals with those people. As I told you, she can live a happy and normal life, just like anyone else."

As Armes finished talking, I could tell that Ffion was feeling reassured by her words, and so was I.

We sat and enjoyed the warm bubbling bath as Argel, came back into the pool and brought us some more wine, and a few snacks to eat.

"My skin is getting wrinkled," Ffion whispered to me, holding out her hand. "We have been in the pool for almost an hour."

"Don't worry," Armes said, having heard Ffion's concern. "This mineral water consists of calcium, magnesium, sodium, potassium, lithium and silica, and it is very good for you and your skin." We sat back on our stone seats again and relaxed.

"Now we need to talk about Rhiddian," Armes said.

"Rhiddian, who is Rhiddian?" both Ffion and I asked.

"Rhiddian is the phantom mare that you call Nan's Nan," she replied. "First you must understand who Rhiddian is. Rhiddian is a Spirit Horse that is able to transform from the physical to the spiritual in appearance and is able to travel back and forth through the Portal of Pennard Past and Pennard Present." Ffion and I looked back and forth at one another, but we said nothing and continued to listen.

"Rhiddian has been protecting our Clan for over six hundred years. She fights off our enemies, whether it be warriors of warring clans, wild animals, or individuals with evil intent within their hearts, and anything else that she perceives as a danger to our clan."

"What does she want with us?" Ffion asked nervously.

"She has an association with you because of Melody, and you must keep Melody away from Rhiddian."

"Why is she stalking us then," I asked, "even when Melody is not with us?"

"It is because she knows your association with Melody; that you and Ffion are her guardians. She can see into your hearts and knows that you love and protect Melody, that is why she will never actually harm you. She is following you to get to Melody and she will keep searching for Melody until she finds her."

"This is crazy!" Ffion retorted. "And if this is true, how can we protect our daughter from being harmed by this creature?"

"Oh Rhiddian will not harm Melody," Armes tried to reassure us, "but she will protect Melody with her life!"

"It still doesn't make me feel any better," Ffion continued, "and I hope the authorities can destroy that phantom horse or whatever it is!"

I looked across at Ffion. "Come on love, just calm down and hear her out."

"Rhiddian is trying to find Melody so that she can bring her through the portal to be united with her family in Pennard Past."

"But we are Melody's family!" Ffion protested. "And that phantom horse is not taking her anywhere!"

"That's right," I said. "Our daughter is not going away with some phantom horse and traveling through some portal that leads to the past! This is crazy! And I will fight any animal or person that dares to try and take her away!"

"She is our daughter," Ffion continued to say, her words pregnant with a protection and passion that made me proud!

Armes could feel it too, revealing to her how much Ffion loved Melody.

"No one is going to separate your family! I am not arguing that." Armes said, "I am so thankful to you both for giving my granddaughter a wonderful life and home that I couldn't give her."

"Then help us protect Melody," I said, feeling angry.

"I am helping you to protect Melody," Armes said. "Rhiddian will never harm her or take her through the portal against her will. It is up to Melody, if she would like to see Gay again, because Gay is alive in Pennard Past."

"Alright, that is enough!" I said. "Come on Ffion we are leaving!"

"What about your weekend here at the commune?" Armes said, "and the things I have got planned for you to enjoy? Don't go, please stay!"

"I'm sorry Armes, but this is all too much, we don't want any more drama in our lives, we have had enough! Melody is happy in her life and has got over the loss of her mother. We are a family again now, and if your daughter Gay ever cared anything about us, then she would not have left her husband and daughter. Come on, Ffion lets go!"

"What about Gay's robe and her certificate? What did you do with them?" Armes called out. I didn't answer, as I remembered that I hadn't told Ffion anything about them.

Argel gave us some towels, and we quickly dried and got dressed while Armes stayed sitting in the hot spring.

"I'm sorry you feel that you must leave," she called, "but don't worry, Rhiddian will not take Melody anywhere against her will."

"Damn right, she won't," I shouted back as Ffion and I headed back across the fields to our car.

Argel followed behind us to see us off the property. Ffion took the opportunity to ask her about the marks on her back.

"They are not from abuse," she said. "They are from a punishment I received from the Ceremonial Priest, for not wearing the right attire during one of our Ceremonies."

Ffion shook her head, and said, "if I were you, I would get out of here before they do something worse to you! Would you like us to give you a ride somewhere?"

"No," Argel said. "I am happy here, and as I said, I am not being abused, I did something wrong, and the stripes on my back are the consequences."

"Come on," I said to Ffion, "let's get in the car," and we started to make our way home to Pennard.

"There is something I need to talk to you about," Ffion said.

"What is it?" I replied,

"What was Armes talking about when she mentioned Gay's robe and certificate?"

"Oh," I replied. "Yes, that. I forgot to tell you, but one weekend while you and the girls were visiting Pearl in Bristol, Armes rang, and asked if we wanted Gay's robe that she wore at the commune, and the certificate she achieved in her training to be a Priestess."

"I knew nothing about them, Kings, why didn't you tell me?"

"I'm sorry," I replied. "I just thought I was protecting you and our family from more trauma around Gay's disappearance."

"I'm upset, Kings, because you kept things a secret and didn't tell me. No more secrets, remember?"

"Yes, I remember, and I'm sorry."

"Well, what did you do with the robe and certificate? I haven't seen them around the house."

"I buried them at Gay's headstone in the churchyard." Ffion began to weep at my words, and I felt like such an idiot!

"I know you hid them because you wanted to protect the girls and I from any more trauma after Gay's disappearance, but you went behind my back and got rid of them, and not even thinking that Helen might want them to remember her daughter."

"I'm sorry my love," I said, pulling the car over to the side of the road. "The last thing I wanted to do is hurt you, and I did!"

"It's alright, Kings," she said, drying her eyes. "I know that you didn't mean to hurt me, and your heart is always in the right place. Can we go and get them? And at least offer them to Helen? They are something Gay worked hard to achieve and I am sure that they would mean a lot to Helen. I have grown close to Helen, Kings, and I regard her as one of my best friends."

"Of course, we can go and get them," I replied. "I buried them in a box, so they should still be in good condition. Why don't we go and pick them up from the churchyard tomorrow before we pick up Melody from Destiny's house?"

"Thank you for understanding, Kings," Ffion replied.

"Yes, let's pick them up tomorrow, I am too tired to do anything else today. It was very emotional listening to Armes and thinking about everything she said."

"It sure was," I echoed back. "I guess we could have stayed and enjoyed a romantic night in the farmhouse with a body servant," I said.

"No, you did the right thing, Kings, I didn't want to stay anyway and listen to any more of that nonsense."

"Thank you my lovely lady," I said, leaning over and giving her a kiss. But inside, I wasn't sure if what Armes had shared was nonsense, a part of me felt that she was telling the truth, and the thought of Rhiddian taking Melody through this so-called portal, haunted me all the way back to Pennard.

"What do you think of everything?" Ffion asked. "Shall we just try and forget what has happened with that horse and the artifacts in the chest, and just try to live a normal uncomplicated life?"

"Yes," I replied. "We will talk of this no more, and I am going to tell Dad that I am not interested in doing any more translation of Taliath's diary, at least not for a while. We will still go metal detecting with Dad, though, I am not letting the encounters that we have had with that crazy phantom horse rob us of having fun metal detecting and finding treasures."

Ffion smiled and took my hand, and said, "us girls are so blessed to have you as a husband and father and the protector of our family." I smiled at Ffion's words and relished the thought of the wonderful honour and responsibility that I had been given as a husband to Ffion and a father to my children.

Once we arrived home in Pennard and Ffion had gone to sleep, I rang Dad to tell him about the ankle bracelets.

"You're joking Kings," Dad said. "By jove you have made another connection then! First it was Armes having other children with the same names as Taliath's sisters in the diary, and now there is a connection with the ankle bracelets! What did she say when she first saw the identification markings?"

"She said one was her mothers, and the other belonged to her grandmother, and she cried like a baby when she saw them. And guess what else Dad?"

"What, Old Son, don't keep your old man in suspense."

"Both Armes' mother and grandmother were Clan Queens of clan number one hundred and forty-two, and were murdered by an evil Priest, just like Taliath records in the diary!"

"My gosh, Kings, this is becoming more incredible by the minute! Yes, Dad it is, but I have something I must discuss with you."

"Okay son, spit it out, your voice sounds heavy, what is it?"

"I need to take a break from translating the diary for a while. Ffion is getting really stressed about it. I'm sorry Dad, but I need to get my wife and family grounded into a normal routine of everyday life again, without all the drama around Taliath and this phantom horse, which apparently is called Rhiddian. It wants to take Melody back through this so-called portal that Armes is talking about, and it's sending Ffion over the top!"

"What are you talking about, Son? Rhiddian, Portal? You mentioned a portal very briefly before, in a conversation that you had had with Armes, and we concluded that she was off her rocker."

"Yes, Dad, we did, but hearing what she told Ffion and I this weekend, I don't think it's all nonsense, and I would like to talk to you about it some time. But for now, I need to keep things low key, because Ffion is stressed to the gills!"

"Ok Son, I understand, you can resume translating when things have calmed down at home, and meanwhile I will keep plodding on by myself. Don't worry, Kings, you made the right decision putting Ffion and your family first, this is a lot for anyone to digest. One more thing before you go, Kings, what did you say the name Rhiddian signified?"

"Armes said it was the name of the phantom horse that we call, Nan's Nan, and that it is after Melody, and wants to bring her back to see Gay who is large as life living on the other side of the portal!"

"Good God, Kings! No wonder Ffion is feeling over the top!"

"Yes, Dad, I've got to go because she's in bed sleeping and doesn't know I'm on the phone talking about this stuff."

"Ok Kings, hang up and I'll talk to you soon."

"Thanks Dad, love you."

"Love you too, Kings, now go and take care of that lovely wife of yours."

⌒∽

On Sunday afternoon as planned, I took Ffion to Port-Eynon Church, to pick up Gay's Priestess Robe and her Certificate that I had buried at her headstone. As we walked through the quiet church yard we could see Gay's stone in the distance, but as we drew near a horrifying site greeted our eyes! There was fresh earth beside the headstone and a hole where I had buried the robe and certificate.

"They are gone!" I shouted. "Someone has dug them up and stolen them!" It was all too much for Ffion, who sobbed and then cried loudly as she sat down on the church yard grass. I hugged and held her tightly, trying to comfort her, but inside I felt like I was falling apart! Who could have stolen them? Who could have even known they were here? There were no answers, only more frustrating questions. I helped Ffion back to the car, and after we had recovered from the shock, we went and picked up Melody from Destiny's house.

Chapter Eleven

Rhiddy-Rhiddy-Bang-Bang!

Weeks, then months, and then a year went by, and we did not see any more of Nan's Nan, or Rhiddian, as Armes had called the mare, and Melody had no more visions or experiences with artifacts or people that had any connection to her.

Life was good! And normal, for lack of a better word, if there is such a thing as normal. Anyway, we were happy and settled, individually, and as a family.

One Friday evening in July, Ffion and I came home after spending a day with friends in the village. Ffion found a note on the kitchen table from Melody.

"Hi all, Samantha, Destiny and I have gone to visit Nan's Nan with our boyfriends. Don't worry, we won't do anything stupid."

"I don't believe it!" protested Ffion. "I thought she had put all of this behind her, and the fact that she is going any-where near that horse is asking for trouble!"

"She probably has put all this stuff with Nan's Nan behind her," I replied, "it is more likely the boys have put her up to it."

"Do you really think so?"

"Yes," I replied, "boys will be boys, and I used to be one."

"Used to be?" Ffion laughed, and she began to relax.

"I would still like to go and make sure that everything is alright," she said, and we got into the car.

"I don't know where they have gone," I said, "but if we start at the valley and castle, that would be a good starting point."

As we drove along, we talked about Melody's boyfriend, Evan. We were both comfortable with him and he treated Melody like the most important person in his life and came from a good family.

Samantha and Cadan had been together for quite some time and were still together, and Samantha always told us that things were serious between them both, but there was no engagement ring on her finger.

"She's still young," Ffion said, trying to reassure me that things were different these days, and most young couples were dating longer before getting engaged, and often had longer engagements before getting married.

"That may be so, but I also have more old-fashioned values," I replied. "My grandparents wrote to each other for two years before ever meeting in person, and they were married for over sixty-five years. Albeit there was a war on at the time. My Grandfather even proposed by letter."

"How romantic," Helen pondered, "writing and falling in love before you ever meet in person."

"Not so romantic when the Germans are dropping bombs on London," I said, "but there is always time for love."

Ffion took my hand and repeated what I'd said. "There is always time for love, isn't there my love?"

"Yes," I said softly, looking into her big blue eyes.

Melody's friend Destiny had a boyfriend too, named Gavin. Gavin was a bit of a loudmouth and had been a bully towards some of Melody's friends in the past. Melody had told me that he was only on good behaviour because he was dating Destiny, and that for me, waved a red flag, but one must be careful when talking to teenagers, and make sure the facts are right. I have learned that lesson well as a youth pastor. Win their trust and you can talk to them about anything, but do them wrong and they will shut you out like the barred windows of a prison, and it's very difficult to win back their trust.

⁓

Ffion and I arrived at Bendrick Drive, and we parked the car.

"Let's hope they are in the valley or castle," Ffion said, as we walked along. "I'm tired after teaching those extra dance classes this week."

We walked along the sandy path beside the golf course, and then started to cut across the fairways towards the castle. We could see the castle in the distance, but we could also hear shouting and screaming. I wasn't concerned at first, as the kids were on their summer holidays, and they often hung out in groups of teens. But as we approached the castle, we could see that it was our girls and their boyfriends, and they were in trouble! Nan's Nan was chasing them fiercely, and the boys were running away as fast as the girls!

"Oh no, not again!" Ffion shouted, giving me a frightened look.

As we observed from our approach, Rhiddian, as Armes had called the mare, appeared to be charging at everyone, and trying to separate Melody from the others. Melody screamed as the horse galloped back and forth between her and the others. And whenever one of them tried to get closer to Melody, the mare gave chase.

"What are we going to do?" Ffion shouted. "We have to try and rescue them."

"I'm thinking," I said, as I wondered what on earth I could do. As the reality of the situation began to sink into my mind and heart, I could hear the words that Armes spoke to Ffion and I when we had visited her at the commune. "Rhiddian is searching for Melody and won't stop until she finds her, because she wants to take Melody through the portal to her mother."

"Ok, let's go," I said, and we walked towards them. My heart was racing, but I had to be brave, there was no telling what that creature might do!

We arrived where everyone was standing together, except for Melody who was already cut off from the rest of us, as Riddian continued to gallop back and forth between us.

"Come on, we have to be brave," I said. "Let's all walk together towards Melody."

Melody continued to shout. "Please, please come and get me! Dad, don't let the horse get me!"

"I won't," I shouted back, feeling the adrenaline fill my veins. We all walked in a line together, getting closer and closer to Rhiddian, who now stopped galloping and stood facing us.

"He is going to charge us again, Dad, I know it," Samantha said in tears.

"We have to stay together and not show any fear," I said, "and shout and wave our arms if she charges!"

Each time one of us stepped forward breaking our line to get closer to Melody, Rhiddian charged us, biting and kicking, and she bit Cadan on the arm, and kicked me, as we tried to break rank!

"She is herding us like sheep," Ffion murmured, hardly able to speak. And it appeared to us that this animal had a superior intelligence for a horse, or any other animal come to think of it! It seemed human like in its intellect. It stood and waited for one of us to make another move towards Melody, and seemed to be contemplating what we would do next.

"Come on everyone!" I shouted. "Run for the church wall, we can take cover behind it," and we sprinted to take cover, looking over our shoulders to see if she was charging.

"She is not chasing us now," Samantha exclaimed, "she has got what she wanted, Melody!"

And we all shouted to Melody to come and join us. Melody tried to make a run several times towards us, but each time, Rhiddian stood in her way, or pushed her to the ground with his nose.

"Help, Dad, help," Melody cried, and I felt my heart tearing!

Melody now ran in the opposite direction, trying to escape Rhiddian from behind her, but the horse gave chase after her.

"Do something!" both Ffion and Samantha shouted

"Alright," I said, "I want the rest of you to stay here at the wall while I go after Melody." And I ran after Rhiddian, as she continued to pursue Melody, chasing her further and further away. After giving chase and shouting at Rhiddian for about 15 minutes, I slowed to a walk as I was out of breath.

Melody had been chased to the other side of the golf course now, and I could no longer see the others behind me at the church wall. I shouted to Melody, "run back to me, Princess! Run back to me, and don't be afraid!" I had remembered Armes' words, when she said, Rhiddian will never harm Melody. I hoped it was true, as I continued to shout, "come on Princess, run back to me, don't be afraid!"

Melody stopped running now and looked back at me as she anticipated the distance she would have to run.

To my surprise, I could see that Rhiddian had stopped chasing her now and was standing in front of her.

Still breathing heavily and feeling my heart in my mouth, I kept walking towards them, until I was about 30 yards away.

"Watch out Dad!" Melody shouted, as Rhiddian turned and started galloping towards me.

"Stop, stop!" I shouted. "Come on girl, I'm not going to hurt you. You are Nan's Nan, remember, and you and I are friends!"

It was no use, she was still charging towards me, and I braced for impact, believing I would be trampled to the ground! At the last moment she swerved around me, and I let out a breath! For some reason, the horse didn't plough me down, and I thought, I might just live to tell the tale.

Rhiddian made a large loop around me, and then cantered back towards Melody. And I cried out to God to protect me, as I started walking back towards Melody. I would try and protect her, even if it cost me my life.

Suddenly, Rhiddian stopped and sat down in front of Melody, and I couldn't believe what was happening. The animal was actually sitting down! Was it injured or sick? I wondered as I walked up within twenty feet of it.

I walked about another 10 feet and then stopped in fear it would get up and charge me again.

It was then that Melody began to speak to me, and I was horrified at her words!

"Dad," she said, "I am aware of Rhiddians thoughts, and what she wants to do with me. And I know that she knows what I am thinking, I can feel it, Dad. We know each other's thoughts."

At her words, I was haunted by something Gay had said to me years earlier when Nan's Nan had led us down the sandy path to find the chest. And Gay's words rang in my heart again today. "I am afraid of Nan's Nan, Kings, because I am aware that she knows my thoughts, and I am aware of what she is thinking!"

Melody continued to talk and said, "Rhiddian wants me to climb on her back, Dad, and she wants to take me through the portal where mum is."

"Don't do it," I pleaded, "don't do it!" But Melody climbed onto the horse's back, and then it stood up. "Get off its back, Melody," I shouted, "get off now or it will take you away!" Rhiddian started to walk away, and I followed behind, still calling to Melody. "Please get off, Melody," I cried, "I don't want to lose you too!"

"What shall I do, Dad?" she called back, and for a few moments I was lost for words. Then suddenly I remembered something Armes had told Ffion and I.

"Rhiddian won't do anything Melody doesn't want to do."

I called out to Melody, "concentrate and think in your mind, and say, 'put me down, I don't want to go with you', say it and think it princess, over and over again, and the horse will put you down!"

As soon as I finished calling out to Melody, Rhiddian began to canter and then gallop, and I shouted, "stop, stop, you must not take Melody away!" My words seemed to have no effect, as Rhiddian and Melody disappeared in the distance. And I shouted in anguish, "no, no, not again! I have lost my Gay, and now my daughter, please God don't let this happen! I will never get over losing Melody as well as Gay!"

As I continued following behind, neither Melody or the horse were anywhere to be seen, and I turned around and started walking my way back towards the others at the church wall. My heart was heavy and torn, and after walking for about twenty minutes, I could see the others in the distance standing beside the wall. And I wondered what I would say to them. There was nothing that words could say, nothing that could explain what had just happened or give us any hope. Melody was gone, and our family would be left in pieces again!

Suddenly from behind me came a voice, and I didn't want to turn around in case it was a dream.

"Dad, Dad," the voice said, and I turned around. It was Melody! Yes, it was her! And there was no horse behind her. I just stood there dumbfounded, as I couldn't find any words, and I began to weep. "It's alright Dad, it's alright, I'm safe," she said. "I did what you said with my thoughts, and I kept saying over again, put me down, put me down, I don't want to go with you, and Rhiddian kneeled to the grass, and she put me down! And then she walked into this doorway with flames all around it, like a tunnel."

"Oh, my Princess," I said, throwing my arms around her, "I'm so glad to see you back, I couldn't imagine my life without you! Neither could mum or Samantha." We walked arm in arm back to the others.

"Rhiddian will try and come back for me Dad," she said. "I could feel her thinking before she disappeared into the tunnel."

"I won't let that happen," I reassured her, and I vowed in my heart that I would kill that horse. And then I said, "maybe we shouldn't say anything to the others, about knowing Rhiddian's thoughts and the doorway of fire, or mum because it will upset her."

"Yeah, I understand, Dad. Mum has had enough of all this, and so have I. And I'm sorry Dad, Nan's Nan came up in a conversation, and Evan and Gavin wanted to see her. Gavin was really pushy, Dad, and I should have said no. I knew better."

"It's alright," I said. "The main thing is that you are back safe, and I'm sure they won't want to see that horse again any-time soon."

When we met up with the others, it was almost a silent walk back to the car, as we all pondered a day that we would never forget. And we stopped in at the chemist in the village to get some ointment for the bite on Cadan's arm, and the kick on my leg which had a nasty gash. Fortunately, Mrs. Mills who owned the chemist store used to be a nurse, and she inspected the wound and bathed it with warm water and antiseptic.

"I don't think there is any need for stitches," she said, "but I want you to bathe it twice a day with this antiseptic until it has formed a scab. How on earth did you do this anyway, you obviously weren't playing football." Mrs. Mills had known me since I was a baby, so there was no pulling the wool over her eyes.

"I got kicked by a horse," I said. "I got too close to it and it let me have it with its hoof." Mrs. Mills took a look at Cadan's arm too, and said it was only bruised. I thanked Mrs. Mills and we got back in the car and headed for home.

I phoned Dad as soon as we got home and arranged a time to see him. I needed to talk to him and ask his help as to how I could destroy the phantom horse.

He invited me for tea on Monday evening, and I told him and Mary everything that had happened.

"I don't know how you can kill that creature," Dad said. "As you know, I've seen it with my own eyes transform into a phantom, and I don't know if you can kill a spirit horse."

"You have to do something," Mary said, "otherwise it's going to kill someone," and I showed her the gash on my leg.

"It's a good job it didn't kick you in the head," Dad said, "or you could easily be dead." He is right, I thought, that horse could have killed me, and I'm going to kill it, before it has a chance to attack me or my family again.

"Let me think things over," Dad said, "and we will come up with something we can do to stop this creature from terrorizing our family!"

"I'd appreciate that, Dad, Ffion has had enough, we all have!"

"Ok, Kings, I will speak to you at the end of the week, when I've come up with an idea."

"Okay Dad, and thanks for the nice tea, Mary."

"You're welcome, my handsome boy. Your father and I will see you soon."

It had been a nice tea at Dad and Mary's, and it felt good to get everything off my chest, but I left without a plan. What would I do if the phantom showed its face again? Or should I say when it shows its face again.

The week went by quickly, and I couldn't say things were back to normal at our home, not after what had happened. Things looked good on the outside to our friends and neighbours, but on the inside, we were all haunted by a horse named Rhiddian, and the frightening thoughts of when it would strike our family again.

Friday night had come around already, and Dad wanted to see me as soon as I could come over to his place. I arranged to go over on Saturday night, as Ffion was tired from a full week of dance classes and had arranged to spend time with just her and the girls on Sunday.

When I arrived at Dad's on Saturday night, I was surprised to see Taliath's diary on the table, as I'd told dad that I wasn't interested in doing any more translation, at least for a while. And after what had just happened, maybe not for a long time.

"I know you told me you weren't interested in doing any more translation," Dad said, "but I have found something in the diary that might help us destroy the phantom."

"You have!" I exclaimed. "Tell me what it is?"

Dad poured us a sherry and asked me to sit down. "This is what I have found out in my latest translation of the diary, here, read this."

❧

Tell me about Rhiddian, the warrior horse, grandfather, and why she is called after our name?

She is called 'Rhiddian of the Sarens', the mare with a stallion's name. She has been the protector and the avenger of our family since before the Beginning. She fights our enemies as brave and fierce as a lion who turns aside from no one. She is as swift as an eagle, and silent as the night flying owl that swoops upon her prey. Neither spear or bow, or a hundred men could ever tame her way. She has killed a thousand foes and saved a hundred friends.

Can she not die, Grandfather, be slain by an enemy clan?

Not while she is a spirit, Taliath, only when she is in mortal form, when her red coat does not glow. It is the Sarens Secret, that no enemy must ever know, that the only way Rhiddian can die is by a spear to her faithful heart, when her body does not glow.

❧

"That is easy enough for us to understand, isn't it Kings?"

"Yes, Dad, it's plain to see. We must attack her when she is not in spirit form, because then she is vulnerable and can be killed, and she must be slain through the heart."

"Yes, Kings, well read. Now let me tell you of my idea to rid us of this cursed creature."

"Please do, Dad, I'm listening," and I took another sip of sherry.

"We will go and find her while she is with the other horses, and sneak up on her before she can transform. You will shoot her in the head with my 12-gauge shotgun, and I will use my rifle and try to hit her heart. The rifle and shotgun together will bring her down and we can pierce her body with your special sword!"

I looked across the room at the old sword that I had found as a boy.

"It is still strong and sharp," Dad said, and I walked across the room and picked it up from the table. "Feel its weight and swing it," Dad said, and I did.

"It feels good and balanced in my hands, Dad, and will do the job I'm sure."

"Good Kings, that is what I wanted to hear."

"When can we do it?" I asked, swinging the sword with both hands as I imagined thrusting it into Rhiddian's heart!

"Next Monday is the full moon," he replied, "and we need the cover of darkness so we are not seen carrying guns across the golf course, and you can wear your sword strapped over your shoulder. The weather is supposed to be clear on Monday night, so the moon will give us enough light to find the horses in the valley or at the castle, and I'm sure that phantom Rhiddian will be there with them."

     Kingsley Ross Hill

"Thanks Dad, I hope the guns and the sword will be enough to kill it, and that we can catch the horse in its fleshly form."

"It's our best chance, Kings, and hopefully Taliath's grandfather is right and the creature can be killed! We just have to make sure we pierce its heart. Look at this, Kings," my Dad said, pulling a book from the shelf. "I've been studying the anatomy of a horse." And he handed me an illustrated vet's poster of the inner organs of a horse.

"Gosh Dad, you are all prepared."

"Here's its heart, and there's its lungs," Dad pointed out with his wooden cane. "And the kidneys are right here. But we want to aim for the heart!" And I felt relieved that we were going to do this, and that Dad was going to help me rid this creature from our lives!

"Did Taliath's grandfather say any more about the animal?" I asked.

"Yes, he said that Rhiddian was the only means of traveling from one side to the other, of this so-called portal, or doorway, as Melody also called it. I think that's what you said she called it, didn't you, Old Son?"

"Yes Dad, she described it as a doorway with flames around it, like a flaming tunnel in the middle of nowhere."

"By jove, what a sight that must have been!"

"Anything more about the horse? It's intellect or intelligence?"

"No, only the part that you already know, about the clan and how it had lost the knowledge of the secret plant to help see where this portal is.

"Maybe Armes isn't as crazy as I have made her out to be."

"Yes, I would agree with you there, Kings, I remember you telling me what she said. And you might be wise to keep her as an ally, rather than making her into a foe."

"I was just thinking the same thing, now that we know she has a connection with Taliath and her diary, she could be a resource of information for us."

"She seems to have a connection to everything, Kings, so I suggest we take her very seriously. She is vital in helping us to understand, and one day solving these ever deepening mysteries, of who Taliath Saren is, and this phantom horse Rhiddian, and now this preposterous doorway or portal that leads to another place and time! Or the same place at another time, where your now ex-wife Gay, is supposed to be alive and well. Poor Ffion must be on valium by now."

"Not quite, Dad, not quite. I try to tell her as little as possible about all the craziness, but she was there as you know when that horse attacked us, and she hasn't gotten over it yet."

"I'd like to know what all this means, Kings? But first things first, Old Chap. We can start by killing this bloody horse that is causing havoc in our family. "

"Well said, Dad. I'm looking forward to blasting that animal back to Timbuktu! Or a portal to a zoo, or wherever the damn thing is from!" Dad laughed and finished his sherry.

After Mary had made us a nice tea, Dad and I cleaned the guns, and sharpened the old sword.

"You always wanted to use that sword of yours on an enemy," Dad reminded me, as he watched me sharpening its blade with the little sharpening stone that we had often used over the years. "I remember you at 10 years old, standing on the end of Burry Holmes, and swinging that sword at Napoleon.

Then you wanted to swing your sword with Wallace, and fight against the English, remember Kings?"

"Yes, I remember," I said laughing, "and then there was that woman and her dog who came along, and you thought I was going to slay them both."

Dad roared with laughter, and said, "the old battleax came back and tried to tell me off once you had put down the sword. She said you were too young to be playing with a sword down on the beach," and we both laughed. Mary came back into the room and told us to be quiet as she was on the phone. "We better keep the noise down, Kings, otherwise we won't get her treacle pudding."

I finished sharpening the sword and lifted up the blade for Dad to inspect it.

"It is nice and sharp," he said, as he gently rubbed his fingers over the curve of the blade. "Yes, Kings, this will do very nicely, you have made it sticky sharp! I taught you well, didn't I!"

"Yes, you did. And I just thought of something else, Dad."

"What is it, Son?"

"Once we kill that horse, there will be no one traveling back and forth through that portal, and we'll all be safe, especially Melody!" In my heart I knew that killing Rhiddian would sever all hope of ever seeing Gay again, but we cannot live with what if's and had to do what was best for Melody.

"I think you might be right, Kings." So, Dad and I had a plan for next Monday night.

"Now don't forget, Kings, I will call on Sunday evening and tell Ffion I need you to come over to my place and move some antiques around, and she won't suspect anything, and the same with the girls, they mustn't know anything. People can get quite upset in the village if they know you're shooting horses with shotguns." I laughed at Dad's words and started the car for home.

"Bye Dad, see you on Monday, and thanks for everything!"

"Bye Kings, don't worry about things, we will sort that beast out on Monday."

Chapter Twelve

Monday Bloody Monday!

Dad rang the house on Sunday night as planned, and Ffion answered the phone. "Dad wants you to help him tomorrow night, love, can you help him move some antiques?"

"Yes," I said, coming to the phone. "Sure, Dad, what time? Alright, I will meet you at your place at 7:00."

"What have you got planned, love," I said to Ffion, making sure she wasn't planning to come with me to Dad's.

"Oh, I have a meeting at Pennard School. I'm advising the faculty on some exercise and dance programs they might want me to do with the students at the school."

"That is exciting," I said, "you are a great dance teacher and I think it would be great if they had a dance program for the students."

Good I thought, Dad and I could keep everything to plan. I would meet him on Bendrick Drive at 7:00, and we would go to the pub and have tea and wait until it was dark, and then go and kill that crazy horse.

Monday evening arrived, and Ffion left the house before me to go to her meeting at the school. At 6:45 I said bye to the girls and went into the garage to get my old 'Bowie knife', the one that Dad had given me for Christmas all those years ago, when I left home to go and live in Bacon Hole. My Bowie Knife had been like an extension of me back then, as I used it for skinning rabbits and spearing skate in the river, and in those early frightening days, Mr. Bowie, as I had named my knife, gave me some security against the dark creatures at the back of my cave that invaded my dreams each night. Would Mr. Bowie help me tonight, I pondered, to kill that phantom horse? It's not as heavy as my sword. I will try and pierce its heart with the sword first, and then finish the creature off with Mr. Bowie! And I headed off to meet dad for 7:00.

He was right on time as he parked the car, and we walked to the Southgate Pub for our evening meal.

"Everything is ready in the boot of the car," he said, as we waited for the waitress to take our order. "A pint of Guinness and fish and chips please, and make that two," Dad said.

"I think we will need more than a pint before this night is over," and I laughed.

We took our time with our food and ordered a dessert and a second drink. Finally, it began to get dark, and we walked back along Southgate Road to Dad's car on Bendrick drive. The moon was rising in the sky which had cleared after some late afternoon clouds that had hung over Cefn Bryn.

"It will be the perfect light to keep our guns concealed," Dad said, "and enough light to find the horses in the valley."

We reached the car, and he opened the boot. "Here," he said, handing me the shotgun, "and here are some magnum cartridges to get some extra power. One shot in the head with one of those, and that phantom mare won't know what hit her!" Dad carried the rifle's in a gun bag, and I strapped my sword over my shoulder, and we made our way across the golf course towards the castle.

"What's that hanging on your hip, Kings, is that your old Bowie Knife?"

"Yes, I thought I would bring it, even just for good luck, if I don't use it."

"I remember giving you that, Kings, for Christmas. Where has time gone? It only seems like yesterday when you were living like a caveman in the wild and living off the land and sea, and that was almost thirty years ago!"

"Yes, Dad, I can hardly believe how quick the time has gone."

As we got closer to the castle a heaviness began to come over me. I was on my way to try and kill a phantom horse named Rhiddian. But this horse was also Nan's Nan to me, whom I'd known since I was a boy. I had put Melody on her back and led her across the beach, less than 7 years ago! Was I doing the right thing killing this horse, or whatever this creature is? I thought about all the times it had chased us up on the hills and charged us just the other day when it tried to take Melody away. And Gay had vanished from our lives ridding on the back of this creature. 'Yes', I answered myself, 'I am doing the right thing, by killing this horse and protecting my family'.

As we approached the castle, the moon glowed like a crown upon the head of Cefn Bryn, and its silver light shone on the grass before us.

"Let's get the guns ready," Dad said, "and leave our bags here on the ground. We can pick them up on our way back."

I took off my backpack and unstrapped my sword from my shoulders. Dad took his rifle out of the gun bag and loaded its magazine with bullets.

"Here," he said, handing me the shotgun. It was Dad's double barrel over and under, that he used to use when he and I went shooting when I was a boy. I had a single barrel in those days. "You use the double, tonight," he said. "You can get two shots off quickly with this, without having to reload like your old single. And I have ten bullets in my magazine. That will be more than enough, even for a phantom. If the creature is still standing after unloading this lot, then we are in trouble Kings!" I laughed as I loaded my shotgun with the magnum cartridges and lifted my gun up and down to my chin to practice.

"I'm sure there will be a good kick with these magnums," I said, lifting it up again and looking through the sites.

"I'm sure there will be," Dad answered, "but you can manage it."

We could hear the horses now in the castle grounds and their shadows moved across the silver light of the grass.

"Remember Kings, we have to shoot it right away, and not give it anytime to change its form, otherwise our weapons will be useless. Be as natural as possible, and hold your gun down at your side, and that way we are least likely to frighten them."

"I can see eight of them, Dad," I whispered, as we reached the castle grounds. "I don't see Nan's Nan, I mean Rhiddian."

"Wait a minute," Dad replied, "there is a horse standing outside the castle room, maybe there are some more of them in there." We walked slowly and calmly between the other horses that were grazing and walked right up to the entrance of the castle room.

"Stick your head around the corner of the wall, and see if it's in there," Dad whispered, lifting up his rifle and cocking the trigger. Slowly I peered around the wall into the entrance of the room, and there was Rhiddian, with another three horses. Slowly I pulled my head back and lifted my gun.

"She's in there, Dad, with some other horses."

"We are going to stand on each side of the doorway, Kings, and as soon as we fire our guns, the other horses are going to come charging out, so watch you don't get trampled." I could feel my heart pounding now as my adrenaline began to rush.

"Slow and easy," Dad whispered, "aim carefully and squeeze that trigger, and fire, and then fire again, and stand back from the entrance of the door as soon as you fire the second barrel! Remember, just aim calmly, and squeeze that trigger, and then the same again."

Dad stood on the left side of the doorway and I on the right, and we lifted our guns to fire. "On the count of three. One - two, three - fire!!!" Boom! went my shotgun, and it kicked back on my shoulder! Boom! went my other barrel, and I could hear several fast cracks coming from Dad's rifle. As we stepped back behind the door, three horses came bolting out like rabbits, and I reloaded my gun. As Dad and I peered back around the doorway, Rhiddian was lying on her side in the sand, and dad shined a light on her. There was lots of blood pouring out of her neck, and several bullet holes in her stomach. I quickly reloaded and fired again, as Dad kept the light on the horse's head, and this time the animal made a low-pitched scream!

"Shoot it again!" Dad said. "It's still alive, let her have another to the head!" I emptied the second barrel now, which peeled the skin off its face, and the animal lay still. "Finish it off with the sword, Kings!"

I quickly ran over and thrust my sword into its side as hard as I could. Then I put down my sword, and pulled my Bowie Knife from its sheath, and I knelt down at the animal's side and stabbed the creature several times trying to pierce its heart until all the life was out of its body. Dad stood over the animal now, with the flashlight, and it was a gruesome site! Its respirations stopped and I looked away.

"Well done," Dad said, looking pale and sweating. "It's dead now!"

I was relieved and sad and my body trembled. We had killed the phantom horse Rhiddian!

"Look, Kings! There is something happening!" And I turned back to look at its body. Its mortal body was dead, alright, with blood and fur all around its lifeless carcass, but an illumined light now covered its form, and it flickered back and forth like stars in the night sky, and then vanished. Dad and I quickly loaded our guns again, in case it was coming back!

"If it comes back, then it's coming for us," I said, pointing my gun to where the body had been lying. "There's still blood," I said. The pool of blood was still on the ground, and I knelt again beside it.

"It's dead," Dad said. "I'm sure it is, otherwise, there wouldn't be so much blood! We killed it, Son, while it was in physical form, and phantoms don't have blood." Dad's words were reassuring, but the tone of his voice said otherwise, and I began to feel afraid.

I stood up and looked around the room pointing my gun, as if expecting Rhiddian to come galloping back through the doorway, but she did not come.

"We killed it," Dad said again, as he looked at the concern on my face. "We have done everything that Taliath's grandfather said in the diary that needed to be done to kill it! We killed it when it was in fleshly form, and we watched it die!"

"Yes, Dad, I know! But where is its body?"

As I was speaking it reappeared, its body still glowing, and lying in the sand where we had killed it. Dad and I watched with pointed guns, as the illuminess light faded back and forth from its body, and then suddenly it was gone again, leaving a dead horse of flesh, blood and fur. I kneeled and touched it, and it was real flesh and bone. And I felt a strange sort of peace, like knowing inside, that it was really gone.

"Come on, Kings," Dad said, "let's get the heck out of here before someone comes and reports us to the police for shooting a horse. There is no way we could talk ourselves out of this one!"

With one last glance back, and a look of relief at one another, Dad and I made our way back across the golf course to the car. We stopped on our way to pick up my backpack, and Dad put the guns back in their case.

"Shit, Kings, I've never seen anything like that," he said. "I think we killed a phantom."

"Me neither," I said, still looking back over my shoulder. We made it back to the cars. After washing my hands with a bottle of water, I changed out of my bloodstained clothes and we put everything into the boot of Dad's car.

"I wouldn't say anything, to anyone," Dad warned, as I wound down the window of my car to say goodbye.

"I won't," I said, now smiling, who would believe it anyway?

"Well, someone is going to find a dead horse in that room at Pennard castle, and I don't want to be around when they do." I laughed at Dad's words and said goodbye.

"I will see you later in the week, Dad, and thank you so much!"

"You're welcome, Kings, I'm glad we got the job done, and I will look forward to seeing you later in the week."

I drove home to Ffion and the girls.

When I arrived at the house, Ffion was home from her meeting at the school, and Samantha and Melody were studying in their rooms. Everything seemed normal in our world until later on in the evening, when Melody invited me into her room to say goodnight.

"You did it, Dad, you killed Rhiddian," she said softly, and I almost fell off the side of her bed!

"How did you know?" I asked, though not too surprised.

"I dreamed it first the other night, and I felt it tonight, in my heart, and I knew she was dead. It's alright, Dad, I'm not angry or upset. I know why you did it, to protect me, Samantha and Mum. There is no way back now through the portal to Pennard's past. We are safe now Dad, and I love you. Thank you for protecting us, you are truly brave."

"Thank you, Princess," I said, still startled, "and I love you too, more than all the bluebells in the meadow."

"Nite nite, Dad, don't let Nan's Nan bite, I mean... We need a different saying now, don't we?"

"Yes," I replied, "how about, don't let Samantha bite?"

"That's a good idea," Melody replied.

I laughed, "and when I say goodnight to Samantha, I can say, don't let Melody bite." We both laughed and I closed the door.

☙

For the next few weeks, Dad and I laid low, so to speak. We didn't go on any walks to Pennard castle or the Three Cliffs valley, and we didn't do any metal detecting in the area either. Not that anyone had seen us with our guns, but the news of one of the horses having been killed was in the local paper. Ffion and Samantha didn't mention anything, although I am sure they had their suspicions. And Melody kept it a secret, not even telling Dad that she knew. After about a month, there was no more talk about the slain horse in the village, and my family and I never saw Rhiddian again. She was finally gone, gone forever.

Chapter Thirteen

An Adventure In Penclawdd

Summer made her slow surrender to Autumn,, and it was time for Ffion and I to go on a little getaway before the next busy school term started.

"Where would you like to go, my lovely lady?" I asked.

"Oh, anywhere love, as long as I'm with you."

"I thought we would take a break from the Salutation Inn, this time," I said. "How about we go somewhere different?" Ffion and I had never stayed overnight in Penclawdd, and I had been wanting to study the marshes there, and in particular, the marsh horses that managed to live out on the salt flats, foraging the marsh grasses for food between the fast-moving tides. And of course, there were the famous Penclawdd Cockle Beds, that were protected by the fierce Cockle Women, who made a living collecting the little cockles from their beds. I hadn't explored the salt flats since my father took me there as a boy, and we were surrounded by angry Cockle Women, when we tried to take some cockles for ourselves.

Ffion liked the idea of doing some exploring out on the marsh, but mostly staying in a Bed and Breakfast, and having a romantic weekend.

"We would do both," I said, and we booked a Bed and Breakfast for two nights.

We booked into our room on Friday morning and went out exploring. I had a secret place in mind that I wanted to share with Ffion, if I could find it. Dad had taken me there only once before, but the memory of what we discovered was still vivid in my mind.

"Where are you taking me?" Ffion giggled, and I didn't give anything away.

"Wait and see, my inquisitive lady," I laughed, and I parked the car at the entrance of a narrow lane.

"Are you going to kidnap me and make wild love to me out on the barren marshes, my sexy man?" she asked.

"I am, if I possibly can," I replied, and Ffion blushed like the ruby on her hand.

"Come on, where are we going?" she persisted, as she took my hand.

"I told you it's a secret," I said, blowing gently in her ear.

Ffion giggled and said, "you are the only person I know who can turn a walk down a country lane into something so wonderfully romantic."

"Why thank you," I smiled. "That is what a man is supposed to do, when he has such a beautiful woman holding his hand."

At the end of the lane, we came to a farm called Llanellen Farm. The farm has several buildings that are solid and white-walled.

"I love the old stone buildings," Ffion shared, "with their white- washed stones and old slate roofs." We could see smoke coming out of the chimney of what appeared to be the main farmhouse.

"I'm sure they are sitting around a nice warm fire," I said, feeling the cool air blowing up the path from the marsh, and I could feel the warmth of Ffion's hand in mine.

Just beyond the farm is the site of a long-lost medieval village and church with a strange, romantic history.

"What is this place?" Ffion said, pulling my arm to stop. "I can feel an ancient past here, and many things that once happened where we are standing." And I thought it rather special that she would feel the presence of this place, as I had not shared with her yet anything of its history. "What is this place, tell me Kings?"

"I will tell you what my father told me, when he brought me here, long ago, and I have always wanted to come back.

"Llanellen once had a chapel here, close to where we are standing. There are records still showing its existence in the time of Edward VI. After that, the church and village disappeared from history. The grass grows over the site of the church and cottages," I said, and we looked around at the scattered stones that were here and there, between the overgrown grass. "Dad said there was a 500 year old Yew tree that is supposed to mark the spot of the old medieval church and village, but we never found the tree around here. We found it further along if I remember rightly." Ffion's eyes grew big with wonder as we scanned the area for the ancient tree. No, it's not around here we concluded, and we continued on, past the scattered stones.

"The story goes that a ship washed ashore on a high spring tide, and those who survived the waves staggered through the darkness and up the steep hill to Llanellen."

"I can really feel that a solemn event took place here," Ffion whispered, clasping my hand more tightly, and the two of us looked around for ghosts.

"The ship's survivors were welcomed by the villagers," I continued, but they were given a tragic return for their hospitality, as the ship's crew carried the plague." Ffion sighed at my words and said, 'how tragic'!

"Yes, it was," I replied, "and in less than a week all the villagers were dead. Llanellen never recovered and the village was left desolate and became forgotten in the winds of time."

"It must be a haunted place," Ffion said, "I wouldn't want to live near here."

"It is haunted," I replied. "My father told me that a ghost of a lady in white haunts the place where the village now lies in ruins, and on still nights she can be heard weeping for the villagers of Llanellen. It is also believed to be very unlucky to touch what remains of the old village. A farmer who lived in the Wern Halog, nearby, once took a stone from the old church, and when he got it home, the stone started rolling around in fury and killed his dog, and he had to return it to the church. These old ruins are not to be confused with the more modern village nearby with the same name."

Ffion and I continued our walk, and we eventually found the Old Yew tree. Its trunk is thick, and it is not as tall as one would think, for a tree that is 500 years old!

"I remember Dad saying that this was the actual site of the church, and in 1975 the Pendragon Society began excavating, and they found the walls of the church and some of the old houses. Another of Gower's 'lost villages' had been found. Some historians believe that the church might have even been built on an older site that goes back to the Dark Ages."

Tis true boy, the Gower, has many secrets! Yes sir, she does!

Ffion and I sat under the ancient Yew and had our lunch. And we heard no sounds or sights of the woman in white, only the sound of the birds and a wind that played gently in the long grasses.

After our lunch we climbed up a bryn known as Cil Ifor Bryn, and to the west we could look out over the marshes to where a long spur jutting out to the sands marks the hamlet of Crofty and the beginning of Penclawdd.

Dad had told me that Penclawdd is the biggest and the most important place in this north-east corner of Gower, as well as the two roads that lead to it from Llanrhidian. Ffion and I could see below us in the distance. From up here we could see a direct wide road from Cil Ifor and a small winding road that went along the edge of the saltmarsh.

"It's such a beautiful view," Ffion exclaimed, and we could feel a fresh breeze blowing in and up over the hills from the marsh. As we looked out across the wide expanse, I shook hands with another memory of a walk I took with my father along the road at the edge of the saltmarsh. It was a secret winding road he called it, where one can look out across the marsh and hear the birds calling. Dad had given me a pair of binoculars to use that day, and we had seen a lot of birds feeding out on the marshes and standing in the mud pools at low water. We could hear the Herons and other wading birds calling from great distances across the estuary and smell the salt wind blowing in from the distant sea. And today, while Ffion and I looked out from our High place, we could see that the tide was a long way out, and the little mud gullies that twisted and turned, made pictures upon the marsh grasses that told stories of the fast-moving tides. Out on the far marshes we could see some small herds of horses that were almost at the water's edge.

"We will have to wait until tomorrow before we can go and explore the horses," I said, as the sun was already westering in the sky, and I could feel that Ffion was getting cold.

"Here, my lovely lady," I said, and I took off my jacket and put it over her shoulders, as we made our way back down the hill towards the narrow lane. As we passed the old farmhouse buildings, there was a heavy silence in the air.

We were cool, and our legs tired as we reached the car, and we both looked forward to a nice relaxing evening at our Bed and Breakfast.

"I brought some of our special wine," Ffion said, "and some bubble bath, and we have a nice bathtub in our room," she reminded me.

"What about tea?" I asked, feeling hungry.

"How about fish and chips?" she said. "I saw a nice chippy on our way from Penclawdd." So, it was fish and chips, blackberry wine, and a bath with a beautiful woman.

"What more can a man want," I said to Ffion, teasing her with my smile.

"What more can a woman want," she teased back, and we arrived back at our room.

Our room was in the back of the house, facing the salt-marshes, and we had a little tea table in front of the window so we could look out. There was just enough light to look out on the tide that was now making its way in, and we sat with a glass of wine and our fish and chips at the window. Sometimes you don't have to travel very far from home to experience somewhere new, and feel the spirit of a place, I thought, and especially on the Gower Peninsula where there are so many special and sacred places to explore.

It seemed like it had been a long time since Ffion and I had spent some time exclusively to ourselves, although it hadn't been very long at all. I felt now that we could put the crazy days of Nan's Nan and Rhiddian behind us, and we were able to return to our normal rhythm of life and enjoy each other to the fullest again, and the wonderful life that was ours.

We watched from our window as the curtains of the day were slowly drawn, and our sweet September evening came to an end, and darkness fell, and it would cloak the marshes with its silent shouting shadows and walking ghosts, until the first rays of the bright singing dawn broke forth upon the morrow.

"I love you, my darling," Ffion said, fixing her lovely eyes on mine.

"I love you too," I echoed back, and we finished another glass of wine as we waited for more exciting things to come. "Are you going to bath me and make love to me?" she asked in a quiet voice. "I have been picturing you touching me all week."

"Of course, my darling, I am so hungry for you, why don't you sit there and finish your wine," I said, "and I will go and run our bath."

"Look in my bag," she said, "and you will find the bubble bath."

Ffion's bag was always full of things that excited me, it seemed. First there were her coloured nail varnishes which she painted her toes and fingernails with, like an exotic bird, trying to attract my praise. She didn't have to try very hard to attract my praise however, she always looked so classy and beautiful to me. I hope there is no cure for what I feel about Ffion's handbags, I pondered, as I stared at her new blue leather one that sat on the table like a mystery novel waiting to be read.

What wonderful things were in there for me to behold tonight? Lipstick to match those fabulous eyes. Strawberry scented massage cream that I can use on her back and toes. And oh yes, a brand new packet of black pantyhose, and white fishnet stockings that start as high as her shapely thighs, and then show off her slender legs and painted toes. Her nightgown is silk and see through, and then there are her high heels that she wears indoors with nothing else on. And eyeshadows that make her look more mysterious, and of Mediterranean descent. Yes, a look in Ffion's handbag is always time well spent.

Today's bubble bath was apple and pear, and if I remember rightly it smells like her hair. And there was her wooden barrette that held up her curls, so I could smell and kiss her long slender neck..

I ran the bath and poured in some bubbles until the smell of apple and pear came into our room, and Ffion let down her long hair, and I tried not to stare as her red auburn colours danced in the air. I took off her clothes and laid them on a chair, and she stood before me with her body and soul bare, and I wanted her so much, that I pulled her long hair, and she pulled me towards her, and then stripped my soul bare, and we stepped into the tub with only one care, I love you my darling, of that I can swear.

As we lay in the bubbles and basked in each other's presence, we were aware of how much our love had grown. 'My love for you is so deep', Ffion shared, as she lay back upon my breast, and I could only echo the same back to this beautiful woman, that my soul kept no secrets from. There is a freedom, I told her, in loving with all that you are. Heart, mind, body and soul, nothing compares when you can love like that!

After our wonderful bath and lovemaking, we fell asleep until the morrow, and we went into the dinning room for breakfast. Mr. and Mrs. Jones owned the B and B, and they were a lovely couple, originally from the midlands in England, and had come to Wales to escape the busyness of the city. And they were not disappointed. They shared with us that Gower and Penclawdd were wonderful. They said, 'we can't imagine living anywhere else, and the only regret they had was not coming here sooner'.

After a lovely British breakfast, Ivan and Sherry, packed us a picnic lunch to take out for our day. And the picnic included a basket of Penclawdd famous cockles, along with some homemade Welsh cakes and bacon and ham sandwiches, and to drink, a bottle of local apple cider. Gosh I love food!

It was low tide and I wanted to take Ffion out on a walk that my father had once taken me on, though many years ago now, and I asked Ivan for directions to where we could walk out onto the sands of the Burry Estuary. We recognized some of the landmarks from our walk out to Whitford Point and the Lighthouse, when we had gone on our hike with Fraser and Lynn, back in the summer.

"You have to go to Crofty," Ivan said, "and if you find the spit of land that runs out a long way, you can by-pass the channels and flats of the marsh and walk out directly onto the actual sands of the Burry Estuary."

"Yes, that is the place my father took me when I was a boy, I can remember walking out on this long spit!" Ivan drew us a map and told us to keep on the narrow road that runs in front of the marsh.

"Keep on that road," he insisted, "and you can't miss it!"

We found the spit and walked out as far as the Estuary. And I remembered my father telling me that this was the path from which the cockle pickers followed the tide out to the biggest cockle-beds in Britain.

"I don't know if they are still the biggest cockle-beds in Britain," I said to Ffion, "but they are certainly one of the biggest in Wales, and the cockles we eat at the Swansea Market come from here." We decided to sit down on the sand and eat our Penclawdd Cockles, and they were delicious!

The cockle pickers are women and are reputed to be the toughest in Wales. And I shared my story with Ffion, about the time these cockle women surrounded my dad and I in his car, after we had been raking cockles and the women had chased us across the sands.

Ffion laughed and said, "I would have loved to have seen that, Kings."

"It is funny now looking back," I said, "but at the time those tough looking women with arm muscles the size of my stomach, were pretty intimidating."

"Hopefully we won't meet up with them today," Ffion laughed as we finished eating our cockles on the sand. "Did you and your dad ever have any more adventures with the cockle women?" Ffion asked, wanting to hear more.

"Not with the cockle women that I can remember," I replied, "but I do remember going out onto the marshes and following the falling tide to try and find the cockle beds."

"A friend of mine and I tried it a few times, but we always seemed to get the tides wrong, and had to wade back, up to our knees through the fast moving water to get back onto solid ground."

"There is a story that my grandfather told me about, that he heard on the BBC, shortly after the war. A man was interviewing one of the Penclawdd cockle women as to what her work was like out on the cockle beds. The woman talked about the great camaraderie there was among the cockle women of Penclawdd. And then she told a story about how she was caught off guard by the tide and almost drowned. My grandfather told me the story because he thought it would make me think twice, before I went out onto the marshes again and followed the tide to the cockle beds. He and my grandmother always worried when my friend Jimmy Rigg and I went out looking for cockles.

Anyway, the woman who was being interviewed said that cockling nearly caused her death a few times. 'The first time was when I was fifteen', she said. 'As soon as I left school, I had a craving to go and work harvesting the cockles. My mother said 'No', but I took a donkey and went out with two friends. We misjudged the tides coming back and got caught in one of the pills. My two friends managed to wade across, but I was left behind leading the donkey. Suddenly I was swept off my feet. I could hear my friends on the bank shouting and saying their prayers out loud for God to save my life! The donkey sounded like he was praying too, and he made the loudest

'Ehaw' I had ever heard! I managed to cling on to the neck of the donkey when he lost his footing too. The poor thing was already weighed down with our two hundred weight of cockle's, but he swam like a trooper and dragged himself and me onto a dry bank. I swallowed so much salt water that I was more dead than alive when my friends strapped me to the donkey and took me home. My mother went wild of course, and the donkey hee-hawed, and I had to say good-bye to the cockles for at least a few years'."

Ffion roared with laughter, and said, "are you serious?"

"Yes," I replied, "I'm not joking, that is what my grandfather told me. And guess what?"

"What?"

"That woman went back to picking cockles, and even owned her own donkeys, one of which always shouted, 'Ehaw'."

As our weekend came to an end and we drove back to our home in Pennard we were glad we took the time to invest in our relationship and we felt refreshed and ready to face the new school term with our girls.

Chapter Fourteen

Ilston Cwms

It was late October, and my brother Fraser rang and asked if I wanted to go for a walk with him up the Ilston Cwms. The cwms was one of my favourite walks so I eagerly agreed to go.

"We can have a pint of beer in the Gower Inn, after our walk," he said. "I want you to try a Three Cliffs Ale."

"I will look forward to it," I said, though I can't imagine anything tasting better than my Guinness.

We met in the car park at the Gower Inn. The Ilston Valley really begins behind the Gower Inn and the Killy Willy trout stream bubbles along under the deeply wooded sides of the cwm. 'Cwm' is the Welsh word for a valley. The streams from the Ilston Valley and the Green Cwm join waters to form the Pennard Pill, which flows under Pennard Castle and enters the sea at Three Cliffs.

An old man once told me that the Killy Willy trout stream becomes Park Mill stream once its waters cross under Park Mill Bridge. Later on, it becomes the Three Cliffs River once it reaches the valley, but that is going in the other direction.

Today we were walking up Ilston Coombs to the little hamlet and the church at Ilston. The Killy Willy stream, she has many secrets boy, yes Sir, I remember! Don't forget boy! No Sir, I won't.

It was time to start our walk, and as Fraser and I passed Old Park Mill School on our left, beyond the bubbling brook, memories began to shake hands with my heart, and again I played in the old school yard with my friends, and a girl named Susan Smith who gave me my first kiss on the bridge. Or should I say she stuck her tongue down my throat, yuk! But I pretended to enjoy it in front of my jealous friends who could never pluck up the courage to talk to a girl! Neither could I, but she just walked up to me and stuck her tongue in my mouth and then felt my privates. And that was my introduction to girls. Mother always said that the boys and girls who come from Sandy Lane are a rough lot. I wasn't going to argue with a tongue in my mouth and a hand on my bollocks.

After walking about a quarter of a mile, Fraser and I came to the old ruins of Trinity Chapel. Before the ruins stands a stone memorial pulpit, and on it is a Bible cast in stone.

I have one vivid memory of the day I discovered the old ruin of the chapel. I had been a naughty boy and had skipped off school to come and fish for trout in the Killy Willy. It was the day I met 'The Old Man' who lived in the Cwm.

"What are you doing boy?" he said, as I sat on the bank of the stream with a worm on my hook. "It's more fun than being in school, isn't it boy!"

"Yes, sir it is," I replied, relieved he wasn't one of my teachers. The old man sat and talked to me for hours that day and walked with me up to the old chapel.

"Stand up on the pulpit boy and give us a sermon," he said, and he looked gruff and serious, so I did. I had seen my grandfather speak from the pulpit at his church in Swansea, but I didn't know what to say. The old man stood and stared. And I will never forget what he said to me that day.

"Speak from what is in your heart, boy," he said, "if you do that, God will always hear you and tell you what to say!" I don't know what I actually said that day, but later on I was to become a pastor, and I wondered if somehow the old man knew? He seemed to know many things, and over the years of my boyhood, I would sometimes see him walking along the cwm or in the village begging for food. He always remembered me and always called me boy. But I never forgot what he told me and that is how I preach and teach all these years later. I say what God puts in my heart!

'Well done boy! God has heard your prayers! Yes sir, thank you Sir! Thank Him, boy, not me, He always has the answer!'

As Fraser and I stood in front of the memorial stone, I read it once again. It records the work of John Miles who was once the Rector of Ilston. He was educated at Brasenose College, Oxford, and lost his living under Charles the 1 for refusing to read the Book of Sports from the pulpit, as commanded by the law of James 1.

"Miles must have been a man of conviction," I said to Fraser, who now stood up on the pulpit, and shouted, 'go forth and multiply'.

"Who said that?" he said, "I'm sure it was one of the Gospelers."

"I don't think so," I said, still laughing. "I think it was Noah, after the ark had landed on Mount Ararat. No, it was God talking to Noah, I remember now!"

We continued our way up the Cwm's until we reached Ilston Church, and as we walked through the old church yard where the gravestones are too old for names, I was greeted with a fond memory. I remembered the time when I was riding my stallion Great Thunder, across the church yard and a cloaked priest came running after us, and shouted, 'get that animal out of here!' And Great Thunder galloped between the gravestones and out through the church gate, as I held on for dear life! Our fun wasn't over yet, as we separated a woman and her dog out on the road. The woman swore and called us names that I hadn't even read in books. 'Don't worry old boy,' I said to Thunder, she must be a Roman Catholic! And we galloped off with the cantankerous priest still shouting at the gate. 'You're not getting a confession from me, you silly Catholic,' I shouted, and we carried on our way.

Fraser and I looked around the old church, and then made our way back down the Cwm to the Gower Inn.

"I can't wait to try that beer," Fraser said, as we arrived at the Inn and sat down.

"Two pints of Three Cliffs ale, please," I said to the waitress.

As we sat and drank our beer, it appeared that at the corner table, a couple were arguing loudly.

"They are not using fists yet," Fraser exclaimed, but their profanity carried across the lounge. Then came a voice from behind the bar, which said, 'take your fighting outside, and don't come back!' And they left.

About an hour later, Fraser and I left the Inn and headed to his car. The same couple were now fighting in their car, which was parked close to ours. The woman appeared to be struggling and started banging at the window from inside the car to try and get our attention.

"Help, help!" We heard her shout, as we approached the car.

"Leave her alone," my brother shouted to the man, "or I'll punch your lights out!"

"Yeah, get your hands off her, punk, or I'll kick you in the bollocks, and call the police!" I added, not wanting to be outdone by my brother's words.

Suddenly the car door thumped open, and the woman came running out into my arms for protection. Her face was bruised, and she had a black eye.

"You stay with her Kings, I'm going back inside to call the police," Fraser said, and the man sped away in his car at great speed.

"He beat me, he beat me," the woman cried, clinging to my waist as I held her tightly.

"What are you doing with a man like that?" I said. "Look at your face, it's covered in bruises and you have a black eye, you don't deserve this!"

"I've tried to leave him, I've tried!" she said between sobs, "but he just won't leave me alone!"

"I've called the police," Fraser said, as he reappeared from the Inn. "They have the registration number of his car."

"He will kill me now," the woman said, as she continued to cry. "He will kill me because you called the police." I could feel her shaking and trembling in my arms as she spoke, and I knew this abuse had been going on for some time.

"Let's take you home," Fraser said, and I walked her to the car. She tripped as one of her high heels came off, and I managed to catch her, so she did not fall.

"Please don't leave me, please don't leave me," she cried, now clinging to me again for comfort.

"I'll sit in the back with her, Fraser," I said, opening the door. Fraser started the car.

"Now where do you live, love," I said. "Where is your home?"

"I live with my father, well he's not my real father, he just looks after me at our cottage," she said.

"Where is your cottage?" I asked. "Is it in Park Mill?"

"It's in Ilston village," she replied, starting to calm down. "I live in the old cottage next to the farm."

"You just relax, love," Fraser said, as we drove on towards the village. "We will soon have you home."

"What is your name?" I asked.

"It's Gwenderwynd."

"Gwenderwynd," I echoed back, "that is a nice name," and through her running mascara, she forced a smile. It was then that something happened, something behind her eyes was familiar, and I had the strangest feeling inside!

Aware of something happening between us, Gwenerwynd glanced quickly across at me and caught my eyes, and then looked quickly away again, as did I. And as we sat in the back of the car, there was such a strong energy between us, pulling like a magnet for us to look at one another again, and we did. The connection between us was so intense that it was frightening, and we had to look away from each other again.

Fraser, oblivious as to what was going on between us, called back from the driver's seat, "is this your cottage?"

"Yes," she answered, "this is it."

"Walk her into her house," Fraser said, "and I'll wait in the car for you, Kings." I didn't want to walk her in, I didn't want to look into those eyes again. "Come on," Fraser insisted, "walk her in while I wait here."

She took my arm, and I walked her to the cottage porch, where she rang the doorbell of a large arch shaped door. We both looked down at the ground and not at each other. Obviously, she was still as uncomfortable as I was, I thought, as we waited for someone to answer the door.

"I hope my father won't be angry with me," she said.

"Why would he be angry?" I replied, still looking down at the ground.

"Because he doesn't like the man I was with."

"I can see why," I replied sternly.

Just when I thought no one was in, the big door creaked open, and a tall older man looked me up and down, and said, "who the hell are you?"

"I'm one of the men who rescued your daughter, Sir!"

"You rescued her, did you?"

"Yes Sir, I did."

"Well, thank you. Are you expecting a cup of tea or something? You are standing there like you want something, what is it boy, cat got your tongue?"

"Oh, don't be rude, Father, this is Kingsley....." and as Gwenderwynd said my name, her voice trembled. The man looked at me strangely now as he heard the trembling tone of Gwederwynds voice, and I felt uncomfortable.

Gwederwynd spoke again, only this time she was composed, and said, "this is Kingsley, father, and he and his brother Fraser, saved me from that awful man, Derek Williams."

"Yes, I heard you the first time, Gwen, that his name is Kingsley. What do you want me to do, give him a medal? By the look of your face, young lady, your knight in shining armor, arrived a little late!"

"Oh, excuse my father, Kingsley, he's in one of his moods."

"Of course, I'm in one of my moods, girl, you keep going off with a man who beats you!"

"Not anymore, father, not anymore!"

"I'll believe it when I see it, woman, now come on in and let's clean up that face of yours."

"I'll leave you to it, then Sir, and bye Gwen," and I turned to walk away.

"Sorry I was rude," the man called out, before closing the door.

"Not at all, Sir," I called back, "take care of your daughter."

"What did he say?" Fraser asked, as we drove away.

"He didn't say anything, the ungrateful git! He just asked me what the hell I was doing standing at his door, miserable beggar!"

"Anyone who allows his daughter to go out with a man like that is a real prick," Fraser added.

"Yeah, you're right, she could have been killed by that loser!"

"Oh well, that is our good deed of the day done, Kings."

As we drove along, I pondered why I had felt so uncomfortable around Gwenderwynd.

"You're quiet, Kings, is everything alright?" Fraser asked.

"I'm just tired," I replied. I dare not tell him what I'm really thinking, I thought, or he will think I'm crazy! I was being haunted by that woman's eyes, and her spirit that recognized me, and she was so familiar to me, but I don't know who she could be? I recognized her eyes, but not her face.

"Kings, Kings," my brother's voice called, as I jumped out of my daydream. "What are you thinking about, man? You have been miles away, like in a trance for about fifteen minutes."

"Sorry Fraser, it's that woman! I recognized her eyes. I've seen her before!"

I wasn't going to say anything more to my brother, because it was all so weird. But I needed to tell someone.

"Tell me about this woman?" Fraser replied.

"It's hard to explain, but in her eyes, it was like seeing pictures of myself and her together, in life. Not like in a movie where you can see physical pictures of people and places, but inside my soul. Looking into her eyes evoked memories of times and events that we had shared together, and yet she was a stranger. I can't remember having seen her face before."

"That's weird, Kings, that's really scary, I can't Imagine what I would do if anything like that happened to me."

"So, you believe me then?"

"Yeah, Kings, I do, if you could see your face, man, you look like you've seen a ghost!" I tried to laugh it off, and then I said, knowing my luck I probably have.

"What do you want to do about it, Kings?" Fraser asked.

"I want to go back, back to her cottage," I said. "I want to find out who this person is!"

 Kingsley Ross Hill

"Alright, Kings," he said, and he turned the car around, "but I'm coming with you. And I've got a feeling that her father will not be particularly pleased to see us."

"No indeed," I said, and I cracked a smile as we headed back towards the cottage. "She said he wasn't her real father," I said. "She said he was like a father to her and looked after her."

"He's not doing a good job of it," Fraser replied, and we arrived back at the cottage.

"Who are you looking for?" a neighbour called out, as we walked up the driveway to the door.

"We are going to see Gwenderwynd and the old man," I answered.

"Not in there, you're not," the man said. "No one has lived in that house for 20 years!"

"Don't be stupid, you senile twat," Fraser called back. "We just visited them less than an hour ago."

"Yeah, I think you have got it wrong Sir," I added, "we talked to the people in the house just a little while ago."

"Don't bother talking to him," Fraser said, "he's obviously off his rocker."

Fraser rang the doorbell and we waited on the porch for someone to come.

"He's a bit slow," I said to Fraser. "Gwederwynd and I had to wait a month of Sundays earlier, before the old git answered the door," and Fraser rang the bell again. We waited another 10 minutes, and still no one came to the door.

"Maybe they went out," Fraser said, "or that crazy guy at the Gower Inn came back and committed a crime."

"I wouldn't be surprised," I said, becoming impatient. "Come on Fraser, we haven't got all night, thanks for coming back with me, but obviously they are out. I'll come back another time."

Just then the man from next door came up the driveway with a key to the house, and he opened the door. Neither Fraser nor I were prepared for what we saw inside. The house was completely empty, just like the man had said. There wasn't a stick of furniture, and there were cobwebs hanging from the ceiling, and paint peeling off the walls.

"As you can see," the man said, "no one has lived here for years."

"Well, who the hell did I drop off here earlier?" Fraser said, raising his voice, and the man looked rather strangely at us both.

"Come on, Fraser," I said, "let's get out of here. You saw the old man standing at the door talking to me, Fraser, didn't you?"

"Yes, of course I did, Kings, and we dropped the girl right here at this cottage. I watched her go into the house," and the old man closed the door behind them. "I watched you guys from the car. Shit, Kings, let's get the heck out of here! Were she and the old man ghosts?"

"I don't know, Fraser, but that man next door was right, that house isn't lived in, not by the living anyway. Did you see the cobwebs on the ceiling and the wallpaper peeling off the walls?"

"Yeah, I did Kings, and there was no furniture in the place at all."

"Are you satisfied now?" the man said. "Now you have seen inside."

"Yes," I replied, "and thank you for showing us, and I'm sorry we called you a twat. I do have a question for you, Sir, you said the house has not been lived in for 20 years."

"Yes, what of it?" Do you remember who lived here 20 years ago?"

"Yes, I do, an old man lived there, who is now long gone, and he had a daughter, who always kept to herself. She seemed a bit strange if you ask me, and I don't know if I can remember her name. I think it was Gwenlyn, or something strange like that. Not your usual name like Susan or Carol."

"Thank you, sir, we won't bother you anymore."

"Shit, Kings, who the hell were they?" Fraser said. "Wait till Dad hears about this!"

"Yeah, I can only imagine what Dad will think," I replied.

"We have to go back to the Gower Inn," I said, "so I can pick up my car. Do you fancy another drink, Fraser?"

"Yes," he replied, "I need another one after that!"

Just as Fraser started up the car to leave, I glanced back at the cottage, and saw an upstairs curtain move and as the car pulled away. A horrible feeling traveled from my gut to my chest, and my heart began to race.

"What's wrong, Kings?" Fraser said, seeing the fear written across my face.

"Don't ask," I replied. "I just saw the curtain move upstairs as you were pulling away, and there was a silhouette in the shape of a person watching us from the window."

"Shit, Kings, I need a scotch!"

We arrived at the Gower Inn and went inside.

As we drank and talked about our experience with the woman and the old man, Fraser seemed as keen as I was now, to know what was going on. Had we seen two ghosts, or was someone playing a trick? It had to be real, we both agreed, we know what we saw, but what did we see?

We talked for about an hour, and then Fraser left for home, leaving me to finish my drink and order some food. Ffion would be out until later this evening, so I may as well order something to eat I thought. The waitress brought over a menu.

"I'll have haddock peas and chips please, and no more to drink, just water thank you."

The lounge was quiet, I thought, and the waitress said, 'this was the quiet before the storm. They will all be in later this evening as we have a pub quiz and a DJ tonight.'

As I was sitting and enjoying my meal, you will never believe what the cat brought in, as my mother would say. Only this had not been brought in, it walked in on two legs, and came and sat at my table.

It was Gwenderwynd, and she asked if she could join me.

"Yes," I said, rather stunned and confused. "I am not sure I understand what is happening," I said cautiously. She didn't answer, she just sat there and looked at me, and I wondered why she was here.

Finally, she said something.

"Hello Kingsley, I had to come and see you. I know you saw me hiding in the upstairs room earlier, when you and Fraser came by the cottage."

"We came round and rang the doorbell," I said, "and no one answered, and the man next door said that there hadn't been anyone living at the cottage for 20 years. That couldn't be true of course, because we dropped you off at the cottage and met your father, or whoever he was at the door. Why are you hiding from us after we helped you?"

"I'm sorry Kingsley. I hid because I was afraid."

"Afraid of what?" I asked, although in my heart I already knew.

"I'm afraid of you," she said, "afraid of what your eyes could see."

"What did my eyes see? Who are you?"

"You knew me as Gay," she cried. "Your wife."

It was then that I fully recognized her. I was looking into the eyes of my beloved Gay! And for what seemed like hours, I just stared into her eyes, and I saw our lives, lives that we had lived and shared together, and I wept.

"How can this be," I said. "How can this be? You are my Gay inside someone else's body, of this, I am sure. You have come back after all this time, but you are inside someone else's body! I do not understand?"

"Yes, I have another body, Kingsley, because the body you knew as Gay, died, but I am still here in this body. It's me, my love, don't be afraid."

"When did you die?" I gulped. "Was it when you vanished on Nan's Nan's back? Or Rhiddian?"

"So, you know about Rhiddian then."

"Yes," I replied, "the phantom horse that is centuries old."

"How do you know this, Kingsley, have you been talking to my mother, Armes?"

"Yes, but you haven't answered my question. How did you die? And what are you doing back in someone else's body, if you are dead?"

"I did not die, I took a body, and there is no such person as Gay."

"What do you mean?" I choked, feeling a sinking feeling inside. "What do you mean that there is no such person as Gay? We had a life together, remember, before you disappeared and left Melody, and Samantha and I to pick up the pieces!"

"I am sorry my love, I didn't mean to leave you, not for as long as I did, anyway."

"Don't you call me love," I protested. "You lost that privilege a long time ago, when you left your husband and daughters, who loved you so much! You were the joy of our lives, and you left us, and I will never understand how you could leave your family! You left me, after we had lost each other once before, and we found each other again after 20 years! Didn't that mean anything to you? And you left Melody, who cried herself to sleep for months, and even now she keeps you alive in her heart."

"Kingsley, there is so much that you don't understand, and didn't you and the girls get my letter?"

"You're damn right I don't understand, and no, we didn't get your letter, not until three years after you disappeared. And you asked Helen to take care of us. Did you have it planned all along? Why didn't you come back to us, why?"

"I know that I can't give back to you what I took away, Kingsley, but there are some things you need to understand."

"Understand! I don't think so. What could you possibly say that I could understand? Your actions in leaving us, is enough to make me understand that you never really loved us, or you would never have left in the first place!"

"Hear me out, Kingsley, just hear me out!"

"Alright, you have 10 minutes, and then I never want to see you again. Melody, Samantha and I have built new lives and are a family again now, along with Helen and my new wife, Ffion. And if you care anything about us at all, you will leave us alone and go back to wherever you came from! You can't just come back in our lives again like some relic from the past. You died, and we buried you! We even erected a headstone next to Maggie's grave at Port Eynon church."

"I know, Kings, that I just can't come back into your lives. And I am happy that you have all become a family again, I really am, but let me explain a few things."

"Go on," I said angrily, "you have 10 minutes, or 5 minutes now!"

"Firstly, I never was Gay. Gay died when she was 9 years old in Singleton Hospital here in Swansea, and I took her body. The person you knew and fell in love with is really someone else named Taliath. That is who I am, Taliath, and I fell in love with you Kingsley, when we were teenagers on Pobbles Beach, you just knew me as Gay whose body I lived in."

"I don't believe you," I retorted, feeling my spirit sinking deeper and deeper inside me. "No, I don't believe you! Taliath! I was wondering when I would hear that cursed name again, and here it is!"

"It's true, Kingsley, I'm sitting right in front of you, I'm just in another body that's all. And do you remember when you gave me this?" She put the Evening Emerald necklace that I had given Gay into my hand. "And I remember when you came looking for me down on the beach, and you met Melody by the Dragon Pool, and you emptied the pool together, and caught some seahorses. Then I gave Melody the necklace to wear, so that you would know that you had found me. Do you believe me now, Kings?" And as I examined the Evening Emerald in my hand, I didn't know what to say. I sat silent for a few minutes, quietly contemplating.

"If you still don't believe me," she continued, "why don't you ask Helen if Gay died when she was 9 years old. She will tell you that she did. It was only for a few minutes, just enough time for me to enter her body. Helen has always known me as Gay, though she doesn't know that at that moment, Gay's spirit left her body, I came in and lived inside her."

"Well, you needn't worry, I'll never tell her, because I can't believe it myself!"

"Can't or won't, Kingsley, which is it?" I remained silent. "I know that it must be so hard for you to even try to understand this."

"Hard! Did you say hard? You have no idea! And why have you come back now, why? And what have you done with Gay? No, let me rephrase that, what have you done with her body? You know, the one I kissed you in? Where is it, and where is Gay's spirit that left her body at 9 years old?"

"Her spirit is in Heaven, Kingsley, with God. You knew me as Gay Tripp, when we met as teenagers, and then my body died, it was killed when I went back to Pennard Past through the Portal, so I took the body of a woman named Gwenderwynd, but you can see that it's me inside, Kingsley. It's me, I'm still the same and I love you!"

"No, no don't talk to me about love, if you loved us, you would never have left the girls and I, but do you know what, I'm glad you left, because Ffion is such a wonderful wife and mother. She would never hurt us like you did, abandoning her own husband and daughters! Oh, and I have a question for you. Why didn't your spirit go up to Heaven like Gay's? No wait, don't tell me. I know why, because God doesn't like body snatchers!"

"I'm sorry, Kingsley, I really am," Taliath sobbed.

"And," I said, "I have to ask, so what are you then a ghost?"

" No, I'm not a ghost, I'm a real person who loves and hurts just like anyone else. I just don't have a body of my own yet."

"Why not, haven't you stolen the right one yet? And did you trade Gay's body in for a new model, is that what you did? Is that how it works?"

Taliath wept loudly, and somehow, I felt pity for her, but I had a right to be angry, didn't I? Yes, I did, I argued with myself.

"I'm sorry for hurting you, Kings. I know you don't understand," and she got up to leave. "If ever you want to talk to me, Kingsley," she cried, "you can find me at Pennard Castle," and she left. A part of me wanted to get up and run after her, but I didn't. I just sat there and drank another beer. What could I say? What was there to say? What has my life come to?

'Hello everyone, I've just been having a conversation with a ghost! And not an ordinary one at that, this one is a body snatcher, and she lives inside my ex-wife. Or at least she did, until my ex-wife's body died, and then she took another one as if buying a new car! Excuse me waitress, I need another drink, and a psychiatrist if you have one! Can you help me? Oh, you don't have a psychiatrist, how about a poltergeist, do you have one of them? One just walked out of the door, and if you hurry, you just might catch her, her name is Taliath, and I can only imagine what her surname turns out to be. I can't wait for that one, can you?'

After three more drinks and a conversation with the exorcist, Kingsley Hill (who lives inside of his own body by the way), called Ffion to come and pick me up because I'd had too much to drink and drive.

And I will give you one guess, dear reader, what I asked Helen next time I saw her. Yes, that's right, I asked her if Gay had died in hospital when she was 9 years old? And guess what Helen said? Right again dear reader. She said, 'yes she did, how do you know about that, I've never told anyone about it..'

'Oh, a little ghost told me.' No, I didn't say that. I just told her that I had dreamed about it the other day.

∾

For the next several weeks, I tried to forget about Taliath, and never mentioned anything to Fraser or Dad or anyone else about my experience in the Gower Inn with the anonymous body snatcher. I did not want Ffion or the girls to have to go through any more than they already had. But as we got closer to Christmas, I began to feel that I wanted to know more about this spirit, that I had loved and lost twice! Why was I even thinking about this Taliath woman, I thought? Maybe it was because of the Christmas Holidays, or the fact that I never had any real closure since Gay's body had not been found. According to Taliath, I never met the real Gay Tripp. She died before I ever met her as a teenager when I attended Dumbarton House

School in Swansea. The Gay I knew was only 15 then, but she was already Taliath, I'd missed the real Gay by 6 years.

Anyway, I felt I needed to talk to Taliath again and find out more about her existence. We had loved each other once. No, twice, and we had shared a life together, so I decided to go for a walk to Pennard Castle. The last thing I could remember her saying to me was if I ever wanted to talk to her, I could find her at the castle.

I waited for Wednesday, when Ffion was in Swansea for a full day teaching her dance classes, and the girls of course would be at school.

I walked to Pennard Castle, and sat on the rocks that looked like an altar in the middle of the castle grounds. Surrounded by the ancient crumbling walls, and my memories, I waited expectantly. What was I waiting for? An invisible person, or a luminous phantom like I saw when she disappeared on Nan's Nan's back. Or would she come as Gwenderwynd as she called herself, who's body she possessed when we talked at the Gower Inn? I waited and watched for two hours, and she did not come. Maybe I had hurt her too much with my words at the Inn. I was angry then, I thought, but I'm not now, and I hoped she would show up soon.

After three hours I gave up waiting and headed for home. I would try and come another day, I thought, and hopefully she will come.

I walked to the castle three more times before Christmas, and twice again in January, and Ffion and the girls began to wonder why I was going on these walks alone. It seemed that Taliath was not coming back to the castle, and I thought about the reasons she did not come. Maybe Gwenderwynd had died, and Taliath doesn't have a body anymore? And if she did appear as a spirit, things just might be too complicated for us to have any communication at all. She had said she wasn't a ghost, but how else would one explain her? Or maybe she has returned to Pennard Past, as she called it, on the other side of the Portal? I don't know, I pondered, but I had an idea!

I would ask Dad and Fraser if they would like to go and look for Gwenderwynd and the old man at the cottage in Ilston. I know that Fraser had told Dad about our experience there with the neighbour, who had opened the cottage door for us and there was no one to be seen. No furniture, just cobwebs and peeling wallpaper. Dad had wanted to go right away and check things out as soon as he heard our story from Fraser, but I hadn't wanted to go. I do now, I thought, and it would be a good way to see if I could find Taliath again, and also have an adventure with Dad and Fraser.

Chapter Fifteen

Two-Stroking

"A great idea," Dad said, and he suggested that we take our motorcycles, and go for a nice ride to Ilston. "We're in!" both Fraser and I said. "It has been a long time since the three of us had gone for a burn on our motorcycles together.

"Let's do it next Sunday," Dad said. "We can all meet at your place in Pennard, Kings, and ride out to Ilston from there." So, we were all set for next Sunday.

During the week I cleaned and serviced my bike, and I made its chrome exhaust pipes shine like new! I hadn't ridden for over a year, so going for a blast around the Gower was going to be fun!

On Sunday morning Dad and Fraser arrived at my place as planned, and I could hear Fraser's two-stroke Kawasaki winding its way through the village long before he arrived. Dad's Honda 750cc four-stroke was a lot quieter and made a deep low throbbing sound as he opened up the torque on the strait, and then geared down for the corners. Fraser and I both had Kawasaki H2 750 two strokes, and at the time Dad bought them in 1972, the H2 750 Triple was in a class of its own! For sheer excitement there was nothing on two wheels to match it!

They were fast, loud, smoky, thirsty, and ill handling, just like Susan Smith, but that's another pair of knickers! The H2 was also known as the Mach IV and was a wild ride that quickly earned a reputation for unmatched speed and aggression.

"It's a deadly bike for rebellious teenagers," my father told my brother and I, and we were not allowed to have the bikes until we both had jobs to pay my father back our loans, and took a motorcycle training and riding test. And even after that we had to prove to Dad that we were competent and responsible enough to ride them. But what a motivation to get a job and be responsible! The old man knew what he was doing when he dangled a Kwacker H2 in front of our faces. To ride anything over a 50cc scooter or moped in the United Kingdom, one had to be 17 years old, and pass their road test. At 16 both my brother and I had mopeds. I had a Puch Grand Prix, which did a maximum speed of 55mph, and my brother had a Yamaha TY 50p, which did a maximum speed of about 50mph, and along with 8 other 16 year old's in our village, we used to race around the narrow roads of the Gower Peninsula like there was no tomorrow! Many of mine and my brother's friends had accidents, and some serious ones and we were all able to learn from everyone's mistakes. I often wondered if we would ever live to be able to ride our H2 750s. We did and had Dad to thank for that. I know that if I had ridden 'Smoky

Blue' as I called my bike, when I was 17, I would have surely killed myself on it.

"Motorcycles can be dangerous," Dad said, "and it's better to crash a few times when you are going a lot slower on a moped, than crash on a larger bike at speed." He was right, and my brother and I learned our road sense with only minor road rash, and a few cuts and bruises.

Well, back to today, and our ride to Ilston Village.

Dad led the way on his Honda 750 K6 Four-Stroker, and Fraser and I dabbled behind on our H2s. Dad refused to ride behind us because of the beautiful blue exhaust smoke which blew from our exhaust pipes to mix with our adrenalin as we banked into the corners and accelerated out of them leaving our stomachs behind.

"If I wanted to smoke," Dad said, "I would buy a cigar, not ride behind you two smokestacks!"

One of the things that Fraser and I liked to do was to slow down and allow Dad to get far ahead of us and out of sight, then we would ride side by side and wait until a car was practically on our rear mudguards, and then accelerate like the stink, leaving the driver of the car in a blue haze of smoke while we accelerated to catch Dad. And we did it again today. What an adrenaline rush! Fraser and I also had Motorcycle Bluetooth communication devices in our helmets so that we could talk to one another. It was like having a walkie talkie in your helmet, and they had quite a range. As we powered our way through Pennard Lanes, and out onto the main South Gower Road, Fraser and I rode close on the straight stretches of the road, and then broke like Spitfires braking formation to take the corners, and it was a good thing that Dad didn't have a microphone in his helmet, as some of our language as we passed cars was as blue as the smoke coming out of our exhausts.

Much as the **H2** is a speed demon, it has milder porting and ignition timing, which helps to give a broader spread of power. But although this means that the triple can be ridden gently, with minimum use of its five-speed gearbox, that is not what this bike is built for. Sheer speed is its forte. Its acceleration enables it to reach over 100mph from a standing start in less than 13 seconds and leaves a line of smoke with its front wheel in the air. I have only reached 95mph from a standing start, and I wheelied the front wheel. I took Ffion for a ride to the Gower Inn last summer, and she loved the acceleration.

"I love your bad boy antics on a motorcycle," she said. "I find it very sexy!"

"Keep talking lovely lady, if this is sexy, I'll keep riding!"

After we rode along the South Gower Road to Park Mill, we stopped at Shepherds general store for a pop, and to admire our bikes, or should I say to allow other people and bikers to admire our bikes. They were all classics now, and especially Fraser's and my Kawasaki H2s that had collector status! We were often asked if we were interested in selling them, and the answer was always no. Dad sure knew what he was doing when he bought these for us. He knew that one day they would become collector bikes, and today we had a crowd of about 10 people looking at them, and several other bikers who had stopped for some refreshments. Dad and Fraser enjoyed talking to the other bikers, and telling stories of their adventures, but I had my mind on Taliath, and whether I would see her again at the cottage in Ilston. She seemed to have vanished. And what was she doing in that empty house in Ilston with that old man she called her father? It was all so weird. Oh well, I would have to wait and see, I pondered, maybe we will see her and her father at the cottage.

After we had finished talking with the other bikers at Shepherds shop, we rode up the steep hill to Lunnon, and then on to Ilston village. Dad now followed behind Fraser and me until we stopped outside the cottage.

"I will go and ring the doorbell," I said," as Dad and Fraser stayed sitting on their bikes.

"Say hi to Gwenderwynd," Fraser shouted to me, as I stood on the porch waiting for the door to open. Just like the first time Fraser and I rang the doorbell, it was taking ages for anyone to come.

"Come on Kings, they must be out," Dad shouted, wanting to get going on our ride.

"Just wait another few minutes," I called back. "It takes the old man a long time to come to the door." Come on you silly old fart, I said to myself, answer the door!

Suddenly the door creaked open just like before, and there was an old man's face, standing there looking at me as if I'd crawled out of a piece of cheese.

"Oh, it's you again? What do you want?" said the miserable old cuss.

'Listen old man, if I had a face like yours, I'd teach my arse to talk!' No, I didn't say that, but I thought it.

"What is he saying?" Both Dad and Fraser shouted from their bikes. I didn't answer as the old man looked at them and then back at me.

"Answer me boy, why are you here?"

"I'm here to see Gwenderwynd, I called around to see how she was doing."

"What are you talking about, boy? She is just fine and does not want to see anyone! Now get off my property before I call the police!" Fraser now walked up the path carrying his helmet and stood at my side.

"What are you trying to hide, Sir?" I continued.

"Get off my property," he shouted again, and this time loud enough so Dad could hear it from under his helmet. Dad took his helmet off and then shouted to Fraser and me.

"Come on boys, leave the old fellow alone, and let's continue with our bike ride."

"I know he's lying," I said to Fraser as we walked back down the garden path, and we both looked up to the room where I had seen the curtain move last time, and it moved again!

"She is up there," Fraser said. "Do you want to go back and knock on the door again?"

"No," Dad replied, having heard us talking. "There is someone else in the house," he said. "I saw the curtains move as well, but we can't stay on his property if he doesn't want us here."

"Come on," I said in a frustrated voice. "Let's get out of here. If she wanted to see us, then she would have come down to the door." At least I know where she is, I thought to myself, as I pulled my helmet over my face and sat back on my motorcycle, and as Dad and Fraser pulled away, I looked back up at the window once more, and there she was, standing at the window in full view. I waved my arms for her to come down, but she just shook her head and then backed away from the window. For several minutes I just sat on my bike feeling bewildered as to what was happening, and I pondered what I should do next. Shall I go and bang on the door until she comes out, and will the old man call the police? Oh, what's the use, if Taliath wanted to see me then she would have come out to meet me, not hide up stairs behind a curtain. What the heck am I doing anyway, chasing ghosts? Much as I wanted to find out what was going on, I was tired of this nonsense!

∾

I clinked my bike into gear and accelerated down the road to catch up with Fraser and Dad. We rode back down Lunnon Hill to Shepherds, and then headed west to Cefn Bryn and the North Gower Road.

There is a wonderful open road up on Cefn Bryn, and we opened up our bikes. Dad accelerated away as Fraser, and I listened to the throbbing sound of his big four stroke until it disappeared into the distance. We sat on our bikes side by side and decided to do a standing start up to 100mph.

"There is no one here, Kings," Fraser said, "only horses and sheep out on the common, let's see how quickly we can reach 100mph." It was on the count of five, and we accelerated together like the stink, leaving clouds of blue smoke behind us. I was now reaching 90mph and I could feel the front of my bike getting lighter, and we were still neck and neck. Suddenly I hit the top of my powerband, and Smoky Blue lunged forward, my helmet shook and my front wheel lifted off the ground momentarily and then came down again, and for a split second I looked down at my clock which read 105 mph! I eased off the throttle and Fraser went screaming past me, and I breathed in the wonderful smell of two stroke oil.

⌁

We reached Dad who had stopped at the top of the Bryn and had seen us accelerating like bats out of hell.

"Good job there wasn't a cow or a sheep on the road," he said, "otherwise they would be digging you out of its stomach." Fraser and I both laughed, and he said, "what a rush, we reached 105mph!"

"You silly boys", he said, "that's a frightening speed!"

"What did you get up to Dad?" I asked.

"Oh, only 110," and we all laughed.

We sat on top of Cefn Bryn for a while and enjoyed the views and wide-open space as always, and there was a herd of ponies grazing nearby. After talking and admiring our bikes for an hour, we said goodbye to the sheep and ponies, and headed for home. Dad headed off in the direction of Swansea, and Fraser took the road south and then west to Three Crosses, Gowerton, and on to his home in Gorseinon. I continued to sit on my bike for a few minutes and thought about Taliath. It had been hard not to say anything to Dad or Fraser, about my discovery of Taliath living in Gwenderwynd's body, but that is how it had to be. I couldn't tell anyone, at least not yet, and Smoky Blue and I smoked our way home to Pennard.

❧

It wasn't until next spring that I went for a walk to Pennard Castle again on my own.

We often went as a family all year round, and a few times over the winter months when I went with Ffion and the girls, once or twice I had a strong feeling that we were being watched. Maybe it was because I was always looking for Taliath and expected her to appear in some shape or form, but I seemed to be the only one that sensed the presence of someone nearby. Melody seemed to have become desensitized to feeling things about people, and even artifacts as she and Samantha went metal detecting with Dad at least four or five times a month and found different things. Ffion and I no longer felt that we had to be on guard protecting her from people or artifacts that might awaken her powers. Destiny and Melody were still close friends, and the girls often had their boyfriends over to visit. Everything was good and peaceful in our home, and I felt so thankful.

❧

It was March 1st, 2022, St. David's Day here in Wales, and Helen, Ffion, Samantha and Melody had been cooking and baking all day so that we could have friends over and celebrate with a lovely meal in the evening. After doing some spring chores in the garden, I had about three hours before any of our guests would arrive for our meal, and I decided to go for a walk to Pennard castle.

Surprisingly, I was the only one there when I arrived. Usually there were a few families or people walking their dogs in and around the castle grounds in the springtime, and especially on St. David's Day as a lot of people were on holiday.

It was a lovely afternoon, and the skylarks were singing overhead, excited about their nests in the grass and heather below. And I felt excited with them, as I thought about my life, and how blessed I was.

Suddenly there was a voice from behind me.

"Hello Kingsley." I turned around and recognized that it was Gwenderwynd, or should I say, Taliath in Gwenerwynd's body.

"I have come looking for you a few times," I said, "but I haven't been able to find you. I thought you must have disappeared for good this time."

"Well here I am, Kingsley, and as you can see I have not disappeared. I'm here as I said I would be if you ever wanted to see me."

"Yes I can see it's you, Taliath," I replied. "I am here because I want to get some final closure in understanding who you are, and why you came into my life in the first place. Was I just some entertainment for you between lives? Or bodies to be more precise. Why did you come into my life when I was a teenager, anyway? Did you seek me out to have a relationship with, or was I some random person that suited your whims at the time we met? Please tell me something that makes some sense to me, Taliath, something that I can look back on in my life and understand, if that is possible. I mean I loved and lost you twice! We were even married as husband and wife and shared what I thought was a wonderful life together!. Who was I married to? And who are you? You said that you're not a ghost, then what are you?"

Taliath was quiet for several minutes, and then she spoke.

"I have not told you who I am, Kingsley, because you could never understand who I am."

"Alright," I replied, feeling bold, "why don't you try me. Who and what are you?"

"I am Taliath Saren, and I am twelve hundred years old. I am the one who wrote the diary that you and your father are translating. I was the presence in the gentle wind that surrounded you when you found the diary in the castle sands when you were twelve years old, remember? And I watched and waited excitedly while you dug in the ground near the altar stones where I buried my diary. For centuries I watched and waited for the one who would come and find it, the one that I could trust to tell the story of my family and I, and our lives in Clan number 142 of the Coastal and Black Mountain Celtic Clans of Wales. Tell our story, Kingsley, tell it! You are the one that my family and I have waited for, the one chosen to find my diary and to tell our story!"

"No, I shouted! No, I won't do it, get away from me, and leave me alone!"

"No Kingsley, you do not understand."

"Damn right I don't! You come into people's lives, and they love you with all their hearts and then you leave them, disappearing on the back of a phantom horse! That is what you did to me and a family that adored you, that is what you do, Taliath Saren, or whatever your name is. And now you want me to tell the story of you and your people! What about the family that you left behind? A family that adored you and loved you with all their hearts! So I was just a pawn in all of this…"

"No, Kingsley, no, you do not understand!"

"Oh, I understand alright!" I wept as I felt pain inside my heart. "Goodbye Taliath, I wish you all the best in your life, or existence. And I do thank you for the life I once shared with you, when I knew you and loved you as my Gay, and thank you for my lovely daughter, Melody. I will always be thankful for her."

"Kingsley, please don't go, let me explain!"

"No, I have had enough! Please leave me alone." Please, if you have any feelings for me at all, please leave me and my family alone, we have had enough!

"Alright, Kingsley, as you wish. Goodbye my love, I wish you all the wonderful things that life can bring, and I will always love you, and always be your Gay."

My heart was torn as I walked away, and Taliath shouted, "I love you my Prince, and remember, if you ever want to find me and talk to me, you can always find me here at the castle."

I kept walking and I went home to Ffion and my girls.

When I arrived home, Ffion and the girls had a lovely St. David's Day dinner all made, and Helen had arrived having brought her famous trifle made with Birds Custard and real Devonshire Cream! We are going to eat well I thought, as we waited for our guests to arrive. It was surely a wonderful meal, and to have our friends share this special day with our family was a special blessing. It was like having a housewarming party, that we had not really had yet since we moved in. With the Joy and Festivity all around me, I felt like someone trapped between two worlds! One was happy and exciting, and the other, painful and confusing, and I tried to just think of my wife and family, and our friends all celebrating around me. But in my heart, I felt a great sadness, and my mind was confused. Taliath had told me she loves me, just like my Gay used to do. She even called me her Prince, which made my heart go out longing for the love I had found and lost twice!

"What is wrong Dad?" Melody asked. "Oh, I just have a headache," I replied. But they knew better, and my smiling face could not disguise my troubled heart. I had loved a woman named Taliath, who I had known as my Gay, and she was lost and alone it seemed, in a world that I could not understand. My mother once told me that real love never dies! It lives in our hearts for the duration of our lives here in this world, and even travels into eternity with us when we leave this life. Oh, Mum, my heart is so troubled. The love that I found and lost twice has come back into my life again, and I don't know what to do? I love my wife Ffion, and our family, but I can feel Taliath's heart, sad and alone.

Come on Kings, I said to myself, pull yourself together man! She left you and the girls remember. She rode off on a phantom horse, leaving you to pick up the pieces and rebuild your lives! I know that, I wrestled, but why does she still live in my heart? Forget her, Kings, forget her! You have a wonderful wife and family, leave the past behind and focus on the wonderful life you have! Yes, alright, I will!

Chapter Sixteen

By Jove It's a Sword!

On the weekend, Dad and Mary invited Ffion and I and the girls to go metal detecting with them up on Cefn Bryn, and he said we would make a picnic out of it.

"We can go metal detecting around Broad Pool," he said, "and then go and have a picnic at Arthur's Stone." Ffion and Mary committed to making the picnic, and we were all excited to see what we would find. I have never been metal detecting around Broad Pool, I thought, but the pool had always fascinated me, and an old man had once told me a story about a sword that had been thrown into the pool by a knight.

'Tis true boy, the Gower, has many secrets! Yes sir, I know.'

Dad and Mary came over to our house at 11:00 on Saturday morning as planned, and we all squeezed into his car and headed off to Cefn Bryn.

Dad parked the car on a pullout just off the main North Gower Road. Only minutes from where we parked is the fine Bronze Age tumulus of Pen-Crug, and we all turned on our metal detectors, except for Mary who didn't have one.

"I will be the Viking digger-upper," she said laughing. I had recently bought Samantha a detector for her birthday, so I helped her to navigate the new technology on the amazing piece of equipment. It was much like Dad's detector in that it could measure size, shape, and density of metal with amazing accuracy. It also could differentiate the type of ground we were covering, such as stony or clay, or peat-based soils.

We all walked in a line about 15 feet apart, except Mary who walked behind us with a small shovel and trowel. It was all very exciting, and we looked like the Six Musketeers on a mission, and indeed we were!

Ffion's detector was first to beep, and she and Mary dug up an old coca cola bottle , with its rusted cap having set off the beep. It was an old bottle, Dad said, and he would put it with his collection. Ffion pressed forward full of enthusiasm while the rest of us waited for a beep, or counted sheep, it all depends on the way you look at things. What I love about detectoring, is that you can be walking for twenty minutes and hear nothing but sheep, then all of a sudden, the beep goes off. And yes, sometimes your heart can skip a beat as you daydream of ancient helmets, and swords and shields from the times of the Knights. And don't forget coins, there are always coins to be found. Modern coins lost from people on walks or picnics, and ancient coins from the time of the Romans. And then there is always the surprise! A lost watch or necklace, or a ring with a story, or maybe even a chest of artifacts, just like the one Nan's Nan led us to. Gay used to say, that if you hold an artifact in your hand and listen carefully enough, it will tell you, its story. Detectoring is the nearest thing to time travel as you are always traveling back to the past.

Ffion's detector went off again, and Dad called her the favoured one! At least today she was, tomorrow it could be someone else.

"I wonder what it is this time," Mary said, using the trowel to gently dig through the stony ground.

"It's an old, curved piece of metal," Ffion said, handing it to me, and I brushed off the dirt with my hand.

"What have you got there," Dad said, having put down his detector to come and take a look. "It's a horseshoe," he exclaimed.

"I've never found a horseshoe before, well done Ffion!" And I gave her a celebratory kiss, while Samantha and Melody told us to get a room.

"It probably belonged to one of the old farm horses," Dad said, pointing to Cilibion Farm in the distance. Rusty old horseshoe or not, Ffion was full of excitement and walked ahead of us swinging her detector back and forth in search of the crown jewels.

Samantha's new detector went off next, and I immediately put mine down and helped her to dig. We didn't have to dig very deep when we found an old bracelet.

"It was only four inches down," I said, "exactly the depth that your sounder measured it." Samantha seemed disappointed as I held it out in my hand for her to inspect.

"It's really dirty," she said, "and we can't tell what type of metal it is."

"It is not iron or steel," I said. "There is no rust on it, and it has a bluey green colour on the metal."

"Most likely, bronze or copper," Dad said, having walked over to us. "Let me have a look," and he held it in his hand to inspect it. "It's bronze," he said rather excitedly! "This tells me that it's likely a lot older and of greater value than an iron one. I think this is a good find, Samantha. Who knows what we have here, it could be very rare." Samantha smiled from cheek to cheek and handed it to Mary to carry. "Another fifteen minutes," Dad said, "and we will stop and have lunch."

We now reached Broad Pool, a charming little lake on the edge of a wide sweep of the commons of Cefn Bryn, and we sat down to eat. Broad Pool is a place I've always liked to come to on my motorcycle. I park old Smoky Blue just off the road, and then walk out and meditate on the banks of the pool. During cold winters the pool freezes, and my father taught me how to ice skate here. I can remember once falling through the ice, and my father's strong hand pulling me to safety. I think he learned a lesson that day, I remember him saying that there were cracks on the ice, and in places it looked thin. 'I should never have taken you out on the ice,' he said, 'I could have lost you under that frozen sheet,' but thankfully he didn't, and I am still here to tell the tale.

Mary passed our sandwiches around, and we all dug into our food. Salmon sandwiches, Welsh cakes and cockles, and three squares of Cadburys Chocolate each and a pop. Gosh I love food!

Sometimes the wild ponies visit the pool for a drink, especially in the summer months, and herons stalk along its banks on the days when no tourists come and disturb them.

Today a kestrel hovered over its banks, looking for its prey. We watched as it folded its wings once or twice, poised to dive into the thicket of bracken.

"There he goes," Melody said, as it folded its wings again, this time diving to the ground and then reappearing with a mouse or vole in its beak.

"There are swallows too," Samantha pointed out, skimming across the water and catching flies. Once or twice, they appeared to be touching the water with their wing tips, before darting up into the sky again.

Dad explained that Broad Pool is a bit of a mystery at first sight, as it is not at all obvious as to where the water comes from or why it should stay in the pool.

"The water comes from the rain," Melody said, with a cheeky look on her face.

"It's not that simple," Dad replied. "The backbone of Cefn Bryn is formed from old red sandstone, but Broad Pool sits on limestone. From what I understand, the water is held by a thick layer of glacial boulder clay which has subsided into hollows dissolved in the underlying limestone."

"You know so much, Roger," Ffion exclaimed, and Mary teased by saying, "he's showing off."

Broad Pool is a Nature Reserve and is rich in insect life, including several species of dragonfly, and today we saw a number of beautiful blue and black and white ones.

"And there is an orange and black one," Melody said excitedly, as it landed on one of the lily flowers that covered about half of the pool's surface.

After we had finished our picnic, we drove to the summit of Cefn Bryn, and walked out across the moorland to Arthur's

Stone. The ground around the stone is rough and stony, and then boggy in other places, and we followed a path beyond the stone, and then spread out with our detectors, walking in our usual line of about 15 feet apart. We covered a fair distance, and there were no beeps from any of our detectors.

"This is the way it goes," I reminded everyone, "but you never know when that beep is going to sound!"

"That's half the fun of it," Ffion said, "not knowing," and we all agreed.

"But it is always nice to find something," Samantha said, and she now led the way across the moorland.

We reached a boggy area now and had to change course, but as I was inspecting my running shoes which were covered in wet mud, my metal detector beeped loudly.

"It's coming from a boggy puddle," I said, as everyone began to walk over towards me. "Whatever it is, it's in the wet mud," I said, kneeling, and Mary handed me the trowel.

I handed Dad my detector and began to dig, but each time I lifted a trowel full of soil, the hole filled with water.

"It's a bog down there," Dad said, seeing my frustration. "Mary, pass Kings the shovel." It was the same challenge, as I lifted out more mud and clay, the water quickly engulfed the hole again.

"We can't give up," I said, now kneeling in the mud. So much for my clean jeans, and I continued to dig.

"Try and push down the shovel as far as it will go," Dad said, "and see if you can feel anything."

Pushing the shovel deep into the mud, I couldn't feel any-thing, and I kept prodding all around where I was kneeling. Suddenly I hit something, and it was metal against metal.

"I can feel something," I shouted, "and it feels quite big!" Everyone gathered around as close as they dared without falling into the mud pool which was now making suction noises as I pushed the shovel deeper into the soft mud and tried to get underneath whatever was down there.

"That's it, Kings," Dad said, "keep pushing the shovel underneath it, and try to lift it to the surface."

"It's heavy!" I proclaimed. "It's not something small, I can tell you that." The foul smell of boggy mud now filled the air, and Samantha and Melody made noises of disapproval of the foul smell, while I grinned and bared it, and kept trying to lift whatever it was up out of the mud.

"It's like quicksand," Ffion said. "Be careful down there, Kings, I don't want you disappearing in the quicksand."

Suddenly with a burst of effort, and the squelching sounds of disapproval from the mud, up came a long metal piece with a handle.

"It's a sword," I shouted, "It's a sword!"

"By jove you're right," Dad said, almost falling into the bog. "Let's have a look, Kings, let's have a look." I handed the sword to Dad, dripping and smelling of mud. "This is a fantastic find," he said, as we all watched in silence, as he examined it from top to bottom.

"What type of sword is it, Dad?" I asked, glowing with excitement.

"I can't tell you until we can wash it off and examine it properly," he said, "but I can tell you this, it's centuries old, it has to be! You would never find a modern sword out here, there would be no reason for one to be out here. It could be from the Iron Age era, or even the Bronze Age, it is the find of the decade, Kings, and depending on what type of sword it is, it could be a find of a lifetime!"

Covered in mud, I stood up like the hero Knight, and everyone said, "well done Kings!"

"Yes, well done Dad!" the girls declared. And we all squelched our way back to the car in our gumboots.

"We better celebrate," Dad said, and we picked up fish and chips, and a Joe's Ice-cream on our way back to our house where Dad examined the sword.

"It is a Bronze Age sword," he said, after we rinsed all the mud off. "A priceless find, Kings, well done Son! This is known as a Leaf Shaped Blade Sword, which is a variant of the European Bronze Age Sword. It was most commonly used in North-West Europe at the end of the Bronze Age, and in particular on the British Isles. What it was doing on Cefn Bryn, is anyone's guess, Old Son. But you found it! And it is the most amazing find for the Gower Peninsula."

"It looks much like a dagger in design," I said, as I thrust it back and forth through the air.

"It does look more like a dagger than a sword," Dad confirmed, "but it is a sword and not a dagger. If you remember, Kings, the swords that we buried and dug up in Mr. and Mrs. Kent's garden were also quite short, and when we first found them when you were a boy, you thought they looked more like daggers than swords back then."

"Yes, I remember, Dad, and they were Carp Tongue Swords, and they were common to Western Europe in the 9th and back as far as the early 8th century. The blades of the Carp Tongue Swords are wide and parallel for most of its length, but the final third narrows into a thin tip for thrusting."

"That's right, Kings, well done!" Ffion and Mary were impressed, and said I was becoming like Dad, in my knowledge of the artifacts we were finding. I felt flattered at their words, but it was Dad who had taught me most of what I know.

After a nice tea of fish and chips, and ice-cream, Dad and Mary headed home to Swansea. I let Dad take the sword home to his house, where he would deep clean it, and keep it safe with our collection of other artifacts. We had all handled the sword before Dad and Mary left, and Melody had made no connection to its origin or past, which alleviated any concern that Ffion and I had about her handling it.

⌯

Over the next few months, life seemed particularly grand as my family, and I enjoyed our life here on the happy healing shores of my beloved Gower Peninsula.

There are seasons in our lives when we are able to stand back and watch, and reflect on where our souls have been, and where we are going in this mystery of life that is both familiar and strange at the same time. As revelations come upon us of awakenings that are stirring in the awareness of our souls, we journey, ever learning and growing as a flooding tide that washes away the old dross, and newness is exposed like the beams of a sunken ship between the receding waves of Rhossili Beach. The wandering albatross sleeps upon the wing, realizes its dreams and wakes, and lands, coming home to where it has never been.

⌯

During our latest family conference which we try to have about four times a year, Helen shared that she wanted to sell her house in Cardiff and move to Pennard so that she could live closer to us.

"I practically spend every second weekend with you in Pennard already," she shared. Of course, we were all delighted at the thought of Helen coming to live in Pennard and being close to us, and she soon put her house on the market. Her property sold within two months, and she bought a house on Heather Slade Drive, close to her friend June.

Almost eighteen months had passed since my conversation with Taliath at Pennard Castle. It was mid June and the weather was beautiful!

Samantha had moved to Aberystwyth in West Wales, to start her master's program in a private counseling office to continue her career in becoming an Art Therapist, and she hopes to have her own practice one day. We are all so proud of her!

The boys also came out for a holiday for the whole month of May, and Ffion and the girls and I, took them on a surfing holiday to Devon and Cornwall. And for the last week of their stay, we rented a caravan near Llangennith Beach. We had campfires at night and went fishing and rock climbing during the day. We didn't get chased by any mad cows this time but we were attacked by a cockerel as we tried to pinch some eggs from a farm.

"Serves you right," both Ffion and Helen said as they dressed our wounds. Nasty creatures those cockerels are. Don't cross one, or they will make you shout cocka-doodle-do! Dad also took the boys metal detecting and they both found some more Roman coins.

It was Saturday June the 11th, and Ffion and I, along with Melody, Helen, and Helen's friend June, decided to spend the day at Pobbles Beach. We all met at Pennard Stores to buy our food and drinks, and then walked along the Westcliff Path to Pobbles.

It was so nice to have Helen living on Heather Slade Drive now, which was right across the road from our house. 'It is perfect,' Helen would often say. 'I am close enough to walk over to the family house and have the privacy of my own home too!' I was happy that she did not have to make the long drive to Cardiff and back anymore, especially on those dark wet winter days.

It is a glorious walk along West Cliff, with the beautiful blue of the sea to your left, and the majestic hill of Cefn Bryn, arrayed in all its glory, standing before you like a King wearing nature's crown. There are grey rocks and brown ferns at its base, and the green of the meadows that wind upwards are dotted with white sheep and clouds that reflect their shadows across its wide expanse. Buzzard's glide and circle, and Kestrel's hover over its heights, while the sun kisses its summit with the different hues of the day, and makes one soul shout, Hurray, Hurray, Hurray!

Once we had climbed down the rocks and along the sandy path to the beach, Melody raced across the golden sand to the Dragon pool where we put down our towels and backpacks, claiming this little nook for ourselves.

"This is where I met Dad," Melody announced to everyone. "Right here at our pool. This is the Dragon pool, and Dad and I emptied it, just using buckets, and we found two sea-horses in here." I felt so proud to hear Melody announcing our heritage to everyone who had a listening ear.

Helen and Melody took a walk to the sea, while the rest of us sat on our towels and daydreamed. There were but a few white puffy clouds in the sky, and the sound of the sky-larks carried down from the heights of the golden dunes that were robed in their long green grasses, that waved to us in the breeze like dancing girls. The sky was a deep blue that matched Ffion's eyes, and her long hair danced across her face, taking me deeper and deeper until I was lost in space.

As I looked across the sand to the sea, I noticed Helen and Melody paddling in the waves, and a woman in a white dress stood talking with them.

I didn't recognize the person as anyone I knew, and I didn't think anymore of it, as Ffion and I continued to sit on our towels and enjoy a conversation with Helen's friend June.

Helen suddenly arrived back, quite upset, and I noticed that Melody had gone for a walk on her own along the beach. This was not unusual, but Helen, still upset, said, "Kings, I think you better go and see your daughter." So, I ran down to the surf to catch her up.

"Dad, I'm so freaked out!" she said sobbing, "and you are going to think I am completely mad, when I tell you this."

"What, me? I won't think you're mad, of course I won't! I'm the only mad one in our family. Come on, what's wrong? We can always talk to each other, no matter what, remember?"

"Yes Dad, I know we can always talk to each other, but this is beyond 'no matter what'. This is different and I am really scared Dad!"

"Scared, my sweetheart, what on earth has happened? I can't help you unless you tell me what is wrong."

As I waited for Melody to speak, my mind flashed back to the look on Helen's face. She was upset too, so I anticipated it being something serious, but what? But nothing could have prepared me for what Melody was about to tell me.

As Melody continued to cry with her face looking down to the sand, I looked around to see if I could see the woman who had been talking to her and Helen while they were paddling in the sea, but she was nowhere to be seen.

Finally, Melody spoke and told me what was wrong, and our world would be rocked to its foundations again!

"I just talked to Mum, Dad."

"You talked to Ffion you mean?" I replied.

"No Dad, I talked to Mum!" At Melody's words, I felt numb inside! Taliath had shown herself to me in someone else's body. And I wanted to convince myself that she wouldn't do this to Melody. Surely, she wouldn't!

"I talked to Mum, Dad," Melody repeated. "Didn't you hear me? It was her Dad, and she was in someone else's body."

"How did you know it was Mum?" I asked. Holding her tightly in my arms, I could feel her trembling.

"I just knew, Dad," she sobbed. "It was her!"

"Yes, but what did she say in order for you to know that she was really Mum? I know that you have your special abilities of knowing and discerning who people are and what a person is like, Melody. Was it an experience like that?"

"No Dad, she asked me things, and talked about things that only she and I could know, and she talked to Grandma the same way too. And Grandma is also very upset."

"I know," I replied. "I saw that she was upset when she came walking back."

After listening to Melody's words, there was nothing for me to say, other than to try and comfort her, so I held her even tighter and told her that I loved her, and that she was safe, and that everything would be alright. To my surprise she stopped crying at my words and began to calm down, and I knew that she would be okay.

"Come on Dad," she said, taking my arm, "Grandma needs you too," and we walked back to the others.

As Melody and I arrived back to the others, Ffion and June were still sitting and talking as if nothing had happened. Helen was standing a distance away, and I could see that she was troubled.

As Melody and I reached Helen, Melody let go of my arm, and said, "I am alright Dad, you can go and talk with Grandma."

"Helen, can you come and walk with me?" I said, and we walked down the sand to the surf.

As we walked, Helen's countenance appeared heavy and strained, and her face was flushed and tense. I put my arm around her waist and said, "Melody just told me that you both had an encounter?"

"Yes," she replied. "It was her, Kings. Melody and I met Gay, and she talked to us. She was in someone else's body! It was awful! My lovely Gay came to see us in someone else's body, Kings! Is she dead, is she alive, what is she? Oh, Kings, I am so upset, and Melody... What a way to see her mother again. Why is this happening to us?"

"I don't know," I replied. "I just don't know."

"And you are sure it was her, Helen?"

"Oh, Kings, there was no mistake! It was her alright, she talked to us as only she could, and asked us questions about ourselves that only she and us could possibly know about."

"That is what Melody said," I replied. "I don't know what to say, Helen, I really don't. I can only say what I said to Melody, and that is I love you, and you are safe with me, I will protect you, Helen."

"I know you will, Kings, and I love you too. A part of me was happy to see that it was her. At least I know that she is alive, but to see her inside another body, frightens me."

Not knowing what else to say, I said, "was she the lady in the white dress who was talking to you in the sea?"

"Yes, that was her. Did you see where she went?"

"No," I replied. "I saw her talking to you both in the waves, and then she was gone. I don't know what to say to Ffion," I said. "If she hears about this, it will send her over the top! She has been worried enough as it is, with Melody having had the connection to the artifacts in the chest, and then when we took her to West Wales, she knew new places she hadn't been to, and people she had never met. Just like what happened when you and your husband John were lost, and Gay knew where you were."

"Yes, I remember telling you that story, Kings. So, what are we going to do?"

"I don't know, I'm puzzled, I don't think we can do anything, other than wait and see what happens, we have no way of stopping her showing up and visiting us."

"Yes," Helen replied, "but a part of me wants to hug and embrace her, and the other part of me wants to run for the hills!

I suppose, we can only do what you said, Kings, just wait and see what happens and try to carry on with our lives."

"But what am I going to say to Ffion?" I said. "She has only just gotten over the encounters we had with Nan's Nan, the spirit horse."

"I hear you, Kings. I think it best that we don't say anything, she is too fragile to go through any more of this crazy stuff."

"That's what I am thinking too, Helen, and I know that Melody doesn't need to say anything to Ffion about it, as long as she can talk to you and I."

"Well, that settles it for now, then, we just won't mention anything, and see what happens."

After our walk and conversation, we rejoined the others at the Dragon Pool, and Melody agreed not to say anything to Ffion. If Taliath continues to come and visit us, then I would have to tell Ffion, I thought, but for now we will just wait and see what happens, maybe she will just disappear. I could only hope.

∽

The following weekend, I went to see if I could find Taliath, however, to see if I could stop her coming and visiting us like this. How can I stop her? She is a spirit, I thought, as I walked my way across the golf course to the castle.

She had said that if I ever wanted to talk to her, then I could find her at Pennard Castle.

This time I found her right away, standing by what I have always called the Altar of Stones, in the middle of the castle grounds, right where I had found the diary when I was a boy. And I had the feeling Taliath was waiting for me, knowing that I would want to come and speak to her, after the episode down on the beach with Helen and Melody.

"What the heck is the matter with you!" I said angrily. "Why would you come and visit Melody and Helen like this? After all this time, you showed up like this, in someone else's body! Do you have no respect? No forethought as to what this could do to Melody and Helen? And to my family? What do you want?"

"I am Melody's mother, and Helen's daughter, need I remind you."

"I want you gone from our lives! We are a family now, and happy, at least we were until you showed your ghostly face again last Saturday."

"I am sorry, Kings, but I needed to see my daughter, and Helen too. I still love you all, and I am so lonely without you, Kings, I miss you all so much! You and mum and the girls are the only real family I have ever known."

"It's too late, Taliath ,don't you get it? For the hundredth time, go away and leave us alone. We have all moved on with our lives, and you must too! Now for the last time, leave us alone and don't come back." At my words, Taliath just stood there, sad and lost, and as always my compassion won out over my anger. "Look, Taliath," I said, "if you promise to leave us alone, I will do what you asked me to do last time we met. I will write the story of you and your people from your diary but you must promise to leave us alone.

"Can't I see you once in a while?" she replied. "You have no idea how hard it is being stuck inside someone else's body."

"You're right there," I replied. "Thankfully I don't know what it's like, but since I have come all this way and I may not see you again we may as well talk for a while. So what is it like?" Taliath walked over to me and we sat on the sand in the castle room.

"The hardest thing is to try and make people believe that you are still their loved one. Each person comes with a family, and I really don't know what the person was really like before I entered their body, so I have to always pretend to be someone I'm not. I have gotten quite good at it over the years, or centuries should I say. Sometimes the body is middle aged and has a big life around them. Husbands, children, I even found myself with grandchildren once or twice. Most often people have jobs or a career in something, and I find myself doing all sorts of things. One woman was a typist before she died, and typed over sixty words per minute, and I couldn't type for toffee, so the boss was suspicious right away. I'm sure he thought I was on drugs or something when he asked me to type out a paper. I was typing as slow as molasses while he stood over my desk. Within a week, he called me into his office, and asked what the hell was going on. 'Have you been drinking, Cindy', he said. 'Something has happened to you over the last few weeks.' As Taliath spoke, I began to laugh.

"I wish I had seen his face," I said, "when you couldn't type."

"I did see the funny side of it," Taliath continued, "and I almost told him that my name was Taliath, not Cindy."

Taliath and I now laughed together, and I said, "please carry on, tell me some more about what it is like."

"Oh, I had one experience that still haunts me, get it Kings, still haunts me?"

"Yes, I get it," I laughed, "please continue with your story."

"Okay, well I found myself having to live inside a 35 year old woman named Debby, and she was very athletic, and she was married to this man who was an athlete as well, and he expected me to go running with him every evening after work. That wasn't a problem because I had a nice slender body and could run as well as he could, but I hated running and I started to let him know how much I hated it. Well, the poor man! I only told him that I didn't want to run about three times, and he thought he had lost his best friend. I mean I thought he was going to divorce me, which wouldn't have been the first time when I couldn't live up to someone else's life."

"Go on Gay, tell me some more," I said, enthralled in what she was saying.

"This man, Nick was his name, he had a mother who absolutely hated me! I had been able to convince Nick that I was still his wife, even with the changes of my personality, and I was even able to convince his friends that I was Debby, even his best friend Malcolm and his wife Lucy, who Nick and I played golf with at Langland golf course once a week. You should have seen me Kings, I couldn't hit a golf ball to save Debby's life, pardon the pun, and you should have seen Malcolm and Lucy's faces as I tried to tee off from number 3, they must have thought I was on magic mushrooms, as I picked out a putter instead of a driver and proceeded to tee off with it."

I was roaring with laughter now, and so was Taliath. "Carry on," I said, "please."

"Well, Nick was so embarrassed, as he and his friends were such good golfers. Nick took me to the doctor when we got home, thinking I was off my rocker. I was, I mean I had never even been interested in playing golf before, and I couldn't hit the side of a barn door. But do you know what the scariest thing of all is, Kings?"

"No, I don't," I replied, "tell me."

"It is when one member of the family knows that you are an intruder inside their loved one. You make eye contact with them, and you know that they know that you are not their loved one, but someone else inside their body. I had that experience with Nick's mother Alice. She had these dark staring eyes, and a contentious spirit, that I could feel inside everytime she looked at me."

"Creepy," I replied, "and did anyone else know that you weren't Debby?"

"No, only Nick's mother, and she tried everything she knew to expose me to Nick and his friends."

"Wow, Gay," I said. "I can not imagine how that must feel when you know someone knows."

"Yeah, it's pretty terrible. I have had to deal and adapt to many different situations and families, Kings," she said, now going quiet as her sadness returned.

The silence between us grew loud and uncomfortable. I felt within my own heart the questions I had not asked Gay, and needed to ask!

"Where did you come from when you lived in your own body, Taliath, I mean Gay," I said breaking the silence. "How did this wandering of your spirit come to be? If I am to understand you, you must tell me."

Gay sat in silence pondering my questions for some time, and then spoke.

"My family was born near here at a small Celtic Settlement close to the castle. You only know this castle as a ruin, but my family knew it in its youth. They lived in a village called St. Mary's which is only a stone's throw away from here. All that is left that you can see is one small piece of the church wall, but it was once part of a vibrant village where my family dwelled. I am the youngest of four sisters, and my mother was the Clan Queen of clan number One Hundred and Forty Two of the Coastal and Black Mountain Clans of Wales. My father was a great Warrior and leader of our people."

"Yes Gay," I interjected, "I do believe you, but how did you get here? How did you become a spirit and come to live in modern day Pennard?"

I traveled here through a portal, in my mother's womb. Our people were being attacked by fierce warriors that came to our land from the sea, and desecrated our people. My father sent my mother Armes through the portal when she was pregnant with me, in order to try and save us, while he stayed behind and tried to rescue my sisters and grandfather." Taliath wept bitterly as she spoke, and I felt in my spirit what she was saying must somehow be true. "My father and sisters have been left behind," she cried, "and I can't get back now to find them. I went many times to try but…I don't know whether they are alive or dead!"

I just sat there and listened, and didn't know what to say. But parts of Taliath's Diary that Dad and I had translated began to come alive! And then there were my visits to Armes at the Commune. Taliath was telling me a lot of what Armes had already told me. She had said that she came through a portal pregnant with Taliath, and that Taliath had been born while her mother Armes lived at the commune. Nothing she was telling me contradicted anything I had already learned, and I began to feel goosebumps as I listened to her story. She went on to name all her sisters, and their names and birth order were exactly the same as Dad and I had translated in the diary. I interjected again, and said, "you're telling me about your family on the other side of this portal, but what is the portal? Is it a time passage, and why can't you get back?"

Gay was silent again, pondering how she could answer my questions so that I could understand.

"Tell me," I said, breaking the silence again. "You can't stop now, I need to know!"

"Alright I will continue," she replied. "You would call the portal a time passage, Kingsley, but it doesn't just connect with the past, it is like a parallel world of everything that is still here in Pennard and around the Gower Peninsula, only the modern buildings and landmarks don't exist there yet."

"What about people?" I asked, only half understanding what she was saying, and I must admit, I was struggling now to believe it all, but I kept asking questions.

"It's the same with the people," Gay continue. "The people on this side of the portal don't exist there, for they have not been born yet. Can you understand what I am saying, Kingsley? Or at least try to."

"I am trying," I replied. "I can understand some of it, like you have left your father and sisters, and your grandfather on the other side of the portal, and your people are under siege from warriors that have come to your land by sea. Knowing history as I do, I would say that your people are being attacked by the Vikings."

"The Vikings!" Taliath exclaimed.

"The Vikings," I replied. I believe they are the great Sea Warriors you mentioned, from Norway, Sweden and Denmark, and they traveled up and down the coast exploring and conquering new lands. We only have a few records of them landing in Gower, but according to what you are saying, their landings and invasions are far more extensive into Wales than our known history tells us. Can you tell me why you can't return through the portal?" I asked. "Why are you trapped here?"

"When my father sent my mother through the portal, she was supposed to try and find my Aunt Tally, who came through the portal before us, several years before. The portal has existed for hundreds if not thousands of years, and my Aunt Taliath or Tally, who I am named after, would travel back and forth through the portal to observe what was going on on this side of the portal which you know as the Gower Peninsula."

"Why would your aunt want to observe what was going on here?"

"The Gower Peninsula is where our clan members fled to,during times of war and unrest to escape being killed or taken as slaves to other enemy clans," Taliath replied. "The Gower has been a place of refuge for our people for centuries."

"I can only understand it as time travel," I replied, "but it seems even more complex than that!"

"It is complex, because time does not stand still on the other side but also continues on, which is why I have not been able to find my family, they have moved on and I don't know where," Taliath replied. "I am so glad that you are willing to hear me out, Kingsley, you don't know how much of a relief it is, for me to be able to try and explain things to you, even though I know there is so much you can't understand."

"So why can't you find your aunt who can help you return to your people?" I asked.

"She became lost to us," Gay replied, "and my mother Armes spent years looking for her, but has never found her."

"Why can't you return through the portal without her?" I asked.

"Because she is the only member of our clan who knows the secret ingredient to mix with a potion that gives what our people call the "Second Sight" which we need in order to be able to see where the portal is and travel through it. Without the potion we can't see where the portal is. It is invisible to the naked eye without drinking the potion. It was my fathers plan for my mother Armes, to find my Aunt and get the potion from her, so that we could travel back to him when it was safe to do so. But Mum and I have been stuck here ever since. Maybe my Father and sisters are still alive, but my Grandfather, he is an old old man by now and likely dead."

"Is there no other way back other than taking the potion?" I asked.

"No, not now, thanks to you and your Dad, Kingsley! What do you mean, not now because of my Dad and me?" I replied, feeling a sinking feeling inside.

"The Spirit Horse, Rhiddian, was the only other way back, Kingsley, and you and your Dad, killed him."

"What are you talking about," I snapped angrily. "That horse tried to attack us, and even tried to steal Melody away on its back!"

"Rhiddian didn't steal Melody," Taliath said. "She was trying to take her back to her family through the portal."

"That's what your mother Armes told Fion and I when we went to talk to her at the Commune. But I wasn't having it. I was just protecting my family, and that phantom horse wouldn't leave us alone so I killed it!"

"I am not angry with you," Taliath replied, "but Rhiddian was the only other way back other than the potion. So Armes and I are stuck here, for who knows how long, maybe forever!"

"Why didn't Armes go back on Rhiddian when she had the chance. This just doesn't make sense."

"I am trying to explain…Firstly, Rhiddian cannot take Armes back. Rhiddian can only take someone who has been born on this side of the portal back in time. Because I was born on this side and also Melody then we are the only ones that were able to go back with her. Secondly, we were limited to the moon phases for passage to the other side. Both the moon phases in each time had to align for the horse to travel through, which did not happen very often so I could not freely move back and forth."

"I'm sorry that you are stranded here," I replied, "but I only did what I thought best to protect my family,Taliath. And don't forget, you had already disappeared once on the back of that phantom horse and there is no way in hell I would ever let it take Melody too! What the heck did you expect me to do!"

Taliath grew silent again and I could see the strain in her eyes.

"Anyway, it's time I was home, it was nice talking to you, Taliath, and please remember what I said, please respect my wishes and leave us alone, and I will tell your story." I paused for a moment and gathered my thoughts. "I have a couple of questions though before I go. You say you came through the portal in Armes' womb so how could you have a diary that is 1200 years old?"

"I know it is confusing to you. It is hard to explain but I exist in both past and present at the same time. In fact, my people call me the Twin Soul. I was sent back to learn the ways of my family once I was out of danger. I was so young I do not remember this but Armes has told me of it. I have come back and forth many times on Rhiddian's back but in each time I can live a whole lifetime, then when I cross over to the other life I start where I left off such as the life I had with you."

"I cannot pretend to understand, I can only tell your story as I know it from the diary. And why can't you tell your own story?"

"You're right, it is my story, but I cannot tell it. Too much has happened and it is too hard. How can I tell my story when I live in both the past and the present. Please Kingsley, tell it for me, it would make no sense if I did it. Besides, you are the story-teller. That is why I chose you. I knew you could give honor to my past and tell it in a way that future generations would under-stand. It is a part of the history of this land that we both love."

I turned to walk away and with each step I felt I was merely a pawn in her complex game, but one thing was true, I was a storyteller and she knew me well enough to know that I would finish what I had started.

"Goodbye Taliath."

"Goodbye Kingsley."

As I reached my car, I was under no delusions, I was sure that I would see her again, it was just a matter of when. Hopefully not for a long time!

Chapter Seventeen

The Latest Translation

Over the next few weeks, our family remained as resilient as always, and although I can't say that we put our experiences of our encounters with Taliath behind us, we learned to adapt to this paranormal phenomena that had dogged our family for so long. To my surprise both Melody and Helen seemed to come through the ordeal they experienced down on the beach relatively unscathed, and none of us mentioned anything to Ffion or Samantha, who remained our reminder of what 'normality and stability' was all about, in the midst of this otherwise crazy time! I am sure that Helen and Melody chose to shut out a lot of their feelings and emotions around what had happened, just as I had done. Out of sight out of mind, they say, I wish it was that easy! But we all had a life to live and a wonderful family to celebrate, in spite of the woman named Taliath Saren.

I asked Melody if she wanted to see her mother again, and she said that she didn't. "I just want to live a normal life, Dad, just like anyone else," she said, "so no, I don't want to see her."

∽

On Saturday morning I decided to go and see Dad in Swansea. It had been some time since I had seen him and it was time to fulfill my promise to Taliath that I would tell her story. I felt that if I kept my end of the bargain that she would respect my wishes and leave us alone.

I arrived at Dad's and rang the doorbell.

"Who goes there, friend or foe," Dad shouted down from upstairs.

"Friend, I shouted back!"

"Hello Kings, it's good to see you Old Son. Mary, can you make us a cuppa tea, while Kings and I talk? Come and sit at the table, Kings, and I will show you the latest translation of the diary. Here, read this. Are you feeling alright, Kings? You look a bit pale, like you have seen a ghost or something."

"Only one," I replied, and Dad laughed. Little did he know! "Yes, I'm alright, Dad, just a bit tired. I have to talk to you about something important."

"What is it?" he said curiously.

"I know I have not wanted to keep up with the translation of the diary but I feel that I am ready now, and that Taliath has a story that needs to be told." I didn't feel comfortable telling Dad what had happened at the castle or down on the beach, knowing that he would want to get more involved in solving the mystery, but I was tired, so tired of the craziness of everything! I would keep my promise and then forget about Taliath Saren.

The harvest moon and three large seas have passed since I last wrote in my diary. My heart sorrows and my spirit is broken as I behold what has happened to Grandfather and me.

Grandfather has been forced to train a Nobleman's Son in the art of shoemaking. There is no nobility in this weak and fainthearted man, who is afraid to fight in battle, or even hunt to provide food for our clan. A commoner would be put to death for such cowardice. This our whole clan knows! But this man is the son of a Nobleman, and that is how the corruption goes! What bribe did the Nobleman give to the priest? Land and title, or female servants to satisfy his lustful appetite? Who knows!

Our Clan Priest has forbidden me to work with grandfather anymore, even though the Ceremonial Slippers that I make are praised throughout our clan as the best! Grandfather taught me well.

Women can no longer make shoes the Priest and Balla now say. And it is going to be written into law at the next meeting of the Nobles and Prince's.

All the women used to lift their heads in pride when I walked through the village. For I made the shoes for the honor of womankind, and celebrated womanhood within my heart, showing the men what us women can do when we are given the chance! Now heads are bowed, and sorrow abounds while I walk past their sad countenance. Another sword has been drawn against us women, my sister Tanwen says. And oh, how I want to draw a sword, and stand up and fight!

I only see grandfather now, after his long day is done. He is old and made one mistake, so now he must teach the Nobleman's son all that he knows of making shoes. Grandfather will not teach him everything, of that I am sure. The Nobleman's son has a mind that is slow and dull.

Once grandfather has trained the man, grandfather will be put to death, for he will have lived out his use and become a burden to our clan, so the priest has said. We all know that this is not true but a lie! The real reason he is to be put to death, is because my mother; his daughter the Clan Queen refused his advances in the temple whilst she was Queen, and now the evil priest will take his vengeance upon the Saren Tribe.

I am already grieving for my loss that is to come. I grieve for the loss of the headship of the Saren's, and the only man I have ever loved, apart from my father whom I have never really known.

My sister Tanwen is my only strength, and at the end of her day in the temple, she comforts me.

The time of harvest, 972 AD.

Our mother Ebrill, [Translated, one born in April] Has been put to death and her body burned, which is our law and custom when a Reigning Queen reaches her 50th year of age. Ebrill, [April] lived to be 53, which is a rare exception these days. If the Ceremonial Priest is occupied with other duties, and the residing Balla [Executioner] is detained with prior executions, then the Queen may continue her reign beyond her appointed term.

Not that our mother living longer made any difference to Tanwen and me. Ebrill was always occupied training our eldest sister Gwenhwyfar, getting her ready to become the next Clan Queen.

Senior Clan Women are permitted to live 45 years, if they are useful to the reigning Queen in helping her with child rearing, advising and ceremonial dress, or are requested by the Queen to be her body servant.

The common clan woman is put to death in her 40th year, if she has no special skills to benefit her clan. Exceptions are made by the Prince's and Nobles, if there has become a shortage of Senior women to instruct the younger women in our laws, spiritual beliefs, and ceremonies of the clan.

My sister Arlias, who's name means 'from the temple', is a Watcher in the temple, and oversees the cremation ovens after the women have been put to death by the Balla, who slits their throats like chickens until their bodies are bled dry. Arlias has told us stories of what the Balla does when the Ceremonial Priest is absent from the temple. The women who are to take part in the execution ceremony are required by our laws to wear the appropriate attire. Arlias has seen the Balla, force the women to participate in the execution ceremony naked, where he has beaten and raped them before slitting their throats. He then threatened Arlias, not to tell the Priest, otherwise she too, would have her throat slit. My body shudders at the thought of that evil Balla.

Our sister Gwenhwyfar, is now our new Clan Queen, and spends all her time in the temple, lusting over the men and participating in the various ceremonies. Gwenhwyfar always wanted power, and now she has it! She chooses who lives, and who must die. She only speaks to Arlias now, and treats Tanwen and me as if we don't exist! Mother favored her, giving her all her love and attention, while the rest of us competed for any little attention that was left. For Tanwen and me, it felt like there was none.

I am mocked by Gwenhwyfar and Arlias, because I do not work within the sacred walls of the temple. Even Tanwen works in the temple as a scribe.

She records the strict order of Dress and Body Jewelry that must be worn for each of our ceremonies, thirty three ceremonies in all. She prepares a script of ceremonial laws and practice for each ceremony, which she copies from the Sacred Book Of Clan Laws, and then gives the script to the Ceremonial Priest. Only the Ceremonial Priest and the Scribe are permitted to even open the Sacred Book Of Our Laws, which Tanwen takes great pride in being able to do. She also scribes an order of Dress Attire for each of the ceremony participants. Tanwen has a very important responsibility, grandfather says, and if she gets the order of Ceremonial Laws wrong, or the attire to be worn by each participant at any given ceremony wrong, the participants can be put to death.

A participant can also be sentenced to death for not following the correct order of ceremony implicitly. What might be permitted in one ceremony, could be forbidden in another.

Tanwen can tell some stories about ceremonial couples that were put to death, because the woman forgot to take off her sandals before the sacred altar, or a man wore the wrong body belt. It all depends on the Priest, Tanwen says, if he is merciful or not, or whether he can be bribed to overlook a mistake. Once she got the order in which a woman was to bow her head before the sacred altar in a love ceremony, wrong, and the Priest slit the woman's throat, and she fell into a pool of blood. Tanwen feared for her life that day. If the priest had bothered to check the order of ceremony which Tanwen had scribed for the participants, he would have found out that she had got it wrong and cost that couple their lives. Fortunately for Tanwen, our Ceremonial Priest, never bothered to check her scribe. It still haunts me, she tells me, if the Priest had found out that I gave the couple the wrong order, there would have been a trial before the High Priest, and the Balla would have slit my throat, and my sister, Arlias, would have burned my body in one of the cremation ovens. And I bet she would have enjoyed it too, because she hates me so much.

Just after the fall solstice, 972 AD.

Today Tanwen and I found out that Ebrill is not our birthmother! We are the daughters of Ebrill's hand-maiden, who's name is Armes, translated, Prophetess. And Ebrill had kept this a secret for all these years!

I talked to Grandfather about it, feeling hurt that he had never told me. I did not tell you Taliath, he said, because I knew you would go searching for your real mother, who is now an outcast of our clan. An outcast, I answered, and I asked why?

Ebrill could not bear any more children after Gwenhwy-far and Arlias were born, so she asked her maid servant Armes to bear children for her. Armes would not agree at first, because she wanted descendants of her own, whom she could mother and love. So Ebrill threatened Armes, and ordered that if she did not bear children for her Queen, then she would be put to death. Armes, not having any other choice, bore your sister Tanwen. Ebrill began to spend most of her time in the temple, teaching Gwenhwyfar what she would need to know to become our next Clan Queen once Ebrill finished her reign. As Ebrill spent long hours in the temple with Gwenhwyfar, Armes was left to mother Tanwen. After a time, Ebrill became jealous of Armes, because Tanwen and Arlias, were bonding with Armes. Ebrill had no time for anyone but her eldest. Your sister Arlias regarded Armes as her mother and not Ebrill. Ebrill became so jealous that she banished Armes from our clan, and threatened to have her executed if she returned. Armes was pregnant again with you when Ebrill banished her from the clan, and one of the temple guards told me that the ceremonial priest had beaten Armes and bruised her stomach, and I feared for her unborn child. I tried talking with Ebrill, but she was too angry and proud to listen, so Armes left our clan and traveled through the portal and never returned. Rhiddian brought you back Taliath when you were still too young to remember and I helped teach you our ways.

As Grandfather spoke, a light of revelation dawned in my heart and mind. I had always known that there must be a reason why Ebrill favored Gwenhwyfar and Arlias over Tanwen and me. And now I know why. Ebrill is not our real mother, Armes is! And something good has already come out of this, in that Tanwen and I are even closer to one another now, knowing that she and I are full blooded sisters and Gwenhwyfar and Arlias are only our half sisters.

Grandfather told Tanwen and I, that the reason Gwenhwyfar and Arlias disliked us so much is because our father loved our mother Armes more than he did Ebrill.

I was still left with more questions than answers but I could not doubt that this was part of an important history. It would take at least another few years for Dad and I to complete the translation of the diary, but that dear reader is another story.

End of Part Five.